BRIAN CALLISON

The
Bone Collectors

A novel of the Atlantic convoys

COLLINS
8 Grafton Street, London WI
1984

William Collins Sons and Co. Ltd
London · Glasgow · Sydney · Auckland
Toronto · Johannesburg

British Library Cataloguing in Publication Data

Callison, Brian
The bone collectors
I. Title
823′.914[F]   PR6053.A39

ISBN 0-00-222782-7

First published 1984
© Brian Callison 1984

Photoset in Plantin by Centracet
Made and Printed in Great Britain by
William Collins Sons & Co. Ltd, Glasgow

Foreword

North Atlantic Eastbound Convoy, Sequence Number SC–7, did exist. Once. And what took place in late 1940, after it had cleared Nova Scotia, Canada; UK-bound at the peak of the U-boat men's Happy Time, became a tragically real event.

Of the thirty-five largely-unarmed and pitifully under-escorted vessels which sailed, SC–7 lost a total of twenty: some with all hands. Sixteen of those were sunk in one appalling night action, on the 18th October, 1940.

There were a great many convoys. And a great many helpless and venerable ships lost which should never have been forced to war, and were offered no opportunity to strike back . . . This is a story of them; of the Merchant Navy; of the Tonnage War and the six-and-a-half knot targets, not of the gallant fighting escorts nor of the U-boats. Others more qualified than I have already written of those.

My slow convoy SC whatever-it-was never did exist, nor did *Olympian* or any of the other ships described in this novel, other than in brief, sad reference to *Athenia*, *Lusitania* and to the real SC–7 . . . or did they? Certainly I have used names for Allied merchantmen which, by the laws of average, must have existed at some time or other because it is virtually impossible not to: there have been many ships involved in war, and the dictionary of gallantry is limited.

And my Chief Officer Ellis? There were all too many Ellises – professional peace-time merchant seamen who unwittingly found themselves embroiled in the early Battle of the Atlantic. I hope I haven't offended any of those who were spared, and have done some small honour to the memory of thousands who weren't.

But for them, and their self-sacrifice, I would never have been permitted to write this novel. Very possibly I, and many of my generation, would not even exist.

I am so very grateful to them all.

Brian Callison.
Dundee, Scotland.
1984.

Prologue

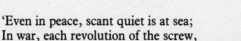

> 'Even in peace, scant quiet is at sea;
> In war, each revolution of the screw,
> Each breath of air that blows the colours free,
> May be the last life movement known to you'.

John Masefield

Her name was *Olympian*. Even by the spring of 1941 she was old, tired, and boiler-scale asthmatic.

She was also desperately needed: but to understand why, to fully explore a complicated issue like that, would demand the use of ponderous phrases like 'Nation under threat', 'Atlantic lifeline' and 'Shadow of the Swastika' whereas, really, it was more a sort of 'Sod the bloody Germans' argument as interpreted by the quite average British seamen who sailed in her.

According to her sailing orders she was nominated as one of the rescue ships – the convoy's rescue ships, that was. Mind you, that was a bit of a misnomer, too: another slightly obscure turn of official phrase. Her designated task wasn't so much to rescue ships as to rescue people when the ships themselves were long past the stage of being rescued because usually – in the North Atlantic War anyway – by the time *Olympian* was needed, their bows or sterns would have already been blown off, their double-bottoms gutted; possibly their entire carcasses vapourised by the monstrous smash of a three-thousand-pound U-boat torpedo.

There wouldn't be much rescuing to be performed in the latter event. Instantly-dissolving ships were invariably petro-chemical tankers or ammunition carriers at risk from

7

a spark struck by a hobnailed seaboot, never mind a deliberate act of war, and any pitiable sailorman surviving the initial detonation was more than likely to be taken shortly thereafter anyway – by thousand-degree surface flames or the inhalation of oil, so emulsified it was like drowning in jet black syrup, or maybe the choked-off-scream variety of surgical shock inflicted when near-freezing salt water encompasses parboiled flesh. Whatever the manner of their going it would be over long before a rescue ship could rescue anything at all, whether or not her sailing orders demanded such a charitable gesture.

While, talking about charity – did anybody's convoy sailing orders specify that they had to rescue the poor bloody crews of the rescue ships if *they* were hit?

But ignorance did offer some blessings to many a man in the middle of the Atlantic in early '41. Take the question of the temporary confiscation of personal radios on passage: seemingly they – 'they' representing, as ever, some faceless scientific authority – claimed that the oscillations generated across the 160 metre band when a cheap Stateside-bought heterodyne set was switched on might just be enough to enable a U-boat direction finder to home in on the convoy . . . OK, so perhaps it did prevent you from listening to a static-tortured Crosby, Glen Miller or Cantor from Station VONF Newfoundland as the Canadian coast faded inexorably astern. But it also meant you couldn't, either by accident or even masochistic design, tune into the Nazi propaganda drawl of a certain William Joyce, professional traitor – Lord Haw-Haw to the irreligious – and grin with carefully-prepared derision around your mates at his ever-escalating claims of bomb damage to London, Liverpool, Glasgow, and at the daily-rising tonnage figures of allegedly sunken merchantmen just like yourselves. And keep on grinning until you went below to your bunk, anyway. Where you secretly lay awake with all your clothes on and a lifejacket for a pillow 'cause the shipping losses had actually

8

scared the hell out of you deep down; staring up at the deckhead with unblinking eyes, wondering if they really *had* hit the Coventry again last night, an' whether or not that meant you were a widower without knowing it because one of them bloody Jerry bombs might just 'ave fell on Number 23 this time, smack atop the tin Anderson shelter shroudin' Aggie an' the kids . . .

You stayed ignorant if that was your way, and slept a little and turned and tossed a lot. You tried to blank out the stories of mummified corpses in ships' boats with claw-bones still gripping the tiller, an' of white-haired mad creatures still alive and trapped in air pockets two weeks after their ships were torpedoed, an' of men jetted vertical from the water all swollen and orange and shrieking in their kapok Board of Trade jackets, spitted like suckling pigs as cargoes of pit props breached while the casualty was sinking and came shooting to the surface with a hiss and a smashing of spine an' gut . . .

Jesus, quite a few of you didn't want to know! Not about anything. Not unless you could eat it, drink it, or look forward to it. Not out here in the bloody North Atlantic when the U-boats were waiting somewhere up ahead.

Because they would be waiting. All of you knew *that* much. No matter how hard you worked at stayin' ignorant.

Talking about lack of awareness, very few of the fifty-three men aboard the Steamship *Olympian* were able to recall the official name – the tactical designator – of the convoy by the time it was entering its eleventh night at sea after clearing the Canadian coast.

Certainly that wasn't through blinkered intent: there couldn't be any predestined significance in a title, though undoubtedly history would disagree when future analysts deliberated in the wake of the cataclysm. Unavoidable battlegrounds would then be accorded the status of 'planned events'; routinely devastated cities would indicate 'turning

9

points of the war', randomly selected convoys of ships and men would assume a strategic prominence never desired by the poor bastards who were just doing an unpleasant job without ever wanting to become legends by the shape of their dying.

No, they wouldn't remember, because it simply wasn't important, their collective cipher. They would never come together again, those who survived this passage. It was a unique event, a convoy which would fragment at its destination and never reassemble in quite the same form. Some of its components might – almost certainly would, in this under-defended phase of the battle – be sent to the bottom of the sea; those ships which made it home would be reloaded and re-routed as parts of yet another whole, and with yet another temporary identity. An as-yet indeterminate percentage of the fleshy sub-components – the seamen themselves – would die by explosion or drowning, or through some messy accident the threat of which hovered constantly at the shoulder of every sailor even when the hazards weren't compounded by war and national hate. Others would split from their voyage partners to sign aboard other doomed ships or hell ships or happy ships; some would retire either gratefully or with bloody-minded resentment as years finally wasted muscle and sinew once toned by the oceans which had been their chosen life. Some would die of heart attacks or be run over by tramcars or be kicked into paupers' graves during pub brawls: some, a very few, would refuse ever to board a ship again once they'd set foot on dry land, preferring automatic conscription into khaki or airforce blue as a less harrowing alternative.

So who the hell cared what this particular convoy was called? The cryptics of war claim low priority in a man's mind when set against the imminent prospect of ceasing to exist at all, even as a marker tally on a North Atlantic tactical trade plot. But still, for the academic speculator who did give the matter of Naval Control hieroglyphics a second thought – and there weren't that many of *those* aboard *Olympian* – it could be confidently assumed that this rag-tag, smoke-emitting rusty-grey flock of ocean-going tramps had to be christened *Sugar Charlie* followed by a sequence number something-or-other, largely because everybody – and 'everybody' included the Staff of Submarine Division, German Naval High Command – knew that all Allied East-bound Atlantic convoys sailing from Sydney, Cape Breton Island, were identified by the prefix SC as opposed to the somewhat more prestigious HX applied to faster Halifax, Nova Scotia outward-bounders.

And there was no way this SC Number whatever-it-was could have been described as 'fast', Halifax or no Halifax: not grinding along at under seven knots despite the moderate weather; barely the pace an elderly marathon runner could maintain without effort. Six and three quarter knots over the past twenty-four hours was the current estimate from the bridge – and *that* didn't even represent the convoy's speed of advance because they'd been zig-zagging part of that time to confuse the enemy instead of steaming on a straight course for home.

Confuse the *enemy*? Can you imagine – especially in the first few days of the convoy's formation – the disconcerted-ness and the prickle-hair an' the sheer bloody ill-temper on a tramp steamer's bridge when the Commodore's 'execute' hoist dropped, whereupon thirty-odd totally incompatible vessels sailing in six parallel columns suddenly tried to make a fifteen degree turn together? It meant anyone on the inside of the turn who wasn't a new-fangled motorship – which meant pretty well everyone in SC something-or-other – had to let off precious steam and drop revolutions, while the poor soddin' firemen stoking the outer vessels' boilers had to shovel like blacks to increase speed just enough to keep up but not so much they'd bloody blow up! And inevitably some rogue ship would fall back on the next astern with suicidal determination, while others shot off at a tangent because the God-rotted steering gear had jammed wheels three spokes to starboard; and yet others boomed or hooted or screeched and belched clouds of steam from their whistles as long-tormented safety valves finally gave up the ghost altogether despite grizzled, unbelievably foul-mouthed Chiefs hittin' them with wrenches and fists an' even black-smeared foreheads . . .

Mind you, they'd have zig-zagged anyway, with or without orders from the Navy, most of them. The two most venerable inhabitants of this convoy had first kissed salt water in a previous century, the majority had limped through one world war already, followed by a depression-plagued peace in which spares had been but a wistful gleam in a master's eye and repairs authorised by the shipowners only when their corroding investments had eventually clawed into port under jury steering or with reciprocating engines leaking steam from so many worn glands they almost refused to reciprocate.

Olympian herself was spawned of that later penny-pinching, sailor-exploiting era. Fashioned on the Tyne in 1922 from 3,946 tons of steel, brass, pitch pine, boiler plate and riveters' sweat she was damn near twenty years clapped-out by the time she found herself last in line in the third column of Convoy Sugar Charlie whatever, in the spring of 1941.

Yet despite all that, *Olympian* did still represent one of the younger elements forming that escort commander's nightmare straggle of dilapidated maritime geriatrics. Which was the main reason why she'd been nominated as the rescue ship for anyone torpedoed in Column Three.

'But *why* demand a slow and ponderous freighter like her to stop and offer herself as an even easier static target?' an innocent soul might ask. 'Why the need to call upon a cargo-laden ship already in grave hazard by virtue of her bulk, her torpedo-attractive draft, even her cumbersome handling qualities to perform a task of mercy difficult and dangerous enough for a faster, lighter vessel?'

Can't gallantry and self-sacrifice be pressed too far? Couldn't one consider it too exquisite a cruelty to place those merchant seamen's lives – to say nothing of the lives of the already-once-stricken crews they were morally black-mailed into attempting to save – at additional risk, some-times for hours by the time they'd caught up with the protection of the convoy again, when even seconds of solitary exposure offered a periscope-certain escalation of the odds in favour of death.?

It was quite simple, really – it was just that no one in government had yet got round to the rather uninspiring secondary priority of producing specialist aid vessels for the Atlantic lifelines, though future plans were rumoured to allow for the inclusion of smaller, more manoeuvrable ships fitted with additional galley facilities, operating theatres, sick bays; even proper gear to lift helpless men from the water. A bit of a luxury in warime, though. Not providing half the propaganda value to the beleaguered shorebound public as a newspaper photograph of half-a-dozen new fighting tanks or a couple of Spitfires that everyone could actually marvel at in the skies above Britain. So the orders for every convoy demanded that the last vessel in the column should act as mercy ship for those ahead of her. And whatever her master might have declared her practical speed to be in early 1941, Admiralty Trade Division records still showed that the good ship *Olympian* had notched up ten knots on her trials; therefore, on paper anyway, she had the power in hand to overhaul the convoy should she fall astern while acting the Good Samaritan to the four ships in line ahead of her.

Ten *knots*?

That had been in 1922, dammit. The only time anyone could remember her having equalled that was when old Nervous Theakstone was panic-dodging into Hong Kong typhoon anchorage before the great blow of '29 – an' only then because he'd ordered them to broach a cargo of first grade smokeless Welsh coal earmarked for Orient Line bunkers instead of the wartime dross *Olympian* then carried.

So they could conceivably end up straggling miles behind the convoy: no escorts, no defensive armament; say realistically steaming at eight, maybe eight an' a half flat out and urged on by a prayer from the crew.

Christ, hadn't it occurred to the Admiralty – to *any* of those pre-war planners – that a V11-C U-boat running on the surface could do over seventeen?

Head-in-the-sand ignorant or merely kept-in-the-dark ignorant, every man aboard the rescue ship designate *Olympian* knew *that* much!

Other knowledge was available to all and sundry who used the eyes God gave them: the number of ships comprising the convoy, for example – more or less thirty-four. More because they'd swept up a paint-shiny straggler on the second day out which had fallen astern from the previous HX convoy and now limped, utterly mortified, on one of two engines in tandem with its scruffier elder sisters: and less because they'd lost three of their original thirty-six during the first night out; their masters either super-optimistic when it had come to declaring their sea-readiness at the pre-sailing conference or, like the Greek which had simply turned around and steamed back in the vague direction of Nova Scotia, because her old man had died of a surfeit of vine leaves or whatever within hours of leaving an' no one else aboard was capable of navigating across the bloody Atlantic; whereupon her already less than war-like crew had point-blank refused to stop and take on a volunteer pilot from one of the other ships.

By the time they'd been eleven – or was it twelve? – days on passage the *Olympian* men also knew the identities of many of their consorts in that ramshackle armada despite

14

the theoretical security requirements to obliterate all names and ports of registry . . . theoretical because not only had most of them surreptitiously reappeared on bluff and battered bows over the months since the war began, but also individual companies' funnel liveries had been repainted: usually by some mysterious agency not too far removed from the Bosun's Crowd in the middle of a night. Now, in every ocean convoy, high above anonymous grey hulls and upperworks rose multi-coloured spindle stacks defiantly proclaiming their belonging to Guinea Gulf Line of Liverpool or Stewarts of Glasgow; Roberts, Newcastle; Denholme or Bank or Shell; Glen, Strick, Ellerman, Coast Lines. *Coast* Lines? Out here in the middle of the North Atlantic? 'Yeah; din't you know there wus a war on, pal?' Then the sad but equally proud owners' colours maintaining allegiance to nations and companies now under Nazi oppression: Ekerholt of Oslo; Koninklijke Paketvaart Maats NV, Amsterdam; Le Borgne, Paris; Norden A/S Dampskibs, Copenhagen . . . And the shipping houses of the Commonwealth and allies: Eagle Tankers of Nassau; Wo Fat Sing, Hong Kong; Chin Seng, Bangkok; Bharat of Bombay and Austasia of Singapore; Smeltzer of Toronto; Thesen's Steamships of Cape Town; Yelkenci Lutfi, Istanbul; Zaphiropoulos Steam Navigation of Piraeus – not all Greeks lacked the fire of hatred in their bellies and the fine-tuned courage of the seaman at war.

So the men of *Olympian* were perfectly aware that they were sailing in company with *Nicodemus* and *Valiant Star; Hecuba, City of Rouen, Joan M* and *Jollity; Antigone, Antisthenes* and *Bubble; Theotokos* and *Stafford Pride* . . . all those lumbering, sagging vessels flaunting their identities with a bloody-minded indifference to officialdom, an' bugger Mister Hitler altogether!

And of course everybody aboard *Olympian* was aware of what was, for want of a better term, the convoy's 'battle order'. Could see that the convoy's ocean formation involved their steaming on a broad front in six columns with the Commodore ship, *Pendragon*, leading the fourth column from port. They could hardly avoid knowing she was the Commodore's ship because she kept running up hoists of signal flags unintelligible to any but the unfortunate officer of that particular watch, whose unenviable task it was to interpret naval signalese from equally unfamiliar convoy manoeuvring orders. Mind you, there weren't any signal flags for the watchkeepers to get hysterical about during the hours of darkness: Good Lord, no! No: then the Commodore hoisted strings of coloured bloody lights instead, which were repeated, sometimes inaccurately to add to the confusion, by nominated ships throughout the ranks.

Of course when you did look outboard there were other factors – more ominous features – about this plodding, terribly vulnerable entity called SC something-or-other, which no eye could fail to miss and no man fail to grasp the import of, no matter whether his resolution was bolstered by blissful unawareness or not. Or was it more a question of what the searching gaze *didn't* encompass: of what was missing rather than of what existed? For where were all the escorts, the warships, the protectors who might stand between your unarmed tortoise hulls and the predatory emissaries of *Gross-admiral* Dönitz – the black U-boats who must be gathering by now in anticipation of SC whatsits coming as the convoy entered this, its twelfth night at sea?

Because there were only two! A tiddley little British corvette about half the size of the smallest merchantman, and an armed Royal Canadian Navy trawler. 'An armed *trawler*, f'r Chrissakes?' 'Yeah – an armed trawler, matey!' Armed with a foredeck gun and a couple of high-angle Bofors which would be splendid protection against aircraft should the *Luftwaffe* happened to send any of their mercifully scarce long-range Focke-Wolf 200's to spy and report their position – which they hadn't done so far, thank God – but which weren't exactly goin' to scare the sauerkraut out

16

of some blood-lusting Hamburger in three million Reich-mark's-worth of submerged *Frontboote* . . . and a slightly more reassuring deckload of depthcharges. Oh, plus a helluva nerve!

But two escorts? While everybody knew the enemy had finally perfected *die Rudeltaktik* – 'the Wolf tactic' in which a U-boat shadowing from eighteen, twenty miles astern would report the convoy's mean course and speed, and then wait for the monstrous ambush to assemble across its estimated track. Slowly, efficiently, the pack would rendez-vous, radio-directed from 'Onkel Karl's' *Operationsab-teilung, Befehlshaber der Unterseeboote* – Operations Divi-sion, Commander-in-Chief U-boats based at Kerneval, Lo-rient. It would be a large gathering when completed, a seething of professional killing machines, and only when everything was ready would they finally attack; fall upon the convoy; worry and tear and rend asunder. Gliding silently under cover of night they would operate on the surface in groups; cut ships out like terrified sheep from a flock and impassively execute them. Six U-boats; ten U-boats . . .Fif-teen, maybe even *twenty* U-boats all at the same time, dear God!

Able to outrun only two fighting escorts, harrassed, by that time, to the limits of human endurance: deaf because ASDIC couldn't differentiate between a surfaced submarine and a scurrying merchantman; virtually blind because only panic-fired starshell and snowflake flares from the convoy would offer all-too-brief illumination of conning towers and pencil hulls barely visible even by day.

You couldn't avoid the knowledge of that promise in store: that it could happen tonight; within the next hour; possibly in the next, the very last, sixty seconds of life left to you. Quite a number of you had been through it all before and seen the ships exploding and heard the shrieks of drowning fathers and sons and brothers keening like a distant wind through the flickering blackness; and watched thirty, forty, fifty thousand tons of desperately needed food and amunition and clothing and aircraft and men swallowed by the sea in the blink of a cordite-dazzled eye. But somehow you didn't – you couldn't afford to – brood too much on it because that way lay a terrible madness which would smother you and deny you ever sleeping again, even fitfully. So instead you just did your job, stood your watch, played cards or dominoes or cribbage; rechecked your convoy bag – the little canvas sack you all kept close to hand which contained the family photograph, the pure silk stockings for a loved one, the cheap wrist watch you'd bought for the kid, the well-thumbed poetry book; those valueless trinkets which meant nothing to anyone but yourself, but without which you would have nothing at all if that torpedo did strike and you ever made it to the boats before she sank.

And then you had an argument or a laugh and a bread and jam sandwich for supper, and eventually eased yourself into that cramped little bunk of nightmares once again; maybe even on to a stinking straw mattress mildewed with damp if she was a very old tramp steamer and you were signed on for the foc'sle, because British ships still had a bitter history of being dirty ships as well as gallant ships . . . and reflected in your curled-up loneliness on all the things about the convoy which you'd learned despite yourself, and which disturbed you.

And about all the things you didn't know. Which frightened you even more.

Maybe you weren't sure of your precise daily geographical position, but you certainly knew you'd been pretty close to the polar mainland. Ever since sailing from Cape Breton and clearing Newfoundland's Cape Race the convoy had described a nor'easterly course towards the Arctic Circle; up past St John's to where the Ocean Escort Group – both of them – had taken over from the four RCN coastal escorts,

18

then onwards and upwards through an even greyer, more desolate sea with the weather growing colder by the hour and the smell of what the older hands said was the ice more evident until finally, some eight days later, you'd had Kap Farvel – unsettlingly apt in its translation to Cape Farewell – and the southern tip of Greenland almost abeam, and were skirting latitude 60 degrees.

There had been bergs around you for a while by then, sometimes black-shadowed, sometimes opaque in green and delicate blue, but not glistening like you'd always imagined; presenting more a matt, irregular beauty quite at odds with the hostile monochrome of the ocean. Soon you'd got used to the novelty of leaning out over the rail and gazing down at the ice spicules in the water – the first tangible sign of the true Arctic. 'Frazil ice', the seasoned North Atlantic men called it, which gave the whole surface of the sea a sluggish, oily appearance over which the columns of ships appeared to move in a hushed, unreal way; almost like waterline models slowly being propelled across an undulating board.

But you'd entered a second new world of terminology by then: you'd already learned the first – the convoy man's – language in which you all referred laconically, if not very understandingly, to WOMPS instead of Western Ocean Meeting Points and to ASDIC, spawned by the initials of the Allied Submarine Detection Investigation Committee; to NCSO's, who were Naval Control Service Officers and CHOP times which had more to do with Changes of Operational Control than with eating.

Now you peeped uneasily into the Ice Man's dictionary: grease ice and shuga; slush and rind, light nilas and dark nilas, pancake and grey and grey-white and floe and brash ice. You learned that an iceberg, after forming off the Siberian coast, could drift for up to five years before it crosses the polar basin and reaches Greenland. You grinned a bit when they told you with a straight face that a hump in sheet ice was called a hummock; the matching extrusion below – under the water – was, honest-to-God, matey, called a 'bummock'.

You stopped grinning when the leather-skinned ex-sealers and whalers among you talked about Arctic survival: about how fresh water ice took only half the amount of heat to thaw out that was needed by snow itself, but that you had to look for clear or blue second and third year ice for by then the salt would have been leached from it, especially if it had thawed and refrozen. You had to remember never to eat snow because it dehydrated the body: that rabbits were astonishingly prolific up there if you didn't fancy tackling a polar bear single-handed, but never, ever eat rabbit for more than a few days no matter how desperate you were because, after that short time, they wouldn't satisfy your hunger; they'd strike you with appalling diarrhoea instead, and you would die within a matter of weeks. You learned how to make a fishhook from a sliver of wood or metal sharpened at both ends and suspended in the middle, and that you could bait it if all else failed with nothing more than a scrap of coloured cloth smeared with grease; but you mustn't eat your catch raw as the parasites in ice-water dwellers could rot human gut as easily as any fish's. And, either way, you should never run when you think you've hooked the wretched creature because exertion made you pant very easily in the Arctic, and a man panting was a man drawing in great gouts of super-freezing air – and then you could die in agony from internal frost-bite instead . . .

No wonder you'd stopped grinning as you tried desperately to hoist all that sub-zero wisdom aboard. It was a lot more pertinent, a lot more vital than trying to remember some official sequence number for the SC whatever-it-was you were currently sailing in.

Because there were other dangers lurking under the waters north of the southern tip of Greenland. Much more threatening than finny things which spread disease; even more potentially lethal than eating a continuous diet of rabbit.

20

There was nothing to prevent the U-boats hunting just as keenly up there as anywhere else.

Of course, as the convoy's track gradually altered east, and then south-east and began its run towards home, you and your shipmates in *Olympian* became more aware that you had moved into the Air Gap by now, on top of everything else.

The '*Air* Gap'?

Yeah, well, that was a factor a bloke had been inclined to overlook while his mind was concentrated on the prospects of being converted to an ice-cube – the continuing non-existence, even by early 1941, of any allied aircraft capable of operating out to mid-Atlantic as the *Luftwaffe's* four-engined FW 200's based in Occupied Norway could.

Yet aircraft would have offered the one effective deterrent preventing U-boats from running on the surface in daylight hours. You, as a convoy man, were intimately aware that the submarine *was* simply a surface ship at the end of the day, with the ability to submerge only for relatively short periods: it had to breathe to live, to communicate, to run its diesel engines, to recharge its batteries. More than that; it didn't have the speed to pursue under water – keep it down and it would be forced merely to wait for, rather than seek out, a target of opportunity such as yourself . . . and even the distant drone of a flying machine was enough to make sure the bastard did dive fast, deep, and frustrated.

Only we didn't *have* any suitable bloody aircraft, did we? Or naval carriers to shepherd us. Which meant air cover for the convoys extended only as far as land-bound flying ranges from both sides of the pond or from British-annexed Icelandic bases permitted, which, in turn, didn't allow them to meet anywhere near the middle. And so was created your lethal 'Air Gap' – miles of exposed sea acrosss which you had to sweat at six-point-somethin' bloody knots, and upon which the front line U-boats cruised and tracked you down with minimal risk. They'd even invented their own cynical-affectionate name for your Air Gap: the U-boat men. They called it *das Todesloch* . . . 'The Death Hole'.

Mind you, the U-boat crews had a language of their own just as you did; an appropriate nickname for everything connected with your mutual North Atlantic fratricide and not without, it had to be admitted, a certain wry black humour. D'you know what they actually called your surrogate rescue ship, for instance; the ordinary merchantman like *Olympian* delegated to stop and pick up broken, fuel-burned men from a sea of floating corpses?

They referred to you as *der Knochensammler*.

. . . the 'Bone Collector'.

So there it was – your situation. You had your Air Gap all right: your own personal Death Hole. As well as your lack of escorts, your pathetically inadequate life-saving equipment and your appalling sea-board conditions, and your consequent need to huddle together for protection because, tactically-speaking, it was the only way even a few might get through to feed, fuel and re-arm an island in hazard. You had all that, aggravated by a nagging resentment towards the blinkered political appeasers who hadn't prepared you in the slightest for this war yet who now demanded that you redeem, with your misery and modest courage, their earlier complacency.

But you kept those morale-rotting reflections to yourself, you tried not to brood too long over them: Christ, din't you have enough to worry about without analysing the reasons why? Already you were in one of those overloaded Bone Collectors called *Olympian*; one staggering antique in a slow march of sitting targets which manoeuvred like steamrollers and offered virtually no defence.

You'd been lucky so far, but now you were entering your eleventh – or *was* it your twelfth ? – night at sea – the traditional hours for ship-killing – and for whatever reason, no matter how hard you tried to ignore it, a butterfly of apprehension was beginning to stir your gut.

Somehow you sensed that, tonight, the U-boats would come.

One

'British merchant vessels at all times and
Dominion vessels, when in British Terri-
torial Waters, shall comply with any sailing
or routeing instructions which may from
time to time be issued to them by the
Admiralty or by any person authorised by
the Admiralty to act under this order.'

Navigation Order No. 1, 1939

8.00 p.m.: Eight Bells in the Evening Watch

'Kippers, Mister Ellis,' the Captain said, staring absently
ahead. 'Right now I could jus' go a nice flavoursome
kipper.'

The Third Mate came from the charthouse and stood at
Ellis's side looking tired; more as though he'd just completed, never mind arrived to take over, the watch.

'We're zig-zagging again I see,' he muttered sombrely.

'Diagram nine,' Ellis shrugged. 'East a quarter north:
timer's set for eight minutes, then one an' a half points to
starb'd. We've been waltzing for an hour. Nobody's hit
anybody yet.'

Third Officer Cowan shivered; pushing his scarf even
further down into his greatcoat. 'Christ, it's cold.'

'There's nothin' quite like a well-smoked Manx kipper,'
the Old Man persisted. 'With bread an' butter and some of
the fat dribbled over it . . .'

'Full moon tonight,' Chief Officer Ellis remarked, staring
out over the convoy as he'd done for the past four hours of
his watch yet still seeing, despite all daylight having faded,

the columns of ships black as tar-paper cut-outs against the stars.

'Hunter's moon.' The Third Mate shivered again.

'What d'you have to say that for', Ellis thought savagely. 'Why *say* a bloody obvious thing like that, Cowan?'

'There's sandwiches in the chartroom box,' he growled. 'Cheese and chutney. McKechnie's on the wheel; Sprunt is stand-by man, Logan an' Edwards are look-outs . . . Your eyes used to the darkness yet?'

'Er, yessir!'

'Then you have the watch, Mister Cowan.'

'I have the watch, sir,' the 3/0 nodded without enthusiasm. He wandered back into the wheelhouse and Ellis could see him staring critically over McKechnie's shoulder into the steering compass bowl, the lamp's dim green glow washing the under-jaws of both men.

'Don't go upsetting McKechnie now, f'r Christ's sake,' the Mate urged silently. 'He took the news bad. He doesn't need a nit-picker when it comes to steering a course . . .'

The cable had been waiting for McKechnie with the agents in New York, before they loaded to sail north as a joiner to the Cape Breton convoy. The Old Man had been uncharacteristically tongue-tied even before the young AB knocked respectfully, then entered the cramped little cabin; Ellis could have sworn he'd caught a glint in Albert's eye when he'd silently handed the lad the flimsy sheet: *Regret Mum and Vie killed in air-raid stop Dad and rabbits recovering OK stop Chin up stop Your affectionate brother Andy. Stop.*

Mum and Vie had been dead for nearly three weeks by the time the telegram had caught up with them. Ellis had felt ridiculously glad that the rabbits were all right, though: and Dad, of course. They – the rabbits – must have held a significance to that little back-street-Liverpool family out of all proportion to their status in the animal kingdom. Perhaps they'd bred them through generations for showing;

25

maybe just cuddled and cosseted and loved them for being the only soft things in a flint-hard seaport slumland. Either way it seemed they were marginally less newsworthy than Dad. Able Seaman McKechnie would obviously never have eaten rabbit if he'd been marooned at the North Pole, whether or not they promised to be lethal.

Vie had been McKechnie's fiancée. They were due to be married next time in.

'She was probably at our house for tea,' McKechnie had explained to his discomfited audience; almost as though apologising for embarrassing them with such domestic trivia as the high-explosive destruction of his family.

Then he'd started to cry.

'. . . or tripe, of course,' Captain Burton mused, leaning comfortably over the bridge rail. 'Stewed tripe and onions, done in a bit o' milk. With salt, pepper and vinegar.'

'Chief Steward's got some tinned pilchards in his store,' Ellis suggested resignedly, finally surrendering to the gastronomic fantasies of Albert Burton. But the Old Man always did tend to go on about irrelevant things until you gave in and listened.

'And what makes you think he'd give 'em special to me?'

Ellis sighed: no wonder he was resigned, he'd played this game before. At the first mention of *Olympian's* Chief Steward, her Master's expansive mood immediately changed to one of masochistic resentment.

'I'm only the bloody Captain, mister.' Burton growled plaintively. 'He hides the extra special vittles from me, you know: it'd take a Chinese pirate with a field gun to drag one crumb more than basic Board of Trade scales out of Henry Grubb an' that's a fact.'

'Oh, Grubby's not too bad,' the Mate temporised without too much conviction. 'He went out of his way to get us those extra eggs in New York, remember?'

'For which he fiddled the Owners five cents a dozen

cumshaw f'r himself – ten split atween him an' the agent . . . and anyway, them pilchards is in oil. I like my pilchards in tomato sauce, Mister Ellis. A nasty Dago habit: tinning 'em in oil.'

'Thought you said Henry had hidden them?'

The Captain smiled cleverly and right on cue; a triumphant, deceitful-little-boy smile visibly crinkling his monkey features in the moonlight. 'I said he'd hidden them, Mister; I didn't say I hadn't found 'em, did I?'

'Christ,' Ellis wearied. 'Here he is, in the middle of a freezing ocean and probably with U-boats watching us from all around, yet he's more engrossed in a pilchard war with his own Chief Steward than any prospect of Hitler's *Götterdämmerung*.'

But he knew that was neither fair nor true. This was *Olympian's* sixth North Atlantic convoy under Albert Burton's command: six voyages in which little Albert had stood fast as other ships exploded, friends of a lifetime had drowned, fellow masters had burned alive in swirling, spreading funeral pyres through which Burton had been forced to steer his own crumbling goliath because she was too bloody unmanoeuvrable to divert in the instant of a torpedo strike. But more than that – for war creates havoc with the laws of probability – each additional voyage shortened the odds against Captain Albert Burton and the good ship *Olympian* until, statistically, Albert must surely anticipate that he and his beloved command were destined eventually to sleep together under the sea forever.

Hadn't, for that matter, most of Ellis's shipmates devised some form of alternative preoccupation? Whether evinced in the Third Engineer's anti-social determination to master the ukelele-banjo or the Cook's fascination with religion; Ordinary Seaman Talleyrand's poetic scribblings, Spark's tongue–protruding devotion to constructing a matchstick model of the ship – Donkeyman Rumbelow's even more enthusiastic devotion to his collection of pornographic post-

27

cards – or the Captain's ongoing kippers versus tripe versus Chief Steward Grubb vendetta?

While Ellis had never been quite certain what manner of diversion he himself should pursue he recognised deep down, that he might be well advised to choose one; preferably before some less-welcome abstraction took precedence – an obsession, for instance, with the laws governing statistical probability?

Already he was becoming ever more conscious that he, Chief Officer David Ellis, had also taken part in those first five North Atlantic convoys in *Olympian*. And was sailing in her now, close alongside a mathematically-doomed Albert, on yet another.

He lit a cigarette, shading the flare of the Swan Vestas below the level of the canvas dodger; concealing the glowing tube in cupped hand as he drew on it. Lord, but it really was a bright night for the time of year: Jerry wouldn't need the minute spark of some carelessly-exposed Players Navy Cut to fix their position; even without the night-coated 7 x 50 Barr and Strouds in the bridge box Ellis could detect white water marking the bow wave of the solitary corvette over a mile ahead, cutting from right to left across the track of the steadily steaming ranks of merchantmen on yet another fruitless ASDIC sweep – fruitless because they needed a hell of a lot more than one specialist anti-submarine hunter like *Apple Blossom* to purify every sector of adjacent sea under which a first-strike U-boat group might be lying in wait.

Apple Blossom? Jesus, some of the names the Royal Navy gave to their little ships were hardly calculated to inspire confidence in the merchant seamen who depended upon them. 'Flower Class corvettes' they were hurriedly being cobbled together as. Yeah, well, there you were then . . . I mean – *Flower* Class?

For no real reason Ellis found himself screwing his head round and gazing up at *Olympian's* funnel, spiralling reg-

28

ularly against the luminous sky. He could even make out the distortion of the stack's circular rim where a gunmetal deadlight from the *Empire Drysdale* had struck it two convoys ago. She'd been a mile and a half from them at the time, the *Drysdale*. The deadlight had been charring steadily through *Olympian's* pine boat-deck planking, still glowing a dull red when they discovered it – the only tangible reminder that eleven thousand tons of structure, ammunition and people had ever existed at all.

Ellis automatically scanned the HT aerial and jumper stay, then ran his eye down the stubby mainmast to the tattered Red Ensign listlessly rising and falling to cut the empty black horizon astern. From their position in the rear rank of the convoy there was nothing out there, only their wake fading into featureless sea and a gathering of heavy, rolling cloud seemingly sliding into place to shroud their passing.

It was as though everything was composed of shapes without any depth to them in the blackout. As if they fought a totally flat war out there during an Atlantic night without steaming lights or deck lamps, not even the warm yellow gleam of portholes and engineroom skylights to give objects substance. The entire ship appeared to have been reduced to a two-dimensional world inhabited by two-dimensional men; characterless silhouettes of rigging and winches and watchkeepers; ventilators and rails; lifeboats already strangely unfamiliar because none of them had ever quite got used to their being swung permanently out-board and prepared for instant abandoning . . .

'Now goulash is nice, Mister Ellis,' the flat Captain Burton murmured nostalgically beside him. 'What d'you reckon to a dish o' proper Hungarian goulash, eh?'

Chief Officer Ellis took it as a rhetorical question and hopefully ignored it. He still stayed out there beside the Old Man though: he felt strangely disinclined to go below despite having spent four hours on that chill open bridge deck already, aggravated by the strains of ocean convoy station-keeping which never eased despite familiarity.

Oh, it wasn't anything to do with statistics – or not in the context of personal fear, anyway. While Ellis's courage could falter as easily or hold as resolutely as any man's, he, at least, had the good fortune to be a fatalist regarding his whereabouts in the ship should the ultimate horror occur. Some men – usually seamen or stewards, for engineers by definition spent most of their lives trapped within a thundering steel cocoon anyway – eventually found themselves unable to face the very real prospect of confinement within a sinking vessel. It wasn't a unique occurrence, especially on deck-rounds in the middle of the night, to come across a figure swathed in blankets and huddling silently in the lee of deckhouse or skylight, whereupon, if you'd any sense at all, you'd pretend not to notice, or merely pass by with some casual comment on the weather or on the ships about you as though it was the most unremarkable thing in the world to meet a man attempting to freeze himself to death.

No: while David Ellis was certainly loathe to retire below because of the butterfly within him, his reluctance on that particular night was caused more by a psychological desire to be ready; to be metaphorically booted and spurred and fully aware of what was happening in the moment that it occurred. To Ellis the real nightmare of an attack lay in not knowing instantly what was happening about you: in the seemingly interminable seconds when you found yourself snapped from exhaustion-induced sleep, eyes staring unseeingly while your drugged senses registered the first slam of a shock-wave against the hull as some ship on the other side of the convoy erupted without warning . . . and then the blood-freezing secondary doubt – *had* it been from the other side of the convoy, or had it been your own next-ahead? Were you, too, targeted in the U-boat's first spread of eels: his initial welcome to *das Todesloch*?

It was the anticipation of that specific moment which

disturbed Ellis: that split second of incomprehension, of ignorance during which the animal fear exploded like a great mushroom within him and he would find himself clawing from his bunk, scrambling for his lifejacket, hurling into the alleyway outside his cabin and into a world of jostling bug-eyed mirror images of himself, each heading frantically for some emergency station until suddenly, guiltily, they all became aware of their collective insanity. Usually dignity – the awareness of image – took control by then and men smiled with self-conscious embarrassment; even made jokes without real humour, forced themselves to move in orderly fashion though they were still screaming deep down . . .

Ellis didn't want any part of that again: tonight he'd determined to prepare, at least psychologically, for what the butterfly told him must be the inevitable. For over twelve days the convoy had pushed its luck: the Air Gap had almost been bridged; Rockall would be but a spit on the bow within another fifty-odd hours steaming, protection offered by the Londonderry-based UK escorts even before then. The trouble was that Dönitz must know all that too: 'Onkel Karl' *had* to have gathered his boats together by now. Experience – the bitterness of resignation – told Ellis the packs just had to be ready and waiting somewhere out there, in the dark sea not too far ahead.

The zig-zag clock tinkled and the Second Mate's low helm order came from the wheelhouse. Ellis felt *Olympian* lean perceptibly to port as her head came round, obediently trailing the column as the massive rectangle of darkened vessels pivoted on its right hand upper corner and continued to move sideways across the ocean. Again it was smoothly done; no panic-inducing rogues, no whistle-blaring runaways: they were all becoming practised, after twelve days of each other's lethal proximity, in the skills of tempting providence.

Or at least in the technical and ship-handling skills

demanded by convoy work, Ellis reflected wryly: presumably only the foolish and the complacent ever graduated in the art of being a collective target. It was never easy to tell how his fellow seafarers were taking the strain – other than when he chanced upon one of these nocturnal deck sleepers, or even some shipmate quietly standing by the rail and gazing out over the convoy with unseeing eyes. The seamen about him seldom dropped their guard, revealed their true state of mind during the vacuum before a half-expected attack. So, in an odd sort of way, no-one was brave, yet everyone was brave – apart from Ellis himself, of course: Ellis knew that *he* wasn't brave; that he just had to be the most unvaliant man aboard *Olympian*; probably the most nervous, apprehensive man in the whole convoy, come to that . . . mind you, Chief Officer Ellis, like nearly every other man around him, was buggered if he was goin' to let anyone else see his weakness!

The Old Man was still leaning easily over the rail, eyes absently fixed on the bulk of their next-ahead, thinking wistfully, no doubt, of galley stores jammed to the deckheads with tasty vittles and of fantasy Chief Stewards who fawned and simpered before their vessel's master; bestowing upon him a thousand gastronomic delights in order to gain his royal favours . . . not jus' slam a cracked plate of curry and rice – 'ratchet and hailstones' to a proper tramp steamer man – before him at breakfast with a curt, 'Thass it, Captin . . . an' if you wants seconds, don't bother askin' cause there ain't none. Oh, an' we run out o' mango chutney, the chef's down wi' food poisonin' again and the bloody spuds is gone rotten in the veg locker!'

Yet maybe, for that matter, little Albert Burton wasn't really thinking about food at all: maybe Albert, too, was only giving a calculated impression of unconcern. In the North Atlantic of 1941, in *das Todesloch* of the Bone Collectors, a British merchant master's courage demanded, above all else, a reassuring face . . .

A splash of white beyond the bow momentarily drew Ellis's attention, but that was precisely what it was supposed to do. Each ship in the convoy streamed a drogue – usually an empty barrel – from its counter to facilitate station-keeping for the watchkeeper astern: keep the skip of the marker discernible even on the darkest night, just over your bow, and you knew you weren't creeping up on your next ahead. That and a shaded blue sternlight was your only defence against an over-running collision.

That particular barrel did indeed trail in the wake of *Olympian's* next ahead at convoy position Number 34, indicating her as being the fourth ship in the third column – a tired old goalposter called *Duella*. By chance she and *Olympian* had become joint veterans of the same North Atlantic convoy trail: this SC represented their fourth voyage in close company and in a strange sort of way this factor had taken on a significance for both complements; each had begun, subconsciously, to equate their own prospects for survival with the other's continuing existence; each crew had watched their opposite numbers sail into a hundred nights of flash-rent darkness only to reappear again as the next dawn revealed stark gaps, sometimes listing hulls, occasionally mute columns of black-coiling smoke in the serried ranks of ships.

Yet *Duella* had always survived. And the fortitude of those aboard *Olympian* had been bolstered accordingly.

But each of the vessels before Ellis possessed some special qualities. Two ahead and leading *Duella*, for instance, plodded an even more exhausted 1905-built *Joan M* at position 33 – column three again; third in line – who, on the fourth day out had fallen astern wreathed in clouds of steam to become a straggler, only to catch up again eighteen hours later, shuddering in every rivet with a great white bone in her teeth, her Old Man looking argument-triumphant on her bridge an' her Chief sitting black-faced on the safety valve, just as everyone was debating whether she'd sunk of old age before – or from surface gunfire after – Jerry's 'Tail-end Hans' had caught up with her.

Three ships up the line from Ellis and *Olympian* wallowed a Scandinavian aviation-spirit tanker called *Tunfisk*, well-decks almost permanently awash under her weight of flashpoint-lethal cargo. A prime target, being one of only two tankships in SC whatever, there were a few men in the dry cargo fleet who'd have changed places with those free Danish merchant mariners in *Tunfisk*. Many were secretly relieved she wasn't their own next-ahead: stricken avgas carriers had an unfortunate habit of involving fellow travellers in their cremation.

Finally, way ahead and leading Column Three was the three-island steamer *Antisthenes* which, in an earlier incarnation as the *Magdeburg* had already survived World War One under the flag of Kaiser Bill only to be seized in reparation immediately after. But a change of identity appeared to be all in a decade's work for the crumbling *Antisthenes* – according to Lloyds' List she'd also sailed the seven seas as the *Eskisehir*, the *São Vicente*, the *Chinghai* and *Lafferty's Pride*.

'Christ knows what Lafferty had to be proud about,' Ellis had reflected disbelievingly when she'd first moved slowly into the Cape Breton assembly anchorage. Dirty, rust-caked, inordinately ugly even to the most generous of seamen's eyes with her spindle stack and her up-and-down stem and her battered slab sides, it was rumoured that the only reason her Old Man could sign a crew was because she invariably dropped out of the convoy within the first twenty-four hours anyway. They'd been trying to get her across the Atlantic for four months now: until this present voyage she hadn't even made it as far as Newfoundland's Cape Race without limping back for repairs.

Yet now she was up there in front, still steaming and somewhat bemused by her own tenacity – to say nothing of the disconcertment evident among her habitually shore-

34

bound complement, unexpectedly betrayed into becoming real deepwater sailormen again.

'Lord, if ever a nation really is scraping the bottom of the tonnage barrel then we are,' Ellis brooded sombrely. 'Forced to depend on relics like *Antisthenes* . . .'

He smiled suddenly, inwardly. It was ironic in a way: crews in the faster, more modern HX convoy ships must have felt precisely the same professional condescension for Chief Officer Ellis's own faded *Olympian*.

'Now Father would've produced some profound observation on those in posh ships, as opposed to us in ordinary down-at-heel ships, as opposed to those poor bastards out there in plain bloody appalling ships!' Ellis deliberated. 'But Father always was a great philosophiser on the Human Condition . . .'

'Never consider yourself the most unfortunate, whatever your circumstances,' Father would have uttered portentously, wisping tobacco-brown moustache still foam-flecked from his nightly jug of penny ha'penny ale. 'A cat may well gaze at a King with reverence, boy; but remember – that same insignificant creature can look with equal contempt upon the mouse which cowers before its glare.'

The young Ellis never did understand what curious impulse prompted Father to offer obscure and, if truth be told, pompous observations on nothing and yet everything in particular – other than, or course, that Arthur William Ellis was a thoroughly pompous man, and one who undoubtedly considered that persistent lessons of that nature could only lead to the future betterment of his children. Neither, for that matter, had David ever quite understood his father's preoccupation with social status.

One might have thought that Ellis senior had made his way in life a long time before; rising above the hopeless poverty of their Salford slum environment by tenacity of purpose. From being the eldest son of an itinerant 'sand

35

bone' man – hawking sand from a handcart for alehouse floor coverings together with brownstone and blue mould for every socially-aware Victorian family's Saturday morning ritual of scrubbing and scouring whatever width of public pavement happened to form their crumbling frontage – he had soon moved to a stall down in the poverty-nauseous Flatiron Market where, as was the custom of his day, he'd sold 'slink' – the flesh of still-born animals – along with 'braxy', the mutton from sheep dead of disease or suffocation, to those even poorer than he.

Even then one might have considered that Arthur William Ellis was in the ascendance. By the mid-1890's, when Father finally deigned to marry the mouse who was to be Chief Officer Ellis's mother, he was the twenty-four year old proprietor, not of one but of two Flatiron stalls, the second purveying a range of comestibles sadly familiar to any impecunious slum dweller at the turn of the century. Parings of tripe, flavourless tinned boiled mutton, black treacle, last week's bread, cotton seed cooking oil, fatty bacon, cups of vinegar sauce and formaldehyde-grey skimmed milk floating with the noxious dust of that northern industrial ghetto . . .

On Saturday nights, in that period while he remained a rising Man of the People, Arthur's local hostelry was agog with reverential listeners – many of them of considerable substance in their own local right: drovers, semi-skilled factory hands; carters with whips still hung around beefy necks . . . all anxious to glean some small pointer to the path of material and social acquisition.

'To *be* successful,' Father would pronounce, by then ostentatiously consulting a genuine Lewis's Five Shilling Watch dangling from a copper chain, 'one must first *appear* successful.'

No-one quite understood what he meant, but it surely must have contained the essence of acumen. In 1901, in the very year in which Victorians became Edwardians and some eighteen months before the embryo that would become Chief Officer David Ellis was conceived, Ellis senior resolutely cast off what he'd considered as the social millstone of his hawker past and opened a Permanent Establishment: a little corner shop, a veritable emporia of food stuffs and patent liniments, of gobstoppers and black twist tobacco and tin cufflinks and grate polish.

Arthur William Ellis had finally become a Self Made Man.

Ellis – the two-dimensional Ellis of Atlantic War '41 – drew on the stub of his cigarette, holding it below the level of the dodger and close to his wrist watch. The fleeting incandescence showed twenty-nine minutes past eight.

The Old Man still leaned, engrossed in thought, over the starboard rail: Ellis knew he'd be going below shortly, but only for a ritualistic change of garments and to freshen for the coming night. Burton never left *Olympian's* bridge for longer than it took to shave, not while they were in the Air Gap. Not while they were in U-boat waters of any kind, and that meant virtually nineteen days of charthouse catnapping for Albert Burton.

'D'you want me to hang on until you've been down?' the Mate asked diffidently.

'You're off watch, Mister Ellis. And Mister Cowan's quite capable.'

'Aye, aye, sir!' Ellis nodded, automatically responding to the Old Man's mood. Normally they had a fairly informal relationship when out of earshot of the rest of the crew but occasionally Albert would inject a note of shipboard protocol, just to maintain a proper balance. 'Then I'll go and tidy up. Hunt a mug of cocoa.'

He hesitated, gazing for the last time over the steadily steaming ranks of silent blacked-out ships before walking stiffly to the head of the ladder. He understood the Old Man's formality then; learned that Albert hadn't really been thinking about food at all. Burton's parting observation followed him through the darkness. Matter of fact; almost an idle speculation.

'I'm inclined to think they'll come tonight, Mister Ellis.'

Chief Officer Ellis didn't need to ask who the Captain meant. He shrugged and said, 'Aye, sir. Probably,' Without turning back. Just as levelly, just as if they were discussing the weather. Then slid calmly down the ladder.

It was half past eight in the evening.

Two

~~~~~~

'Convoy composition now reported as
30-plus coffins: 2 pall-bearers. U-boat
Operational Groups *Seeräuber*, *Kriegführend*
and *Jagduhr* will close and engage. Message
ends.'

8.30 p.m.: One Bell in the 8 to 12 Night Watch.

Ellis paused at the bottom of the flying bridge ladder,
briefly captured by the continuous background of twitter
and squeal filtering from the radio room. He'd always
hesitated there, and in his other vessels before *Olympian*,
when the Sparks was on listening watch. In peacetime a
ship's bi-valve receiver had acted as a comforting reminder
that another world did exist outside the confines of their
immediate horizon. The simple act of eavesdropping still
intrigued him, only things were different now: the exigencies of war prevented all but emergency traffic from ships at
sea; each careless radio transmission offered an electronic
invitation from a potential target. While operators aboard
every vessel still maintained listening periods, radio silence
was mandatory unless attacked. Now only occasional staccato bursts of keyed morse interspersed the Harpies' song
from the ether. Only too often, even then, they would
project a cry for help rather than reassurance . . .
    . . . *pedoed and sinking 28 miles WNW Rockall . . . ! . . .
ire out of control in engineroom: bomb damage to bridge . . . !
. . . RRRR – am being attacked by surface raider. Master
dead; 4 officers, 7 ratings missing . . . ! . . . AAAA – estimate
12-plus aircraft in second wave. Escort burning fiercely . . . !*

*SOS . . . SOS de MV Segura Star. Bows blown off by mine in
position 56 deg 23 min nor . . . ! . . . forward bulkheads going:
all lifeboats destroyed. Am abandoning. My positio . . .*

Two convoys ago Ellis had actually been present in the
radio room when Willie Pemberton – *Olympian's* only
wireless officer – had stiffened abruptly in mid-conversa-
tion, pushed his little matchstick model away and leaned
forward with fingers lightly compressing his earphones.
Then he'd begun to scribble with a frown which was
perplexed at first, before slowly deepening.

Finally Willie stopped writing and just sat there looking
sick. Ellis had wondered why at first: while, even to
untrained ears the signal strength was obviously fading,
nevertheless the static-tortured bursts of morse were still
crackling through the speaker. It was a long time before
Sparks handed him the signal, yet Ellis never pressed for
it: the expression in Pemberton's eyes had been too
harrowed.

The anonymous telegraphist hadn't been sending in
message format: he'd just been talking aloud; chatting,
really, to any other operator who happened to be listening.
He wasn't asking them to take any action – there wasn't
anything they could do – while it couldn't have mattered
any longer whether or not he was offering himself as a
target.

*. . . timber deck cargo lifted over WT room by blast. Think
everything's burning . . . lads forced to abandon: not much time
lef . . . I can see the moon through the fracture . . . she's lying
over faster; aerials will short out soo . . . surance policy in top
drawer of dresse . . . ell her I still love he . . . orty degree list
now. More rumbles from belo . . .*

'It's my nightmare,' Willie had finally muttered in dull
recognition. 'Jesus Christ, Dave – that poor bastard's
actually living *my* own personal nightmare . . .'

'Dying it, too. Now! In this very moment while we stand
here,' Ellis amended silently, helplessly, as the transmission

40

had ceased abruptly and only the mocking ether chorus remained.

But he'd never said it out loud. Not to Radio Officer Pemberton. It seemed that Willie had been trapped in that capsizing radio room too many times already.

Second Engineer Ballantyne was playing draughts with Cadet Moberly when Ellis stuck his head into the dingy compartment on the lower bridge deck euphemistically known as the Officers' Smoking Room. The other apprentice, Junior Cadet Westall, was pretending to study at a battered writing desk while the Second Mate's long legs stuck out from under a yellowed copy of the *Scottish Daily Express*, the only tangible proof that a newspaper hadn't suspended itself in mid-air above the leather-buttoned starboard settee.

Ellis knew Cadet Westall was only pretending to study. Just as Westall knew that *Olympian's* Mate invariably glanced into the smoking room on his way to his cabin after he'd been relieved from the evening watch and had calculated, therefore, that Mister Ellis would note his academic application and be impressed by such assiduity.

What the precocious young Westall didn't know, or didn't have the brains to realise, was that Ellis was equally aware of the ploy: that the Mate had taken his measure within twenty-four hours of his joining as a first-tripper prior to their last Birkenhead sailing, and since confirmed him as a useless, scheming little bastard whose father had wasted a whole fifty pounds by indenturing him into the service of *Olympian's* Owners. Conscious of what was, at most, a thoroughly petty triumph, Ellis still felt a glow of satisfaction – Westall had wasted an extra half hour of play- acting tonight through his late arrival from the bridge.

He liked Moberly though: the senior apprentice had the right stuff in him to make a good ship's officer. *If* the war and the U-boats didn't get him before he could sit his ticket. Moberly looked up from the draughts board just then, and smiled a timid acknowledgement – whereupon suddenly, and for the most fleeting of moments, Ellis imagined he saw a drowned man's head bobbing on Moberly's nineteen-year-old shoulders: a grinning, vacuous mask of bone-yellow putrefaction with bright green seaweed entangling Moberly's floating yellow hair, and sea-worms pulsing and writhing within Moberly's empty eye sockets . . .

'Ohhh, *Jesus*!', Ellis postulated with a barely-restrained start, for what macabre trick of light had compelled him to visualise young Moberly like *that*?

Then the butterfly twitched once more to remind him it was the convoy's last night in the Air Gap and his unease, further reinforced by the Captain's parting prediction, welled to the surface. It was time to fight The Shivers again . . . He seemed to be fighting The Shivers a lot recently.

'Steady, Mate', Ellis told himself, smiling back at Cadet Moberly. 'Steady as you go, Mister. They look to you for reassurance every bit as much as you look to little Albert . . .'

Maybe . . . yeah, maybe he *should* take up a hobby at that. Then he recalled Sparks' shocked recognition – his haunted expression of *déjà-vu* during the electronic requiem of a lonely telegraphist – and realised that becoming absorbed in making a matchstick model still didn't prevent the mind of Radio Officer Pemberton from being trapped in a sinking ship every night he was at sea.

'Evenin' Dave,' the Second greeted him, and took one of Moberly's crowns with a superior flourish. Moberly sprang his trap, demolished three of Ballantyne's in return and won the game hands down. The Second Engineer looked piqued.

'Evening, Alec,' Ellis grinned.

Obnoxious Westall screwed his head round, gave a start of amazement that the Chief Officer should have caught him

42

studying yet *again*, and offered in modest confusion, 'Just glancing over densities and block coefficients, sir . . .'

'Try glancing *at* them, Westall,' Ellis retorted shortly. 'That way some of it might stick.'

The headlines across the Second Mate's *Scottish Daily Express* said 'Vichy orders reprisals: 100 BOMBS ON GIB IN FOUR HOURS: Dakar battle still raging: submarine sunk – Nazis at airfields'. Other masochistic front page news proclaimed *Butter ration 2 oz.* and *Fire shower on London: Bombs on SE Scotland: Mothers will be evacuees now*, plus the casual and uniquely British daily observation in the bottom-left corner – INVASION WEATHER: CALM. A further throw-away item in the red-printed Stop Press noted laconically: *German troops land in Finland.*

Sandwiched between imminent defeat and national disaster the Ministry of Information had fought back with stiff-upper-lip encouragement – *Banks to stay open during air raids . . . RAF batter Nazi invasion ports again . . . Girls ignore the sirens to help RAF!*

A fuzzy picture of rather bored figures wearing coalscuttle helmets and leaning on shovels amid what could just as easily have been a municipal rubbish tip was headed: THE RAF GIVE BERLIN ANOTHER TASTE OF IT!' the sabre-rattling sub-heading – *A shattered smouldering roof-top in Berlin after a British raid . . .* had been hurriedly qualified by the addition of . . . *the RAF would claim this a 'miss', as they aim their salvoes to hit military objectives only.*

The virtuous qualification was rather undermined in the final sentence, though. Some jubilant sub-editor hadn't been able to resist adding, . . . *but 'miss' or 'hit', it made a mess of this part of the German capital.*

David Ellis hadn't actually needed to refer to the column headings: he'd read them a hundred times. The one-penny Glasgow edition of the *Express* was months old already, dated Wednesday September 25, 1940. Mind you, the war news hadn't improved a bit since, so far as anyone knew.

Neither, presumably, had the Ministry of Information's clumsy propaganda techniques.

The yellowed pages lowered to reveal Second Officer McKerchar's expressionless gaze meeting his. 2/O McKerchar could surely have recited the whole text of that particular newspaper without batting an eyelid: he retreated behind it every evening after tea without volunteering a word to anyone in the smoking room. He'd been scrutinising all that had happened to an unhappy world on Tuesday the 24th of September, 1940, for weeks now, but maybe that was just McKerchar's form of psychological defence; a lazy man's alternative to making model ships or learning to play the ukelele-banjo.

Or maybe it wasn't. Maybe Second Officer McKerchar was simply, well . . . crazy? McKerchar had already been torpedoed once before – off the coast of Brazil, that had been. Fifty-eight days and nine curiously mutilated shipmates later they'd picked him off a hatchcover, reconstituted his dehydrated skeleton and sent him back to sea. Mind you, it was only rumour that the fleshy wounds gouged from sole survivor McKerchar's ghastly complement of cadavers had suggested more the slicing cut of a seaman's knife than the tearing of crustacean claws in the dark of the tropical night.

Ellis always felt disquiet in Second Officer McKerchar's company. He wouldn't have taken to him anyway: an abrasive, uncompromising man considerably older than Ellis even though his junior in rank, McKerchar never seemed to offer conversation. Any contact, no matter how casual, with *Olympian*'s Second Mate always left the impression of having been a confrontation while the legend of the raft didn't help either, rumour or not. Every seaman rating carried a sheath knife as standard practise when working on deck, but seldom did a ship's officer wear one – yet since his appointment to *Olympian* McKerchar always had: razor-honed and only loosely concealed under the folds of his brass-buttoned reefer. Even off watch. Even while staring cold-eyed into a bloody newspaper.

'By God,' Ellis acknowledged, forcing humour nevertheless, 'you spend a helluva lot of time on that crossword, Two Oh.'

The ship lurched on to yet another zig-zag course, lifting to a bigger than average swell from the nor'east. The suspended *Express* never faltered. Neither did McKerchar's masked stare.

'Ah checked the boat compasses this morning,' he said, the Glasgow accent harsh with bitterness. 'Some bastard's been drinking the alcohol out've Number Three's.'

'You sure?' Ellis responded wearily. 'Couldn't it have evaporated through the filler screw? You checked the leather washer, did you?'

'Ah checked the whole bluidy compass three days ago. It was fine then.'

So that was that – they had a real nutter aboard. Those boat compasses could represent the difference between survival and a lingering death for fifty-odd men should *Olympian* go down in mid-Atlantic – yet it seemed some irresponsible rummy had preferred the foulness of compass alcohol to hanging on a few days longer for a drink; had even been prepared, for that matter, to risk the violence of a focslehead lynch mob if he'd been caught red-handed while robbing the lifeboat. Not that he was likely to be: the blackout – Ellis's two-dimensional, featureless world of war – afforded privacy to the thief as well as to the fearful. It was only the work of moments in the middle of the night to drain a shipwrecked sailor's guide to salvation.

Ellis could only feel frustrated anger. Even discounting the ship's officers, there were still too many potential suspects among the crowd. Merchant seamen all too frequently drank themselves to the stage of leglessness when ashore; it provided temporary anaesthesia against the misery of their focslehead existence. The squalid conditions offered in any ship as old as *Olympian* – the lousy food, the cockroaches, the occasional bullying, the animal stench caused by the lack of hygiene: all that living and eating and sleeping and hating the Owners within a roller-coasting, condensation-beaded steel box with roaring sea the mere thickness of a rusted iron plate away and only a mildewed bunk clamped to the frames plus one dank drawer to call your own . . . Jesus, any man faced with surviving the truth, rather than the romanticised image of the sea, who kept on coming back for more, must have been tempted at some time or other to steal a little extra anaesthesia. It only required one rogue hard-case.

And hard cases? By God but there were plenty of them in the British merchant fleet; enough aboard *Olympian*, come to that. You only needed to watch the black gang signing on: the firemen and trimmers sent down from the pool; clambering bleary-eyed up yet another anonymous gangway clutching their pathetic fifty-three pieces – their pack of cards an' their discharge books representing the only worldly possessions they hadn't pawned for booze, to know what hard cases were. Scrawny undernourished little men most of 'em, but wiry as steel-stranded rope with the coal-dust engrained like tattoos under their eyelids and inside their ears. Hard cases? Jesus, some of those guys, you'd need the Brigade of Guards backing you before you'd take 'em on in an argument. Some of them'd sink the alcohol from a boat compass and then wash it down with a brasso an' bootpolish chaser.

'I'll talk to the Bosun,' Ellis growled. 'Maybe he can name a deckie. Can you finger a possible in your boys, Andy?'

'I c'n pass the word through the stokehold.' Ballantyne was noisily re-setting the draughts board, more preoccupied with scowling fiercely at Cadet Moberly as a psychological preliminary to round two than searching for a needle in a haystack. But then again, Second Engineer Ballantyne had never been adrift on a limitless ocean without a compass.

Yet.

'Ah'll just gut the bastard,' Second Officer McKerchar promised without a flicker of emotion, 'if ah find out who it was. Ah'll see the bastard sign off this ship in a wooden suit.'

The *Scottish Daily Express* rose into place, blanking off McKerchar's star and terminating the discussion. Ellis shivered: he must have got colder on the bridge than he'd realised.

He glanced at his watch as he left the absorbed occupants of the smoking room. The time was seventeen minutes to nine.

The Chief Officer's cabin in *Olympian* was situated starboard side forr'ad within the after funnel deck accomodation, a few feet abaft the slender stack itself. Number two lifeboat station lay directly above on the boat deck, its 23-foot, 30-person capacity boat war-ready and suspended in quadrantial davits. The rivet-punctuated inboard bulkhead of Ellis's berth formed part of the engineroom casing, his forward ports looked out over the bleak vista of the starboard coaling hatch, past the coaming of the Number Three hold and into the after face of the three-tiered bridge housing. That area of rusted deck separating the two main midships structures presented an obstacle course of derrick posts and funnel guys, bollards, coiled wire ropes, fire branches, ringbolts, vents for bunkers, vents for water tanks, vents for the paint store and the carpenter's shop and the barren two-bed hospital . . . the tarpaulin stowage . . . the machinery workshop – even vents ventilating spaces undreamed of by anybody other than *Olympian's* apparently vent-fixated designers and, of course, Chief Engineer Gulliver, keeper of the ship's plans and most intimate bodily secrets.

The door to Ellis's cramped living space opened on to the head of the starboard alleyway serving deck officer country. Immediately adjacent lay the Second Mate's even smaller cabin, then the Third's, with Cadets Moberly and Westall sharing what was little more than a two-berth cubbyhole squeezed between 3/0 Cowan and the steel box which – along with a red cracked-tile deck, three wash basins, one lavatory, one lion-footed cast iron bath and a web of dank, corroded piping – formed the mutual washroom.

The engineer officers lived along the port side alleyway in a mirror-image warren, with the Chief's cabin a handed copy of Ellis's; all lit by low-wattage bulbs protected behind wire grids and further depressed by the same monotonous livery of dark and light brown enamel. Only the Master's accomodation forward, within the bridge housing itself, boasted a few square feet of scarred wooden panelling, a private bathroom and the luxury of a separate bed and 'stateroom'. Grubby Grubb the Chief Steward lived up there, too, in metallic hutches along with the Bosun, the Carpenter and Robbo the Christ-oriented Cook while, as king of the centrecastle, high above everybody else in *Olympian* resided Radio Officer Pemberton; crammed into his squeal-filled box on the pilot bridge deck next to the telegraph room itself.

Ellis left the door ajar as he began to shave: Ellis always left his door either on the hook or dogged wide open now; privacy wasn't worth the risk of being trapped by an explosion-distorted cabin door. Oh sure, kick-out lower panels had been fitted for just such an emergency when the war began: Fred Knox, the Fourth Engineer, had even survived by scrambling through one when the *Malay Princess* was mined off Beachy Head. Knox had been changing his socks at the moment she blew – barefooted, he'd run all the way to his boat; the *Princess* had gone down, and they'd actually started to pull for the shore before he discovered that most of his right toes were fractured.

'Improvidence is the cancer of Life's grand endeavour', Father would have undoubtedly said of anyone so unprepared as to need to kick out a kick-out escape panel in the first place. 'Foresight and planning, my boy: the very rungs forming the ladder to success'.

That represented perhaps the only philosophy of Father's which Ellis *had* taken keenly to heart: planning for his future even as a child. Admittedly the means had been a little sketchy at first, but the intention had hardened from a very early age – to get as far away as possible and as soon as practical.

From Father himself!

The whole family – David's mother, his two sisters and himself – had lived unhappily in the autocratic shadow of the self-made Arthur William Ellis during those early years leading to the First World War.

It wasn't that he'd been a violent or deliberately cruel man, certainly not by the standards of the Edwardian under-privileged in which drink-inflamed child or wife-beating was an all-too-commonplace event. A moderate tippler, never exceeding his one quart of best ale on every week-day evening, Father had seldom laid a hand on any of his offspring: never once, in David's memory, had he physically harmed his wife.

But as the baby David became the child David, and then the schoolboy, he began to appreciate there were other, more subtle forms of cruelty, albeit unintended. Curiously enough success had appeared to temper, rather than fuel Father's early emphasis on the practical virtues of foresight and diligence and owning a Five Shilling Watch. David never quite understood why but it seemed that, despite the undoubted commercial success of the little Salford corner shop, a growing insistence on humility began to emerge as the dominating factor in Ellis Senior's paternalism – humility before God, humility before one's elders, humility in receiving food and clothing . . . even humility in being 'permitted' to work in the corner shop six nights per week after school; David running and fetching and sweating without payment in his tight-buttoned jacket and corduroy knee-breeches with the curled celluloid of his yellowing Eton collar burnishing a livid patch under his chin, while his sisters scrubbed and tended counter. Sometimes, domestic drudgery completed, the children were allowed to help maximise Father's profits by such prudent acts as trimming the maggot-infested parts of poorly cured ham before displaying it for another day's vending; penny-gains further enhanced by Arthur William's own sleight of hand, acquired from the Flatiron market, whereby he secreted a few ounces of fat bacon in the palm of his hand until, at the critical moment of weighing, he would stick it under the down side of the shop scales.

Perhaps most hurtful of all, was that 'Thank you very much, Father' was expected of the increasingly resentful David when Father occasionally, after a particularly satisfying day's trade, allowed him to open one of 'Waldo's Giant Ha'penny Lucky Bags' while Mother, flustered and suddenly guilty, busied herself in the back shop – knowing full well that Father had already searched to ensure that no surprise gift from Waldo would find its way into David's eagerly exploring fingers.

Later as he grew wiser, the adolescent David guessed that too, and looked appealingly toward his mother for an end to the cynical game. But Mother always avoided his mute appeal, for Mother was a sad, permanently forlorn creature who had adopted humility as a less contentious substitute for maternal protectiveness and thus had surrendered to, rather than curtailed, Arthur William's egocentricity.

He never perceived that there was a sad and very real desperation underlying Arthur William's despotism. In David's immature eyes Father's double-edged benevolence, his hypocritical exploitation of his issue, his insistence on familial humility within what was already a more than adequately humiliated community, appeared merely as calculated cruelty. Yet had the maturing David been a little more perceptive, a little more aware of the sociological pressures which the pre-First World War ghettos exerted on men desperate for pride – he might have understood that Father himself had learned that success had proved an empty triumph – that Arthur William Ellis discovered, too late, that no matter what material progress he made in life, the rigid social conventions of his own close society never would permit him to rise above the status of a jumped-up itinerant 'sand-bone man' in the eyes of his neighbours . . . and that his authoritarian bluster simply camouflaged a harsh kindness and was a misguided attempt to prepare his offspring for what he'd sincerely believed would also prove their disillusionment in later years.

Perhaps . . .

It was a cruel irony, had such been the case, that all Arthur William Ellis's paternalistic pressure ever accomplished was to turn his only son against him. And convinced the young David Ellis of the need to sever himself not only from his roots but also from that poverty-stricken shore before he would learn anything of significance.

In the event, it was to take the monstrous power of the sea to teach Chief Officer David Ellis the true meaning of 'Humility'.

The wind was freshening from the nor'east as Ellis stepped out to the funnel deck and walked forward to the galley. It was such a clear night he could see a face on the moon as it swayed across the sky in time with the gentle roll of the ship. Around and ahead of him the convoy looked peaceful and still: there was hardly any sense of forward motion; just bluff, clear-cut images of plodding merchantmen rising and falling, and rising again to the swell. There was little sound, certainly no evidence of there being two thousand living men within those battered shells; only the sigh of water passing along *Olympian's* hull and the occasional muffled rush as a wave larger than the rest curled back on itself in an

51

effervescence of excitement. Just that and the reciprocating pulse of the engine – nothing tangible, more an awareness as familiar, and therefore as unremarkable, as the steady beat of your own heart.

Robbo the Cook was still in the galley, chatting idly to Bosun Leather as he stirred something unspeakable in a great iron fanny. The Bosun was eating a bacon sandwich built like a block of flats. No-one else in *Olympian* got bacon other than for Sunday breakfast, and that included the Old Man. In fact, with Grubby Grubb sailing Chief Steward, that especially included the Old Man!

The heat from the coal-fired range struck Ellis when he stepped over the coaming and pushed through the curtained light trap. He noticed immediately that both petty officers had kept their life-jackets with them; they lay close to hand – grubby orange cushions with worn tape ties and *Board of Trade* stamped across them. Alf Leather and the Chef were seasoned convoy men – like Albert's prediction, their caution provided a further unsettling omen.

Leather's slab-cut sanny waved in shameless greeting. Bacon may well have represented the nectar of the Gods aboard hungry ships like *Olympian*, but any man as capable as Bosun Leather when it came to controlling her harder-boiled elements was worthy of deification.

'Evenin', Mister Ellis.'

'Bose . . . Chef.'

'Tea, coffee or a nice mug o' kai, sir?'

'Kai, please. Your own special brew.'

'Ask, and it shall be given you; seek, and ye shall find,' Cookie bowed cheerfully. 'Saint Matthew: seven, seven!'

'I wus an hundred, an' ye gave me meat; I wus thirsty, an ye gave me drink,' Leather intoned sonorously. '. . . thass a better one, Robbo – Matthew as well. Twenty five, thirty somethin' or other.'

Ellis grinned. The Chef looked flabbergasted. ''Ow d' you know, you bloody heathen? You ain't got religion.'

Leather poked his bacon wad at the ready-use Bible lying open on the chopping block. 'Some chefs,' he said caustically, 'would've been readin' a *cook'ry* book while they wus spoilin' tomorrow's dinner.'

'I don't use no cookery books,' Robbo retorted equably.

'That's f'r bloody sure,' the Bosun growled, squinting into the pot.

Cookie took a mug like a chipped white dustbin from the fiddle, spooned three ladlefuls of cocoa into it, added enough sugar to sweeten a barracuda's rage, topped up with boiling water from a soot-black kettle and stabbed two holes in a tin of condensed milk with the point of Leather's marline spike. He handed the tin and the mug of brown sludge to the Mate with a flourish.

'You might care to add your own connie, sir. I doesn't want to overdo it.'

'Positively cordon bleu, Chef.' Ellis sniffed uncertainly.

'I wus with Cunard White Star, you know,' the Cook admitted modestly.

'As a coal trimmer,' the Bosun reminded him.

'Now *there* is a friend, which is only a friend in name,' Robbo sighed, more in sorrow than resentment. 'Ecclesiasticus thirty seven . . . ah . . . one.'

Chief Officer Ellis lifted the steaming mug to his lips. The Cook would've got on well with Father. He blew cautiously, anticipatorily . . .

The first explosion, when it came, sounded a long way away.

Ellis was more than thankful that he hadn't turned in. That distant overture to the long-awaited attack scared the hell out of him enough as it was.

Three

'Unless you are signalled to do otherwise, all merchant ships will maintain rigid station in the event of an attack. Notwithstanding that, gentlemen: should you be torpedoed and find it impossible to save your vessel . . . then you have my reluctant authority to sink!'

Convoy Commodore: pre-sailing conference

9.00 p.m.: Two Bells in the 8 to 12 Night Watch.

When the group in *Olympian's* galley heard the U-boats' greeting – physically sensed it for that matter, as little tinkles and movements came from pot lids and saucers and dangling utensils while the expanding shock wave from the still-anonymous casualty raced excitedly across the ship in convoy – none of them moved quickly. There wasn't any point in moving quickly. Nothing could be done which hadn't already been done; it hadn't happened to them, and there wasn't anywhere to move to which offered greater safety. And anyway, if such a refuge *had* existed, then it would have been bloody well full to capacity long before now.

The Cook just muttered 'Shit!' – but in the most Christian manner, mind. Perhaps not even swearing so much as indicating a sudden need.

'Port side. Up among the leaders,' Leather speculated levelly, sandwich crust doubling as a compass needle. 'Someone near the Vice-commodore, I'd reckon.'

The Cook replaced the lid on tomorrow's dinner, then

54

began to slip his lifejacket over his head: still not hurried, almost with casual resignation. Ellis kept his voice under control. 'Now it's started the Captain'll want an extra couple of hands turned out for submarine watch. May as well anticipate him, Bose.'

The Bosun grinned: it helped Ellis's jangling nerves a lot. 'You'll 'ave two dozen pair o' eyes up there already . . . But I'll see to it anyway, sir.'

Ellis still held on to the mug of steaming cocoa as he moved towards the curtain: he didn't want them to guess how nervous he really was. Leather and Robbo stood calmly by the range, waiting for him to step on deck first – not wanting the Chief Officer to see how nervous *they* really were. The Cook was grumbling under his breath, struggling to cross the tapes of his lifejacket behind him and tie them at the front all at the same time. It wasn't easy, with the Cook's stomach.

'You should leave that, Robbo: take yer Bible instead,' Ellis heard the Bosun observe bitterly as he followed him over the coaming. 'The way you taken to that religious stuff: if we do cop it tonight – you'll be able to bloody *walk* home!' He noticed that Bosun Leather had brought his lifejacket too, though. Dangling loosely, a bit self-consciously, by its tapes.

Initially, even when their eyes had grown accustomed to the darkness, they could detect nothing untoward as they leaned over the rail to peer tensely ahead, out towards the port corner of the still steadily steaming rectangle. At first sight, Convoy SC whatever-it-was appeared to be continuing its silent progress as if nothing violent had occurred at all.

Ellis knew the attack *had* begun, though. And that a lot of things were happening simultaneously even though they, aboard the majority of the merchant vessels, could only wait.

★ ★ ★

For one thing, he knew that somewhere over there and not much more than a mile away, seamen – carbon copies of himself – would almost certainly be stumbling shocked along blast-contorted and suddenly unfamiliar decks; bleeding, scalded, choking in the after-reek of high explosive; wrestling with religiously-tested lifeboat falls which Sod's Laws of the sea endowed, nevertheless, with the unyielding properties of steel-stranded wire at the moment when you so desperately needed them. That other men – sinew-bulging, coal-blackened men in frayed canvas trousers and sweat rags and sudden pitch darkness – could well be fighting waist-deep through roaring water while Chief Officer Ellis watched with a mug of cocoa in his hand: hopelessly clawing for oil-shiny ladders lying further and further towards the horizontal with every nightmare tick of a doomed ship's chronometer.

Ellis could also guess from past experience at other events gathering momentum outwith his immediate vision.

The convoy escort commander would have reacted instantly, automatically. Little *Apple Blossom* would already be slicing towards the U-boat's estimated ambush position, her echoing electronic pulse of ASDIC probing the cold waters for what would almost certainly have been a hit and dive Hun in this preliminary stage of the battle; hard-eyed young officers on the corvette's postage stamp bridge praying tensely for an all-too-infrequent *Submarine contact, sir! Range and bearing* . . . Aboard both her and her Royal Canadian Navy counterpart – that outrageous armed trawler *Trois-Rivières* – the watches below would be racing to action stations; special sea dutymen closing to wheel and engine controls, gun decks, depth charge racks . . . alarm bells strident with urgency; crisp, economic commands; seaboots thumping on ladders as steel helmets clamped yet again to weary heads, salt-stiff oilskins dragged for the hundredth time over aching limbs. Not for the Fleet the soul-destroying passivity forced on the merchant ship crews: the misery for the North Atlantic escort matelot was a different kind of suffering; an endurance of exposure, of alarm-shattered cat naps and the stress of unremitting vigilance.

One merchantman's bridge would have 'closed-up' in the military sense as well by now – Archie Mulligan's veteran *Pendragon*: Convoy Number 41; lead vessel in the fourth column. The ocean-scarred Steamship *Pendragon* carried the Commodore, Rear Admiral Sir Joseph Edmund Chanders, KBE, CB, RN Ret'd, and his Royal Navy signals staff of five. They, apart from a handful of war reserve gunners spread through the few cargo vessels fitted with any form of weapon, were the only professional fighting men in SC whatever's mercantile lines.

Unusually for a run-of-the-mill convoy Chief Officer, David Ellis had met this particular Commodore. Albert had suffered one of his occasionally-recurring bouts of malaria on the eve of departure – twelve hours of sweating, bunk-bound, childishly ill-tempered protest – and as a consequence, Ellis had been required to deputise for the Old Man at the Master's pre-sailing conference in Cape Breton. It had been the first time he'd been given an opportunity to observe at close quarters the man who would carry the responsibility for himself and his two thousand fellow merchant seamen during the forthcoming nineteen days.

He'd seen a bluff-bowed seahorse of indeterminate years, recalled like many senior ex-Naval officers at the outbreak of war, given the temporary appointment of Commodore, Royal Naval Reserve, and despatched to sea in command of equally elderly Trade convoys: sailing this time not in the giant battleships or cruisers which had befitted their previous rank but in the cramped, miserable accomodation offered by the very tramps they shepherded. Salty, bulldog-tenacious men were the Convoy Commodores; literally commuting back and forth across the lethal North Atlantic with their temporary charges; living almost permanently on open bridge wings in conditions which taxed men twenty years their junior, with the arthritic squeaks ignored in their knee joints and their white hair fuzzing from under their once discarded uniform caps . . . and the pure joy of being wanted once again in eyes wise and experienced.

They'd had to develop a unique sense of humour too, the Commodores; pitch-forked into the sterile, sometimes even hostile environment of the average cargo steamer after lifetimes as socially sophisticated warship officers. The traditional suspicion of the British Merchant Navy for anything which dressed posh and saluted made bloody sure they'd needed to.

Archie Mulligan of *Pendragon* had been like that: unwelcoming. He hadn't wanted to be no flag-wagging Commodore Ship. He didn't want to sail in no bloody Grey Funnel Line convoy at all, come to that. Archie was living proof of the maxim that the only thing containing more obscenities than a Royal Naval officer's opinion of a Merchant Navy officer is a Merchant Navy officer's description of an RN officer.

'So what do you do for on-board entertainment in the long winter evenings, Captain Mulligan?' Rear Admiral Sir Joseph Chanders, KBE, CB, RN not-quite-retired-after-all, was reputed to have asked jovially, probably trying to break the ice as he'd slung his kit up the gangway of Archie's ocean-going scrapyard before sailing.

Mulligan hadn't smiled a bit. From cabin boy all the way up to master in two million miles of deep sea steaming Archie Mulligan had never been known to smile at another human being; sure as hell there wusn't no brass-bound adm'ral goin' to spoil a record like that.

'I lies in me bunk, mister,' Archie retorted pithily, as full of fun as a Chinese undertaker. 'An' the ship's orchestra plays me off ter sleep. Wiv a lullaby.'

The Commodore returned Mulligan's stare with equanimity: not revealing the slightest hint of discomfiture. 'Your

First Mate?' he'd interpreted solemnly. 'You mean he really *can* play the banjo?'

Captain Mulligan had eyed his Very Important Guest for a full expressionless minute before a crease – a completely virgin and never-before-observed crinkle – appeared at the corners of his mouth.

'Me Chief Engineer. 'E's a bloody virtuoso on the jew's harp. Welcome aboard, Adm'ral!'

They usually got on very well together in the end. The Merchant Navy and the Commodores . . .

Commodore Chanders up ahead in *Pendragon* would be playing a very different psychological game now, even as Ellis waited for confirmation of a ship's death. Metaphorically, the Rear Admiral had been forced into the situation of a goalkeeper preparing to defend against a penalty kick: no certainty as to which way to leap to intercept his opponent's ball; no way of anticipating him. Had, for instance, that explosion represented an initial strike by a full attack group, or merely a feint intended to divert them into the jaws of the real U-boat trap? Where might the main pack of predators be gathered – to the north, or to the south of the convoy's present track? Should he order an alteration of course to port or to starboard in order to avoid or at least minimise, the promised holocaust?

And what should the Commodore order his flock to do if there was a whole pack of wolves out there in the night? If *die Rudeltaktik* proved totally successful this time? If it had spawned an assembly numerous enough to lie in wait for them both to port *and* to starboard?

'Sir!'

Bosun Leather had tensed. Ellis followed his pointing finger. One of the black paper ships in the port column had perceptibly begun to fall astern. Even as they watched a red light snapped on at her masthead while the first of two rockets soared from her bridge – the prescribed: 'I have

59

been torpedoed' signals. Whatever nationality her watch-keeper, Ellis took his hat off to the man: that was calm professionalism being displayed out there ... Simul-taneously the victim's siren began to boom ominously in short bursts, warning her trailing sisters to keep clear. No flames, though – no firm indication yet of a mortal wound.

'*Naiad*?'

'I'd guess at *Hecuba*, Mister Ellis. Next astern of the Vice. Dutch flag.'

Ellis felt relieved it wasn't *Naiad*. He'd known her Mate, Jim Skelly, for years: they'd even had a drink together as recently as Sydney, baiting each other about *Naiad's* master being appointed Vice-commodore.

'You've got to admit it's a compliment to Naval Control's perception – recognising superior seamanship and ability,' Jim had jeered cheeerfully.

David Ellis hadn't been able to help feeling a little bit piqued. Well, it *would* have been nice just for once – Mate of the Vice-commodore's ship. 'Crap, Jimmy! It's only 'cause you happen to be the largest of the five Glasgow-bound leavers. They don't give you any Naval staff, nothing special.'

'There's no getting away from it. Some of us are simply destined for greatness,' Skelly parried loftily.

'. . . some have greatness thrust upon 'em! You'll be right in it if the Admiral goes bang and your Old Man has to take command of the whole convoy. He'll ask questions: you'll have a pile of indecipherable confidential books, a frozen brain, an' no bloody answers.'

Presumably only four leavers now for Jim Skelly's ship to lead whenever – or should it be 'if' ever – they reached the Glasgow departure point off the UK. Certainly it seemed that *Hecuba's* sailing orders had been violently amended.

A low warship profile slid in the opposite direction going fast, shaving the northern perimeter of the phalanx: the corvette making her brief defensive lunge for the U-boat.

No doubt the *Trois-Rivières* was out there too; an ill-equipped warrior yet still momentarily forcing the hunter into the role of the hunted. Abruptly the deck below their feet began to throb with a new urgency; steadily climbing to a level of seldom-felt vibration. The forgotten mug in David Ellis's hand started to rattle against the scarred rail; juddering, concentric rings of syrup-thick cocoa expanding to reflect the waxen moonlight. The convoy was increasing speed. At the same time he sensed the ship leaning to port. They were turning; the Commodore was diverting south and away from the source of the attack.

'Maybe there's just the one sub,' Robbo muttered. Only the Cook could've made it sound quite so much like a prayer.

The casualty was rapidly falling abeam of *Olympian* now, the optical effect created by the convoy's turn to starboard giving her the illusion of actually sailing sternwards. For the first time they could observe her overall silhouette, clearly detached from the huddled protection which her scurrying sisters had proved unable to afford her.

'Aye, it wus the Dutchman, all right,' Leather confirmed. 'Didn't *Naiad* have two sets of samson posts forr'ad of the bridge?'

'She's down by the head already,' Ellis muttered. 'Well down.'

The Bosun started to say 'Them poor bastards is goin' to nee . . .' when a sharp report cracked across the lines of black ships and a great white spluttering light exploded in the sky, abruptly slamming Ellis's two-dimensional world into glaring incandescent relief. Moments later there was another, and a third, until the whole sea area was illuminated in eerie flickering detail.

'*Jesus!*' the Chef snarled involuntarily, then tacked on a hurried, '. . . Christ our Saviour an' Protector.'

Ellis had to smile. Strained, but he had to smile to himself.

'Snowflake, yer great Nancy,' Leather growled acidly.

'You seen it often enough – snowflake an' starshell. The boys is gettin' trigger-happy. Merchant gun crews. Bloody show-offs! They gotter put on a Brock's firework benefit if they as much as suspect a U-boat in the bloody Atlantic! Never seems to strike 'em that Jerrie c'n see us now better'n we c'n see him.'

It was only jealousy. He'd have loved to own a gun himself, Bosun Leather, for all his show of disgust; even an antiquated 4.7-inch stern chaser like the lads across in *Stafford Pride*, Bone Collector to the next column to starboard, had acquired. The old reprobate had hung around *Olympian's* foc'slehead all that day while the Canadian Ministry people had fitted her with it in Sydney; pretending not to watch as the ugly weapon, still congealed in its preservative coating of World War One grease, swung tantalisingly overhead before being lowered and sited on their berth neighbour's poopdeck.

He'd hovered and overtly spliced an end of wire even after the fitters had gone; one furtive smouldering eye on the rival crowd as they'd gathered with proprietary delight around their Frankenstein monster: prodding and whizzing various wheels, polishin' it with cotton waste and peering through its sights like they knew what they wus doin', an' then goin' round to the front an' ostentatiously sponging out the barrel – just as soon as they'd figured out which bit of the bloody gun the bloody barrel *was*!

Half a mile astern the stricken *Hecuba* wearily lowered her face into the water; swirling foam clearly seen in the moonlight, breaking at the base of her centrecastle. They wouldn't save her now; not with all the guts and seamanship in the world. As if confirming defeat the sliver of one starboard boat began to ease slowly towards the surface of the sea. Even the act of abandoning held an unreal quality: somehow *Hecuba's* going seemed leisurely and quiet; so lacking in drama. Not at all like a proper war in which men died, or were mutilated.

Within minutes the ship bringing up the rear of the port column began to fall astern too, narrowing in form as she turned away from the convoy to pick up survivors. The Bone Collectors had received a summons at last: first short straw drawn by the unhappy samaritans of Column Number One – illuminated like that, her rusted grey isolation plainly revealed beneath the too-slowly-fading glare of the snowflake there couldn't have been a man aboard who didn't carry his heart in his mouth at the invitation they presented to a trailing U-boat.

Her name was *Theotokos*. From master to galley boy every last one of her crew was Greek. It more than squared the account; made up for the absconder who'd scurried back to Canada before the sinkings had begun. Now a voluntary straggler separated from the main body of the convoy, probably with little speed in reserve, the Hellenic tramp had marked herself as a potential target for a long time before she could regain the dubious safety of the herd. For the moment she was probably safe: those searching fingers of ASDIC would deter the lurking U-boat from returning to periscope depth, but only temporarily. Soon the hard-pressed escorts must abandon their needle in a haystack operation to race up front again; sweep the track ahead and the Devil take the hindmost.

The hindmost?

Olympian might well have to drop astern as a rescue ship – a U-boat humorist's *Knochensammler* herself before morning. Oh, ships had been known to ignore their Commodore's request in previous convoys: ships had been seen to sail on without the courage to stop when panic set in and the going got really bloody – but with brother seamen drowning back there in the darkness, and Albert Burton taking the decisions? Ellis drained the mug without really tasting it. 'I'll be on the bridge if you want me,' he said quietly.

Casually he turned away from the galley rail: neither Leather nor the Cook would have guessed his unease was stronger than ever. It wasn't usually like this when first blood was spilled – this . . . almost this *tedium* of stress? Not that anyone was complaining . . . Dear God but Ellis knew only too well how time would cease to drag on leaden feet throughout the rest of this night should the hours suddenly begin to explode, rather than whimper away.

Not if the undertakers of *Gross-admiral* Dönitz really were out there in force. Numerous enough to thrust their way in among the lines of coffins . . .

The last of the flares had flickered and died as he climbed the ladders of the forr'ad housing. The moon still smiled brightly to light their passage, though; and the sea gambolled and chuckled as if genuinely amused by their rag-tag company.

Why couldn't it have been the *real* North Atlantic on this of all nights? Why couldn't they both have been their usual bastard selves with the moon a fleeting pallid mockery glimpsed only through scudding tattered blackness, and the ocean a giant force bearing down like rows and rows of thundering mountains concealing man-made insignificant things like SC whatever's tired ships behind its icy spindrift mantle?

It wouldn't deter the U-boats: their crews had proved themselves men of fanatical resolution. Crucified by discomfort far worse than that endured aboard any steamer quarry; lashed when necessary to periscope standards or rails to counter their being swept from streaming open bridges, they still watched and waited on the surface for the convoys, through all but the most impossible weather. But a submarine conning tower provided too low a sighting platform in heavy weather; targets were revealed only briefly between massive breaking wavecrests; torpedoes ran wild in fifty-foot seas, the odds for once mounted reassuringly in favour of the clients of the Bone Collector. To a peacetime merchant sailor the North Atlantic's violent moods were a foulness: in war its savagery became the unbegrudged ally of the convoy men.

But not tonight. Tonight *das Todesloch* was ominously docile. Tonight, as SC whatever-it-was crawled nervously across the Death Hole, it seemed to Chief Officer Ellis that even the sea itself had sided with the hunters.

Shadows were still grouped along the after rail when he climbed the lower bridge deck. They showed little inclination to go below: after the torpedoing it appeared that Ellis wasn't the only one foregoing sleep in favour of preparedness. Oh, occasionally someone did laugh, but it was forced, nervous humour: most of the watchers talked in low voices while gazing covertly astern to where stricken *Hecuba* had been swallowed either by distance or by water. It was impossible to tell which: even lonely *Theotokos*, her blue sternlight prudently extinguished, was now lost against the sombre clouds piling the western horizon.

A voice called: 'That you, Mate?'

Ellis halted as the portly figure of the Chief Steward materialised from the shadow of the captain's gig. Ellis noticed Grubb was carrying his lifejacket too. And wearing his best uniform under an old civvy overcoat, rather as if he didn't expect to have time to change. Jesus, the signs of apprehension – of almost resigned anticipation – were becoming more apparent all the time. So much for occupational therapy . . .

'I put a few extra stores in the boats like you asked.' Grubby hesitated, looking pained: for some there were worse things than only being torpedoed. 'Portuguese tinned pilchards; horlicks tablets; barleysugar; a few cans o' fruit. There's a few bob's worth involved. I'll need a receipt.'

'Did you put a tin-opener in each boat with 'em?' David Ellis asked gravely.

'Shit!' the Chief Steward muttered.

Second Officer McKerchar's boat would still be OK.

Second Officer McKerchar's knife would open more than a tin of Portuguese pilchards, and sure as hell he'd have it with him whether they had to leave in a hurry or not. Ellis shook his head wonderingly. 'What happens when the ship goes down with all her stores on board, Henry? Are you going to insist on a receipt from the U-boat *Kapitan*?'

Why did he say '*when* the ship goes down . . .'? Why in God's name didn't he say: 'if'?

'The Old Man's been at you, hasn't he?' Grubby demanded obliquely. 'About them bloody pilchards.'

Out of the corner of his eye Ellis was aware of the corvette racing abeam again; eastwards this time, retiring in frustration to continue her sweep ahead of the convoy. There hadn't been any depth-charging; presumably no contact. An uneventful affair, as placid and unexciting as *Hecuba's* going itself. Unless, of course, you happened to be one of those trapped in that self-same steamship *Hecuba* while Grubby Grubb was going on about pilchards: perhaps sinking to the drifting slime at the bottom of the ocean at this very minute, with bulkheads collapsing like thunder and the eyeballs protruding from your black-purple face as life's bubbles were compressed out of you . . .

'No, the Captain hasn't been on about pilchards,' Ellis lied wearily. 'And how many suitcases have you hidden in your boat this time, Henry? While you were stowing the extra stores?'

He'd sailed into convoy actions with Grubby Grubb before. Grubby was a man of considerable prudence and foresight. Just like Father.

The Chief Steward suddenly looked shifty, a bit defensive. 'Only one. A few odds an' ends.'

'You know no one's allowed to take personal gear in the lifeboats – only their convoy bag.'

'It's jus' one little suitcase, Mate. All I got in the world,' Grubby wheedled pathetically.

Ellis pretended to consider. 'Do you think *I* could have a tin of pilchards for supper, Henry. Just one?'

'Go to hell,' the Chief Steward retorted automatically; forgetfully.

'See what I mean?' Ellis said. 'So get your bloody suitcase out of that boat. Now!'

It was funny – the way he'd thought of Father again. After all this time.

Chief Officer Ellis never had quite decided whether he'd become Chief Officer Ellis because of Father, or because of something that happened during the First World War or, come to that, because of a combination of both.

Certainly the Martyrdom of Mister Neugebauer had created a significant breach in his relationship with Father. And that awful event *had* occurred during the Kaiser's war when David was only twelve years old. Yet it was to be some considerable time before Ellis actually left home and, to be honest, they hadn't been all bad, those teenage years in Salford. To begin with, it wasn't as if David had known any other way of life. For instance, there had been positive advantages reflected in being the son of a corner shop owner.

'Waldo's Giant Ha'penny Lucky Bags' proved a great source of goodwill from his school contemporaries. David quickly discovered that it was possible to mark the contents of each new stock of treasures and, armed with such privileged intelligence, it only required a discreet nod; a warning shake of the head to assure the juvenile purchaser of a prize beyond all dreams: a false nose, a stink bomb, a lifelike rubber eel . . . perhaps a real imitation-silver lucky charm. Once, possibly motivated by ambitions more mature than the callow David realised, he directed a particularly pretty young damsel towards a bag containing a genuine ruby-glass finger ring which sparkled and flashed almost as much as the dark-eyed gratitude of the

Primary Standard IV fellow-pupil he'd previously admired from afar.

So David, armed with this awesome power of benefaction, never ran short of camaraderie in the brief evening periods which Father allowed him to call his own. Sometimes he and his cronies would dare to attend the local church hall where the juvenile temperance movement's Band of Hope meetings were held; ostensibly singing hymns and listening attentively to homilies on the evils of drink in adulthood while all the time giggling silently at the back, finger-wrestling and digging each other in the ribs until one or other exploded in a hysteria of purple-faced merriment, and everyone was thrown out.

Sometimes – special times – they would hear of a local death and venture in a tongue-tied, cap-twisting group to the hurriedly polished front door of the deceased to ask, with much shuffling and meek humility, if they might be permitted to view the corpse and pay their last – and usually their first – respects. They were seldom refused. Dumb and wide-eyed they would troup in to stand for an all-too-brief moment, secretly thrilled, frantically absorbing every detail of a waxen cadaver dressed in Sunday best: the minutia-laden recollection of which would fuel their playground conversation for days after.

But the winds of change were already blowing through the Edwardian society which had defeated Arthur William's own claims on recognition. By David Ellis's twelfth birthday the Kaiser had become the Devil, the country had become a warrior nation and poor men became important for the first time ever. The British Lion roared a hysteria of patriotism and stirring sacrifice whereupon the already tenuous social barriers of the post-Victorian ghettos were breached for ever in a welter of anti-German brotherhood.

Actually, it had been one of the most exciting events of David Ellis's brief life – the Martyrdom of Mister Neugebauer. At first, anyway . . .

Mister Neugebauer had emigrated from Bavaria at least a decade before David had even been born, and had been in business as a pork butcher in the next street for almost as long as anyone could remember. A kindly man, he had supported whole Salford families with credit when times had been hard, but, while Arthur William's sand-bone hawker antecedents were merely Anglo-Saxon disreputable and, as such, had become less important in the new wave of community tolerance, the Good Mister Neugebauer's were unarguably Teutonic.

Along with his friends David watched with bated breath while the mob gathered outside Mister Neugebauer's tiny shop on that 1914 winter's night.

Two caped and helmeted policemen had looked on, yet miraculously saw nothing as the rabble shouted, chanted, bellowed epithets at the monstrous enemy aliens within. The Monstrous Enemy Aliens, meanwhile, revealed white tearful faces from the upper floors; the hastily barricaded refuge to which Mister Neugebauer had numbly retreated along with Mrs Neugebauer and all his screaming little Neugebauers as disbelief turned first to shock, and finally to terror of his dearest neighbours.

Young David Ellis had cheered as loudly as anyone as they smashed one window, and then another, before the frenzied lunacy of the crowd beat down the door itself and poured into Mister Neugebauer's shop, flinging pig's heads and chopping blocks and pork carcasses and baskets of jellied trotters, and parsley and scales and glistening strings of pork sausages into the street.

And then they built a fire with the stuff of Mister Neugebauer's trade and danced around it, old and young alike, until the madness had at last subsided into shuffling realisation of what community ignorance had done. But by then the Salford cobbles were heavy with the smell of charred bacon, and echoed dull with Neugebauer sobs.

The Family Neugebauer had left the area shortly after. They had never been heard of again.

'Good riddance, say I,' Father had pronounced with enormous satisfaction. 'There's room for none but decent law-abiding Englishmen here!' – apparently forgetting, in his blinkered self-righteousness, that the self-same Mister Neugebauer had once lent him three hard-earned sovereigns, on trust, in order that he might stock his very first stall in the Flatiron Market.

Well, the adolescent David hadn't felt too badly about that – all said and done Mister Neugebauer *had* been a Hun. According to the Government, who knew about such things, all Huns laughed as they tossed French babies into the air before spitting them on their bayonets and therefore, quite clearly, no Salford mite could be safe while the evil Neugebauers were in residence.

But it was only later that David discovered what decent law-abiding Englishmen had done to Mister Neugebauer's much-loved German daschund at the height of their patriotic fervour. Overlooked and abandoned by the Neugebauers during their hurried retreat upstairs, the wretched little dog had been seized by the rabble, trussed by its hind legs from one of Mister Neugebauer's own meat hooks – and then gutted while still alive.

They'd even used Mister Neugebauer's favourite skinning knife to butcher the animal . . .

Worst of all, Father had found *that* a very rich joke indeed!

Ellis wondered morbidly whether the Nazis spitted babies on bayonets in *this* war as he climbed the final ladder to the bridge. 'Or was atrocity confined to the sea nowadays? Were they just content to let their U-boat crews fry merchant sailors like him in blazing oil or drown them without warning in their ventilated steel coffins . . . ? Did they, for that matter, perpetrate these horrors because they *were*

Germans, or for a much more simple reason – because they feared the convoy men as much as the convoy men feared them?'

An exquisite irony occurred to David Ellis as he breasted the top step.

'The *Kapitänleutnant* in command of the U-boat out there – the one which just sank helpless *Hecuba* and could very well sink me in the next split-second – could his name possibly be Neugebauer? And if such an irony existed – then might *Kapitänleutnant* Neugebauer still carry a distant boyhood memory of a tiny little dog hanging from a meat-hook, with its entrails sliding to the floor?'

The Old Man had been joined by another casually hunched silhouette at the rail. It had to be Chief Engineer Gulliver: nobody else aboard *Olympian* would have felt that relaxed in the Old Man's company. As Ellis approached, Third Officer Cowan stuck his head out of the wheelhouse and called, 'Jus' coming up to three bells, Cap'n . . . Zig-zag pattern four on the *'execute'*.'

'Thank you, Mister Cowan.'

Young Able Seaman McKechnie, who loved rabbits and almost certainly did hate Germans by now, had been relieved from the wheel and stood right out at the wing on submarine watch; night-glasses constantly vectoring from a point forr'ad of the beam to the port quarter. The additional look-outs posted up in *Olympian's* bows and on the poop would ensure all-round coverage if they didn't fall asleep, betrayed by the warmth of their kapok-filled lifejackets.

Ellis didn't anticipate they would fall asleep, though. Not tonight.

Seen from the bridge there were two gaps in the port column now, though one of the remaining vessels had moved up to fill the blank directly astern of the Vice-commodore. Otherwise black velvet ships still covered the ocean ahead and to either side of them: blockish, unpretty shapes as ever, with their stubby vertical masts and pipecleaner funnels; all sighing in long, slow dips through the oily swell and still emanating that dogged fortitude.

'Evenin' Davy lad,' Bill Gulliver welcomed, patting the rail beside him. Chief Engineer Gulliver was a nice man. A big comfortable West Country man who liked people almost as much as triple-expansion steam engines.

'Up to see where the real work's done, Chief?'

Gulliver grinned. 'If it weren't for us skilled engineers down below, you navigators wouldn't have nothin' to navigate.'

'*Hah!*' little Albert sniffed acidly, barely resisting the temptation to be drawn further. It was an argument as old as the first day they ever put a paddle wheel on a sailing ship.

The Mate smiled back. Somehow, in the presence of those two, the proximity of a U-boat didn't hold quite the same fear: not even one commanded by a Neugebauer. But that didn't alter the fact that they still existed; still fired torpedoes. And could still obliterate grand old seamen like Burton and Bill Gulliver with a random hiss of compressed air.

Ellis turned to frown astern. 'No sign of the Greek catching up yet. Last we saw from aft, they were abandoning *Hecuba* – most of our own crowd are still on deck, by the way.'

'Chief here, reckons we're pessimistic,' Burton growled. 'Reckons, as nothing's happened for half an hour since the Dutchman went, it could just've been some rogue Jerrie trying to win an Iron Cross.'

'Bill, I hope to God you're right,' Ellis muttered with feeling.

'One swallow don't make a summer, does it?,' Gulliver argued reasonably. 'No more than one U-boat necessarily makes a . . .'

The flash as U-boat number two struck somewhere out on the starboard side of the convoy snapped every outboard plate, every wire, every stay and ventilator and white staring face in *Olympian* into split-second, gut-clutching brilliance. On the bridge they whirled: glimpsed a creaming, sallow-red fireball mushrooming skywards . . .

Just as the third detonation occurred. Actually within the stunned centre ranks of SC whatever-the-hell-it-was . . . and suddenly there were *two* burning, reeling ships – *Gotterdämerung* in duplicate, this time. All in the wag of a Neugebauer daschund's tail.

'. . . wolf-pack?' Ellis heard himself finish for the Chief. It should have sounded an example of enormous self-control – to be able to respond as logically as that – but, with the bile already curdling inside him, it expressed itself only as little-boy petulance: virtually accusing Gulliver of lying about something terribly important. 'You *still* say one U-boat doesn't make a wolf-pack, do you?'

Snowflake went up. Almost as frightening as the torpedoes. Etched under the glare they could see a blazing ship already running wild in among the convoy. Sirens began blaring in an urgency of panic. Then someone else fired starshell. *An'* someone bloody ELSE . . .

The tedium of apprehension was over. The undertakers had finally arrived

Four

~~~~~~~~~

'That's my leg on the hatch-cover down there
– Jesus CHRIST, mate . . . that's *my* bloody
LEG!'

Torpedoed seaman: SS 'Valiant Star'

9.30 p.m.: Three Bells in the 8 to 12 Night Watch

Someone was cursing, 'Kenny . . . Gie's a hand wi' this
fuckin' LIFEjacket, Kennie!'

In the chromatic glare of the snowflake Ellis could see most
of the off-duty foc'slehead crowd milling starboard side on
the forr'ad well deck, black gang and seamen alike. Most of
them were already wearing their jackets. The vociferous
'someone' obviously intended to – just as soon as he could
figure out which bit to tie to what; the whole ship practised
'abandon' drill regularly, yet there was always one who never
learned a bloody thing until practice became reality.

It was the same casual attitude to survival which had
prompted whoever had drained the boat's compass alcohol.
Suicidal irresponsibility – murderous irresponsibility it
could well have proved, in that particular case.

Even as the fireball from the first stricken vessel turned to a
pall of smoke with its base reflecting some deeper-seated
blaze below, the Old Man had crossed the wing to gesture to
the stunned Third Mate.

'I'll take her for the moment, Mister Cowan – I have the
watch. Keep your eyes peeled for signals from the Commodore: have the manoeuvring card ready to hand. Mister Ellis?'

'Sir?'

'Get one . . . nay, both apprentices up here if you will. They've got young eyes and it's as safe a place as any.'

'Or as dangerous,' Ellis thought bleakly. He'd seen whole bridge structures weighing hundreds of tons flung into the air like paper boxes by torpedo. Usually from tankers, though. *Olympian* was carrying mainly powdered milk, powdered eggs and powdered God knew what else on her general cargo manifest. There was a sardonic rumour in the British fleet that it came from powdered American hens and powdered American cows. Still, he didn't think *that* would blow up like high octane fuel.

He had a sudden idiot vision of a giant omelette rising into the sky above Convoy SC whatsit; all yellow and creamy. 'Old *Olympian's* gone then,' they'd say aboard the other ships. 'Scrub sending back the Bone Collector – jus' get the knives an' forks out, lads.'

'Aye, aye, sir!' Chief Officer Ellis acknowledged, hauling his Mate's whistle from his side pocket and blowing two long blasts: 'Cadets to the bridge.'

The two lads had been standing near Grubby Grubb and the other officers on the funnel deck. Swollen like penguins in their lifejackets they both came clattering up the ladders at his summons; healthy, wind-burned features now unusually pale in the light of the anxiety-triggered flares. Their solemn, enquiring gaze was unable to conceal the conflict of emotion: natural nervousness balanced against – with their innocence of inexperience – the sheer euphoria of it all.

As soon as he caught sight of Senior Cadet Moberly Ellis noted that pyrotechnic-bleached complexion and was again reminded of his vision in the smoking room earlier; of the awful rotting skull he'd imagined as replacing Moberly's own bright visage.

'Up to monkey island, both of you,' he ordered crisply, trying to look self-confident. 'Keep a lookout for anything unusual: ship's boats, rafts; particularly men in the water . . .'

75

'U-boats, sir?' horrid Westall piped, eyes enormous with earnestness.

'You see a U-boat, you holler straight away, Westall,' Ellis retorted gravely.

'Aye, aye, sir!'

'Dear Lord!' Ellis reflected as he watched them swarm agilely up the vertical ladder to the standard compass platform above the wheelhouse itself. 'Please protect me from fools, children . . . and most especially from a combination of both: Cadet bloody Westall!'

'Two ships torpedoed, sir!' Westall screamed the instant he got up there. 'Broad on the starb'd bow!'

The spasm of collective hysteria was at its peak by then. All across the horizon vessels were releasing rockets, starshell, snowflake. Hooters were blaring; safety valves blowing off steam – someone out on the port flank had even begun rattling away with a Hotchkiss gun; more than likely at some mythical submersible spotted by a look-out with an identi-kit brain to Cadet Westall's. It meant that, in all probability, the one and only thing everyone in the whole bloody convoy *did* know already was that two SHIPS had been torpedoed!

'Thank you, Cadet Westall,' Chief Officer Ellis acknowledged politely.

With every bit of self-restraint he could muster.

The Chief had hardly budged, still leaning over the forward rail and watching the fireworks with evident absorption. Quite probably there were chief engineers within the convoy lines running round in circles down below by now, shouting unnecessary reminders to be alert, to stand-by for manoeuvring orders. Not Chief Gulliver, though. Gulliver had enough self-restraint to accept that the routine watchkeeper – Fourth Engineer Knox, as it happened – would have been at the controls from the moment the underwater explosions had rattled *Olympian's* hull; white boiler-suited figure tense, eyes fixed unblinkingly above him for any change of revolutions demanded by the bridge. And anyway – Fred had been torpedoed before: you didn't need to remind a man who'd already had to kick out a kick-out panel in a foundering ship to pay attention. To have his Chief agitating at his shoulder would only make a junior more nervous; subject him to even greater strain.

While the Chief's being in the engine room itself wouldn't help Fred Knox or his four-man watch of sweating, half-naked firemen and trimmers much if a German eel penetrated *Olympian's* rust-fragile plating to mark the termination of their lives.

No. Ellis guessed that Bill Gulliver would force himself to wait awhile and then ever so casually stroll below to what was an engineer's death hole within a Death Hole, and probably tap his pipe out on the control platform and shout, 'Everythin' all right, Fred?' above the thunderous clamour of the engine. Just to be seen to be calm and untroubled by any below-waterline man who desperately needed to draw on courage.

Chief Officer David Ellis *was* glad he hadn't decided to become a ship's engineer instead.

Really, he hadn't even cherished any long-term ambition to go to sea at all – other than as a means to sever himself from Father and the corner shop, of course.

Certainly the teenage David had been captivated, like many of his generation, by the false image then presented of Jolly Jack Tar's life on the ocean wave: their geographically-limited imaginations inflamed by lurid comics and penny-dreadfuls detailing Gallant Deeds and Romantic War Stories bearing little relation to the discreetly underplayed slaughter of Jutland and the Gallipoli landings; the first Atlantic crucifixion of the pre-1914 British Merchant Fleet. Even the sinking of the *Lusitania* had emerged in the popular press as a triumph of British seamen's pluck once its anti-German propaganda value had been extracted in full, the daily body-count exhausted, the 'eye-witness' accounts of seeing children's pathetic corpses drifting as victims of the dastardly Hun published in every hate-formenting detail.

But that had been during the war to end all wars, while David Ellis had still been too young, too uncertain to go his own way. And after that war the Royal Navy, like the Army and the Flying Corps, had found itself with an embarrassment of surviving cannon fodder, while social status had once again become a qualification in the process of selecting officers. It was highly unlikely that the son of a Salford corner shop owner could have attained entry as a midshipman RN even had that self-same corner shop owner supported his son in his attempt.

Father didn't. Many times a hesitant David approached the subject only to be rebuffed out of hand. 'Thy place is in the business, lad. Honest toil, not fancy ambition, will be your heritage from me.'

The irony was that David had only been luke-warm about entering a seagoing career when its possibilities for independence first occurred to him. It was really because of Father's paternal arrogance, his refusal to consider the matter – and very likely, through sensible discussion, to have quashed such a half-informed intent – that David Ellis's childish enthusiam to become a sailorman had hardened first to vague determination and finally, to blinkered resolution.

Fortunately – if such a term could be applied to Chief Officer David Ellis, now committed to the bloody prospect of night convoy battle in early 1941 . . . fortunately his gateway to the seafaring profession, when it finally opened for the sixteen-year-old David of 1919, had been that for an apprentice seaman or nothing. He'd never even been offered the opportunity to sign on as a ship's engineer in his first vessel.

While he was secretly relieved now, he'd been a little disappointed then. He'd rather fancied the idea of working with engines and, without Father's guidance, had never been advised that the only entry to a seagoing engineer's career was through the shipyards.

But, qualifications apart, that disappointment had typified young David's ill-informed approach to the career which was to be his life. He hadn't even gathered enough knowledge of the sea to realise that his first employers wouldn't have wanted a ship's engineer anyway – not even a very cheap if somewhat inexperienced engineer. Largely because *his* particular maiden voyage had been aboard a sailing vessel.

The last flare sizzled and died, and the temporary madness of SC whatever was over yet again. On the port flank the anonymous Hotchkiss gave up trying to riddle a ghost, while up ahead the plodding ships became silent, orderly and withdrawn in their moonlit apprehension once more. Only out to starboard were the sights and sounds of war, the myriad permutations of a sailorman's dying still evident for all to see and hear if not to comprehend.

'No one ever does understand what the hell's going on when the U-boats hit us!' Chief Officer Ellis brooded as he returned to the wing beside comfortable Chief Engineer Gulliver. Certainly those in the merchant ships didn't. Oh, no doubt the Commodore had the professional ability to hazard a guess at the local situation; the Escort Commander had his intelligence reports supported by hard-won knowledge of U-boat tactics to form some overall picture . . . but not those such as Ellis: not the poor ordinary blokes driving the actual bloody targets. They just saw flashes in the night; heard their consorts' fading desperation over the WT; smelled the acrid burning and their own fear; trembled over the nightmares conjured in their minds and the second-by-second waiting for the unthinkable to happen –

79

and exchanged careful small-talk in between spasms of horror at what other men were trying to do to them.

'Did you know, Davy lad,' Chief Engineer Gulliver mused, 'that the Great Spotted Woodpecker lays between five an' eight eggs, and eats suet?'

Ellis blinked. The burning ship was falling abeam now; too far to starboard to make out detail other than a red glow throwing her forward bridge structure and masts into flickering relief. Her identity would be contained in the confidential papers in Albert Burton's safe but security was tight: the rest of the crowd aboard *Olympian* might never learn her name other than through post-voyage comparison with crews of other surviving ships. Column Six's nominated Bone Collector – Kerr Steamships' *Halcyon*, was it, or the Belgian, *Meerops*? – was also dropping slightly astern of the last rank, her master no doubt reducing speed in anticipation of a quick pick-up . . . a bloody quick pick-up!

'Suet' Ellis queried tonelessly.

'Beef suet. The fatty bits o' beef, eh?'

There was no sign of the second casualty, the one that had run wild within the convoy itself. Column Five seemed to have a blank space as well, though . . . Lord, she must've gone down like a stone in a pond when she went. One minute ploughing crazy through her sheering, scattering sisters: too much way on her to launch any kind of boat – and then gone. Just like that! A bulkhead, a cofferdam imploded; or had she simply snapped in two like rotten driftwood and . . .

Fifty men? Sixty?

'No. I didn't know they ate suet, Chief.'

'What do?'

'Birds. The . . . ah . . . Great Spotted Owl?'

'Woodpecker!'

'Woodpecker, then.'

'Do they?' Chief Gulliver said, surprised. 'Eat suet, eh? Well I never . . .'

'*This*' Ellis muttered to himself, feeling a bit faint, 'is bloody *silly*!'

It also proved that what men said didn't truly reflect what was in men's minds when the other men were drowning. Not even, it seemed, in the case of Chief Engineer Gulliver.

Above and behind Ellis the funnel swayed against the starry sky, puttering a gentle stream of smoke which whorled and spun astern on the freshening breeze. Low voices filtered down from the two cadets on monkey island; the wash of the compass bowl touched the face of little Albert Burton in the wheelhouse. The crowd were still out on the foredeck, leaning over the side or standing in idle black-shadowed groups. Here and there a glow-worm sparked briefly as a cigarette was inhaled below the level of the bulwarks. It was the same aft, on the funnel deck. They were all waiting again.

Ellis lit another Players himself and cupped it, drawing gratefully. His watch said 9.47, only three quarters of an hour since the first torpedo took *Hecuba*, yet three ships gone already. He lifted the Barr and Strouds and turned to scan the horizon astern. Still no sight of *Theotokos*, but she had to be back there somewhere, presumably shuddering and wheezing in every tortured Greek rivet as she struggled to regain the protection of the herd.

'Come on, lads,' Ellis urged in tight-lipped silence. 'Beat the bastards. Please. Because you could be ourselves, and your survival can only underwrite the prospects for our own.'

A bit like the faded *Duella* up ahead of them: their oldest travelling companion. It was strange how, after the first few days of a voyage, they came to identify themselves with random ships within each convoy and how, from the moment they did so, their opposite number's continuation held a quite illogical but encouraging significance; its loss a personal blow . . . Rather as an ant in a rainstorm to a fascinated child. If the ant survives the deluge, then the child is temporarily free from fear; but should a raindrop crush the ant, leave its minute perfection floundering and broken, then the child will feel a deliciously breathless shiver; be come briefly aware of its own mortality.

Chief Officer Ellis was becoming rather too aware of *his* mortality. He'd seen too many ants crushed. But then, he wasn't the child in this particular rainstorm. He was one of the ants.

The Captain came out of the wheelhouse and stood beside them. It was the first time Ellis realised that Albert had been below to change while he was in the galley – now, even through the darkness, he could see Burton's pyjama bottoms peeping below his trousers. And he wore his brass-buttoned reefer with the four gold rings and Merchant Navy diamond on the sleeve, too. Plus his battered uniform cap with the salt-green oak leaves around the peak. It was Albert Burton's night-fighting gear. All day long the Old Man stumped around the bridge dressed as a tramp steamer man sporting a stained trilby, a pair of ancient flannel bags and a tatty old overcoat to cover a once-white seaman's jersey. But after darkness fell, whenever the convoy was at sea, then Albert uniformed for the coming fray.

No one, not even Chief Gulliver, had ever dared challenge the logic which prompted the Captain to wear flannel pyjamas at the same time; presumably because Albert Burton had always been a creature of habit, and it just happened to be night.

'A different U-boat got her, I'd say,' the Old Man growled, jerking his head out to where the blazing casualty had fallen well astern. 'That's Ericson's Steamers' *Valiant Star* out there. Benny Falconer's her skipper.' He grinned severely. 'E'll be fit to chew nails if they sunk 'im.'

'Just one more?' Gulliver's tone was bland. 'While there you was, Albert: talking in whole packs of the little devils earlier. Yet now we got two ships fished simultaneous and you grudge allowin' Jerrie more'n one extra boat?'

It was only a conversational ploy: Bill Gulliver knew all about German submarines.

'Overlapping targets, Chief.' Ellis volunteered. To him as well as to Gulliver' talking, even about U-boats, still held more attraction than thinking his own thoughts. 'The bastards let the escorts run ahead – wait until *we're* passing; until they have a few ships at an angle where their hull silhouettes overlap – then they loose a salvo. Better chance of hitting somethi . . .'

A sullen detonation shattered the peace: then two . . . three . . . a fourth practically merging into the first. One long pulsating flash like subdued lightning, followed moments later by a geysering curtain of spray over to starboard: catching the moonlight; throwing the banks of stolid freighters between the tumult and *Olympian* into sharp relief.

A youthful voice from monkey island squeaked: 'Oh, Lord!,' followed by Moberly's more mature, 'Shurrup, Westall!' Someone more experienced from the foredeck jeered, 'G'wan, Navy – lay doon yer pink gins an' gie it tae the bastards!'

Depth charges. So at least temporarily they were going on the offensive – but to what end? A solid ASDIC contact? Or were they just trying to keep Jerrie's head down . . . maybe boost their own morale as well as the merchant sailors'.

'I never seen a U-boat sunk,' the Chief mused, scratching his head as he watched the distant activity. 'It can't be easy, mind you. Yon's a three-dimensional world down there, and they say a charge has to explode closer than a couple of hundred feet to do owt to an 'Atlantic' class hull. Did you know the Great Spotted Woodpecker eats roast lamb, Albert? The Mate here was tellin' me.'

'Suet,' Ellis corrected with an effort. 'Beef suet, Chief. And it was you telling me.'

'Roast lamb, eh? the Old Man muttered, triggered into immediate fantasy. 'With garden peas an' mint sauce. Or beef, as you say – proper rib o' beef: all bloody inside, wi' Yorkshire pudding an' gravy.'

'Oh, *bugger*! Now you've started him off again,' the Mate gloomed.

Gastric juices revitalised, Albert stamped to the after rail and leaned over, bellowing.

'Chief STEWARD!'

Grubby's equally aggressive shout came ricochetting back.

'*Wot*?'

'Send me personal steward up to the bridge!'

A second pattern of depth-charges erupted out to starboard, killing a trawler-full of fish. Not many bothered glancing at the secondary war: not then; not if the Old Man was proposin' another set-to with Grubby.

'You 'aven't *got* a personal steward. You shares Slimy Weston like everybody else.'

'Well, send 'IM up. I want sandwiches. Beef sandwiches!'

'Sanwichis?' Grubb's voice cracked with incredulity. '*Beef* sanwichis, did you say?'

'Sandwiches!' the Captain confirmed with heavy irony. 'Bits o' bread. Wi' fresh beef an' mustard in the tween decks.'

'FRESH beef?'

There was true anguish there: an outrage of bare credulity.

'It comes from cows,' Burton explained triumphantly. 'It's called *meat*, Chief Steward – somethin' we don't 'ardly 'ave on this bloody skeleton ship.'

There was a hushed pause while Grubby fought for equilibrium in a world going insane. The Old Man had to be delirious, that wus f'r sure. Finally gone doolally: ready f'r the yellow trolley. *Beef*? Jesus, this wus the British Merchant Navy – *Grubby's* merchant navy! No one ever got beef aboard one o' Henry Grubb's tramps unless it was pickled in brine or so green it had to be camouflaged as lobscouse, or curried 'til you couldn't taste the insipient putrefaction.

Caution, to say nothing of uneasy deference towards the mentally afflicted, inspired the Chief Steward to clenched-teeth compromise at first. 'Look, there's extry cheese sanwiches up there f'r the watchkeepers, Cap'n. I might even find a bit more pickle to put onnem.'

But then it got too much, being generous – especially to Albert Burton, crazy-mad or not! Secure in his support from the Owners, Grubby's olive branch withered into bitter hostility. '. . . but there ain't no bloody BEEF! An' what's more, you ain't never goin' to see beef onna sandwich as long as I'm Chief Steward an' that's flat. *Captin*!'

More depth charges exploded on the quarter, ignored by all. The crowd listened to the more crucial battle, enthralled.

'Cheese sandwi . . . CHEESE?' Albert was getting apoplectic now: jumping up and down in his pyjamas and peaked cap. 'If I 'ad a pointed nose an' bloody whiskers I wouldn't eat one o' your cardboard-cheese bloody sand-wiches, Mister! Not if I wus adrift onna hatchcover wi' me bones stickin' through me ribs an' the crew beggin' an' pleading with me to open me mouth, I wouldn't . . .'

'Remember the pilchards,' Chief Officer Ellis whispered urgently. Now was the psychological moment for the Captain to exploit a compromise. Vittling wars were never won or lost with Henry Grubb, only turned to temporary advantage.

The Old Man hesitated, considered the matter in depth, then looked crafty. Far too mild.

'All right – I'll settle for pilchard sandwiches. In tomato sauce: none of your oily-bound Dago rubbish.'

'PILCHARDS?' Christ but Grubby was predictable.

'With real butter on the bread. Not yer usual scrape o' Maggie-Annie!'

'I'll report you to the bloody Owners. You bloody see if I don' . . .'

'And a nice pot of tea. *In* my silver teapot, if you please.'

'It's *not* silver: it's jus' electro-bloody-plated!' Grubby's voice fired a spiteful parting shot from the darkness but Albert turned away from the rail with enormous dignity and vanished into the wheelhouse. Round four hundred and thirty six to him.

Cabaret over, Chief Engineer Gulliver tapped his pipe in the palm of one leathery hand and turned for the ladder. 'Think I'll . . . ah, maybe take a stroll down below. Have a bit of a chat wi' the lads,' he said as if it had just occurred to him.

Ellis smiled softly to himself. Chief Steward Grubb wasn't the only one aboard *Olympian* who acted predictably.

The side show – the world war affair – seemed to have ended as well. There had been no further depth charging; no remaining sign of either escort out on the starboard flank. Presumably they'd returned to their sweep in the track of the convoy, frustrated by lack of numbers. Presumably they hadn't sunk any U-boats.

The unpretty ships sailed on in that eerily silent array. Far astern the torpedoed *Valiant Star* presented a lonely pyre. Above her, across the ocean at the end of a twinkling ruby path the sky seemed to shimmer; dyed in wavering strands of gold like the reflected lights of a city seen at night. Suddenly *she*, unlike the rest of her sisters, had become very beautiful.

Why was it – if ships had to die by violent hands – that they couldn't all go with the ugliness of rage? Did they really have to touch so poignantly upon the already ex-quisite sadness at abandoning them to the sea, that of those who were at one with them? And what of their murderers – the men in the black sliding hulls below . . . ? Weren't they seamen too? Could any one of them, on seeing such a splendour of destruction, not feel a certain guilt: a fleeting regret for what might have been . . . ?

No sign of the straggling *Theotokos* yet. Already the

rescue ship for Column Six had collected whatever bones still had life in them from *Valiant Star* and was hastily moving back into last position; but still no sign of the solitary Greek.

Nearly 10 p.m.: two minutes to go and it would be four bells. First shots fired, first blood drawn; the first watch of the night half over . . . and now they waited once more for the next phase, perhaps the really determined phase of the attack to begin.

Albert Burton re-appeared from the wheelhouse. 'Still here, Mister Ellis?'

The Mate shrugged. 'It's as good a place as any.' He didn't quite know why he added the next bit, but he did. 'It's this suspense that gets me. Time hangs heavy when you're scared.'

He'd never confessed to anything as embarrassing as that before. Not to anyone. The Mate was always 'bucko': always bloody fireproof.

'We're all scared,' Albert said. He smiled briefly: a crinkling of weathered skin around puppy-bright eyes. 'But don't you go tellin' that to Grubby Grubb.'

'You too?'

'Aye: often. In much the same way as you – as wi' most of us out here, I'd venture.'

Ellis frowned absently at the skip of the convoy barrel streaming from *Duella's* counter. 'Why do we do it?'

It was a rhetorical question. He was already aware of the answer. Intangible motives like duty, tradition, even patriotism had a certain bearing – rather more than many of them would openly admit to, perhaps. But, more practically, sailing the merchant ships happened to be their job, and in that context bloody-minded stubbornness came into it as well: the sea was a formidable enough mistress at any time; you had to be either romantic-stupid or blockhead-stubborn to stay bedded with her in the first place.

So just to produce a strutting megalomaniac called Adolf;

turn Germans into something called 'Nazis': give 'em guns and torpedoes and mines and order them to impose their fanatical prejudices on you . . . well, that was hardly going to prevent you from doing something the winds of the Horn, the awesome fury of an Atlantic winter, the hell-screech of a China Seas typhoon, the prowling ice-packs of the far latitudes had all been trying to deter you from for most of your grin-an'-bloody-bear-it life, was it?

Lord, no! It never really occurred to you to stop. You just got that bit more frightened that little bit more often, and carried on anyway.

'He can't be very bright; not much of a psychologist when you come to think of it,' Chief Officer Ellis decided as he looked out over those doggedly-plodding ships in the night.

'. . . that Adolf Hitler man.'

'Grin and bear it' had been the watchword for the fledgling seahawk Ellis right from the start; from the moment he'd first set foot on that windjammer gangplank back in 1919 without knowing enough to realise she didn't even have such a thing as an engine. As far as being romantic-stubborn was concerned, it could hardly have applied in his case – him having embraced an apprentice seaman's life more as a means of escape from Father than out of starry-eyed idealism. So it must have been the alternative: the block-head-stupid motive that had kept him going.

She'd been a full-rigged four-masted barque. Her name was *Miseria*: it had proved a very apt title indeed. David Ellis's first voyage in her had lasted three and a half years and in that time he'd learned what misery, cruelty and semi-starvation really meant. He'd also learned the myriad faces of the sea in its every mood; the exhilaration of driving at sixteen knots before the Roaring Forties; the enchantment of the dolphins in the quiet hours of morning. He'd seen a man beaten to death with a holystone by a drunken second mate in Iquique; heard the last screams of three others as they were plucked from the yards by the talons of God off the Ildefonso Islets; watched a potential mutineer hoisted fifty feet aloft by his ankles to swing and slowly revolve throughout the whole of a tropic day until he had gone insane with the heat and been conveniently discharged ashore to a Peruvian madhouse.

He'd never gone down to the sea in a sailing ship again. Even then in those early Twenties the windjammers were dying. Perhaps he'd glimpsed the future; perhaps there was rather more of Father's self-proclaimed virtues of foresight and planning in him than he realised. Perhaps he always had been a steamship man at heart. Certainly he never felt the loss of the cruelly beautiful wind-ships as many of his generation did . . . but he never recaptured the awful excitement of those early days either; never became quite as aware of the magic of the sea from the bridge of a rumbling hull.

For some reason David Ellis never felt the desire to tie himself down; never did become a contracted 'Company Man'. But then, perhaps Father bore some responsibility for that, too: perhaps his seed had caused a reversion to his own hawker roots, contained the very stuff of vagrancy which Arthur William senior had dedicated his life to disclaiming. It must surely have proved the ultimate irony, had that really been the case – that in his son he had merely created yet another Sand-bone Man: only one belonging to the blue green oceans this time, not of the poverty grey streets.

Whatever the reason, the wandering sailor Ellis eventually found himself drifting from one shipowner's house flag to another. He just did his job: as fourth, third, second, then finally as chief officer – as Mate – in an indifferent variety of Red Ensign trampships. He hauled nitrates from Valparaiso to 'Frisco; shale from Sydney to the Channel; guano from Lima to Antwerp; general from Shanghai to Port Swettenham to Bali to Taku Bar to God-alone-knew-where . . . yet in all that time he never did find a sense of true vocation, a real calling for his craft: simply an undeniable competence.

And *that* was the reason why the thirty-eight year old David Ellis – during this North Atlantic night of 1941, which tendered such promise of his sudden violent end – was sailing only as Chief Officer Ellis of the rusted Steamship *Olympian*, Bone Collector to a procession of equally senile targets, rather than as a senior officer in, say one of the newer, sleeker motor vessels forming those fast HX convoys.

The point was that he still did it. It had simply never occurred to him to deny his profession because there happened to be a war: no more than it had to most of those two thousand-odd seamen out there with him in the shooting gallery of *das Todesloch*.

It certainly proved that, despite all his mistakes in life, Ellis had been right about one thing.

When it came to the rag-tag Merchant Navy – that Adolf Hitler bloke had proved himself a bloody *useless* psychologist!

'. . . your tea and pilchard sanwichis, sir,' the hoarse voice of Steward Weston echoed behind them.

Albert carefully cradled the plate and stood there for a long moment: eyes dreamy, sniffing like a Bisto Kid. Each limpid slab of bread was the thickness of a man's wrist and literally swimming in a sea of scale-glinting tomato sauce. Uncertain in the darkness, Ellis still swore he could detect a fish's tail protruding in mute despair.

'I tell you,' the Captain eventually pronounced with deep reverence, 'there isn't one o' your Crowned Royal Heads o' Europe could ask f'r a more appetising dish than this, Mister Ellis.'

Third Officer Cowan came out of the wheelhouse, eyed the culinary massacre in the Old Man's hand, muttered

'Jesus!' in a shocked tone, then got a grip on himself and said, 'Four bells, sir: and all seems to be well again.'

'Thank you, Mister Cowan . . . I shall be having my supper in the chartroom. Call me if you feel the need.'

'Aye, aye, sir.'

'I'll hang on out here,' Ellis volunteered.

The Old Man hesitated, then muttered grudgingly, 'You . . . ah, don't want a bit o' sandwich first, do you?'

'I c'n bring another bucket,' Slimy offered, then made a convulsive wheezing sound while his old shoulders heaved beneath the dog-eared, barely-white steward's jacket. 'Jus' my little joke, sir. No offence meant.'

'Thank you Steward,' the Captain snapped coldly.

'No' Ellis refused hastily. 'No, you enjoy 'em, sir.'

'You gets a nice view from up 'ere,' Slimy Weston remarked conversationally. apparently quite happy to settle down and study the ships waiting to be torpedoed.

'Leave the Captain's tray in the charthouse, Weston,' the Mate suggested nicely. 'Then bugger off!'

'Chief Steward set it 'imself, personal,' Slimy volunteered, completely unabashed.

Ellis could see that. Oh, the electro-plated metal teapot was there, all right – pointedly flanked by a tin of condensed milk with the lid wagging like the top of a tramp's hat and the barest scraping of damp sugar in a battered aluminium dish . . . but it was the cracked earthenware mug that betrayed the double-edge of spite. Hardly silver service to begin with, it was even larger than the teapot itself: a massive receptacle; a gargantua among mugs. Probably purchased from some Coney Island gimmick stall, undoubtedly with malice aforethought, it screamed the legend: *I'm made for a BIG mouth!*

Ellis hoped the Captain wouldn't think to read it until he was in the chartroom. Round four hundred and thirty-seven coming up: a technical knock-out to Grubby Grubb.

Unwittingly Albert marched off in the wake of Slimy's

shambling gait, pleasurably savouring a communion with pilchards long denied. He'd very nearly got there; arrived at the wheelhouse door, as it happened.

The tanker *Tunfisk* – that Danish aviation-spirit bomb only three ships ahead and in the same column as themselves – took a torpedo. Directly forward of her bridge.

Five

10.00 p.m.: Four Bells in the 8 to 12 Night Watch

It was an odd event, particularly at first – the destruction of the *Tunfisk*.

She didn't suddenly erupt as one might have expected: like many of those volatile tankships did. In fact, steaming in her convoy station some three-quarters of a mile ahead of them as she was, and more or less blanked by two vessels separating them, only Senior Cadet Moberly, from his loftier viewing point up on monkey island, was immediately able to hazard an educated guess at the identity of the latest casualty.

Cadet Westall was up there too, of course, but novice Westall wasn't yet capable of making an educated guess. Come to that, in Ellis's jaundiced opinion Cadet Westall wouldn't have known a tanker from a tugboat. Not unless it had 'Tanker' painted on its side.

All most of them saw was a bright flash directly forr'ad of the bow; sheet lightning slamming the silhouette of next-ahead *Duella* into momentary blinding relief which hung for moments as a black impression on the retina of the eyes – followed by the muffled detonation and what appeared initially as a cloud of dust hanging above the source, clearly discernible against the lighter night sky.

The succeeding blast wave twitched signal halyards and dodgers, touched cheeks with the faintest breath, rattled the ancient railway-carriage-type windows on leather straps which fronted the wheelhouse; then Moberly's shouted alarm: 'Explosion dead ahead, sir. Think it came from the tanker!'

The Captain roared 'Ter hell an' BUGGERY!' and ever so carefully placed his pilchard plate on a mushroom ventilator abaft the wheelhouse door before charging to the front of the bridge, hands clutching the dodger.

'Where away?'

Ellis said, 'Up ahead in our column. Sounds like it's the avgas tanker.'

'No it doesn't,' Albert snapped contrarily. 'She'd've made a bang like the crack o' doom! There isn't even a fire, Mister Ellis.'

'It IS the Danish tanker, sir,' Moberly confirmed, right on cue.

'*Bloody* U-boats!' the Captain snarled furiously. Ellis wasn't certain whether he meant because of being proved wrong, because of the pilchard experience now frustratingly delayed, or because of sixty Danish seamen so abruptly placed under tick-of-the-clock threat of cremation. Burton whirled and shouted at Third Officer Cowan's white moon face hovering uncertainly in the wheelhouse.

'Ring the engine to proper 'Standby'. Then phone down an' explain what's happening – tell 'em we'll be maneouvring almost immediately. Who's on the wheel?'

'McKechnie, sir,' McKechnie's shout came. 'Jus' relieved Able Seaman Sprunt again.'

Ellis was glad to hear the animation in the young seaman's tone. Maybe he'd briefly forgotten Mum and Vie under the adrenalin of fear – or maybe he hadn't had

94

enough time yet to neutralise his grief; to consider his own death an unattractive prospect once more.

'Then keep her steady as she goes f'r the moment, lad,' Albert said, gruffly reassuring. He turned back to his Chief Officer.

'Where's your life preserver, Mister?'

'In the chartroom,' Ellis retorted mildly. 'Next to yours.'

'*Bloody* U-boats,' the Old Man exploded again and hurriedly dropped the subject. It was two minutes into the second half of the watch. At the convoy's painfully slow speed they would take approximately another five minutes to reach the point at which *Tunfisk* had been torpedoed . . . only, where would the stricken tanker be then, in relation to her current position in Column Three – what, come to that, was happening right now: blinded as they were by the bulk of the apparently oblivious *Duella*?

'And where, for that matter' Chief Officer Ellis speculated edgily on that blacked-out bridge deck, suddenly feeling even more vulnerable than ever, 'is my *Kapitänleutnant* Neugebauer at this very moment, or whoever-else of his Ilk?'

For he knew his enemy must be very close; possibly right *underneath* them even, as they waited. In that very second – because he had to be a cold calculating bastard to have penetrated the convoy so early in the battle; before the panic really set in and the escorts were driven to distraction. Presumably he had the courage to stay submerged and silent; risk detection while the probes of ASDIC actually passed on either side of him before coming to attack depth – perhaps even surfacing in the half mile gap between their columns of ships.

It underlined Ellis's previous sombre reflection: that while the North Atlantic was the U-boat's frustration during its raging moods, so was it equally a confederate on any night such as this. For now it was the good fortune of the submersible to become a barely perceptible shadow,

95

merging against the dark gleam of the sea when viewed fron the high bridge of a freighter whereas, in their turn, the merchantmen steaming on either side would tower above it, clearly delineated against the lighter sky.

Three minutes gone. Yet no fire, no subsequent explosions: not even a flicker of light ahead – certainly no suggestion that a fuse had been activated to a monstrous high-octane petard within their midst. Even without ignition by the torpedo strike itself there were still sources of naked flame to trigger her lethal vapours: stokehold fires; a short-circuit from surely-damaged electrical systems; even her open galley range burning in innocent domesticity. Yet to all intents and purposes Column Three of SC whatever continued without alarm or diversion.

The Old Man was trying to peer ahead while hanging precariously out over the end of the starboard wing agitating and fractious. Briefly his Chief Officer considered gripping him by the tail end of his reefer but decided against it – deliberately to commit an act like that demanded courage greater than facing any *Frontboote*.

'What's happenin'?' Burton fretted. 'Is 'e stopped? Is 'e goin' to sheer out of line? Is 'e still under way? Isn't NONE o' them blind bats up ahead goin' to alter round 'im?'

'Whereaway the casualty, Moberly?' Ellis called. The apprentice's voice came back uncertainly. 'Can't make much out, sir. Not in the dark.'

'Bloody TYPICAL!' the Captain roared. 'Oh, give them bloody DEMS gunners a bit of a scare an' they all go trigger 'appy: snowflake; rockets; pyrotechnicals . . . but now – when we *really* needs some light – they've all gone to bloody bed. S'as black out there as a whore's ass in Addis Abbaba!'

'I'll nip over to the port wing,' Ellis broke in. 'See if I can make anything ou . . .'

The whistle blast from ahead was unmistakable: a

wheezing, asthmatic splutter finally converting to a tremulous screech: immediately followed by another – *I am directing my course to port!*

'Hardly a breath of extra steam – bound to be the *Joan M*,' Ellis interpreted. 'Next astern of the Dane.'

'Meaning the tanker's falling out of column to starboard,' Albert said, suddenly mollified. 'Though I still say it's bloody peculiar: full to the gunnels with aviation spirit, yet we haven't seen a lick o' fire yet.'

'God help 'em when we do,' the Mate thought. He didn't have to voice his foreboding aloud: they'd both watched avgas carriers blow.

'We'll need to be quick about it,' Burton said as if reading his mind. He didn't elaborate on what 'it' was, but his meaning was implicit: there had been no discussion, no debate on whether or not it was prudent to heave-to beside a floating bomb. Ellis wouldn't have expected there to be.

'I'll take charge on the well deck mysel . . .'

'There she IS, sir!' Moberly yelled from above. 'Coming clear to starboard now. She seems to be stopped, sir.'

The Captain spun. There was no irascible little Albert now: only a master mariner going about his trade, formal and competent.

'Mister Cowan.'

'Sir.'

'Ring us to half speed. We'll be taking survivors aboard shortly. Mister Ellis.'

'Aye, sir.'

'My compliments to the Chief Steward' – the professional Burton managed even that without the slightest hint of vitriol. 'Ask him to make sure he has plenty o' spirit to clean them poor fellows up: and to break out every spare blanket he has.'

He hesitated, sniffing. Abruptly he crossed to the forward dodger and pulled it down, scenting over it like an alerted gundog with creased brow and narrowed eye.

97

'D'you smell it? Can't you *feel* it out there, Mister?'

The Mate hurried over and faced the freshening breeze from ahead, from the direction of the torpedoed tanker. By God but Albert Burton was right this time: Ellis could sense it himself now; even detect the gentle speckle of wind-borne particles upon his inverted face.

Suddenly he remembered the curious cloud at the moment of the torpedoing; that haze of dust suspended in the night sky above the stricken tanker.

'Petrol, Mister Ellis,' the Captain said. 'Even the very air we're breathing is thick with it.'

As he slid down the bridge ladders Ellis heard the telegraph clang again for 'Stop Engine!', answered by the jangle of bells from below. Almost instantly the vibrations in the deck ceased and for the first time in eleven – or was it twelve? – days *Olympian* became a passive leviathan merely coasting through the night sea.

Second Officer McKerchar's gaunt shadow met him at the foot of the ladder. The two gold rings and the diamond around McKerchar's sleeves gleamed in the moonlight: that, and the fact that they only ran half-way around the cuffs as one of the pettier economies of war reminded Ellis that the uniform was almost brand new – and of the grim circumstance by which Second Officer McKerchar had lost his old one.

Even if it hadn't, then McKerchar's seeming fixation would have. 'Did you tackle the Bosun then, Mister – about whichever wee bastard was in at the boat stores?'

Ellis snapped, 'Jus' go to hell, Second' and shoved angrily past. He'd no concern right then for stupidities past; only for monstrous events about to happen.

'Gie' me a name an' *someone* will, right enough,' the Second Mate called, surprisingly mildly. Ellis heard the footsteps clattering behind his own down the next ladder to the funnel deck. For the first time the crippled vessel had drifted clear and into the full view, lying dead and black in the water. The cloying stench of petrol vapour was stronger than ever.

'So it's the Scowegian, is it? That's the hurry.' The Glasgow voice suddenly understood.

'She's a ticking bomb,' the Mate snapped.

'They're lucky then,' McKerchar said softly, unexpectedly; almost too low for Ellis to hear. Taken aback he halted abruptly, rounding on the angular man.

'Meaning?'

McKerchar dropped his eyes, just for a moment. It was the first time he hadn't stared Ellis out. 'Meaning just that: they're lucky. Either they get picked up – or they're dead. There's no middle ground: no . . . memory.'

Ellis felt embarrassed: he'd never heard McKerchar talk in a gentle way like that. He'd never thought of sailing aboard volatile tankships in quite that way before, either. But then, Ellis had never spent fifty-eight days on a hatch cover under a tropical sun with nine steadily-diminishing corpses as crew.

He felt the shivers again and forced concentration on the problems of recovering survivors from the sea heaving some fourteen feet below the level of *Olympian's* lowest deck. Ellis wasn't sure those Danish seamen ahead would see the advantages of being torpedoed aboard a giant Roman candle through quite the same philosophical eye as Second Officer McKerchar. Not right now, as the seconds for their survival slipped away.

The Second Mate's gaze locked back, his tone grew harsh again: maybe he, too, was surfacing from some macabre and better-kept-secret vision. 'Say what ye want. Ah'll see it's done. Smartly.'

'Just take charge on the after well deck like we agreed. Chippie'll have his recovery party there already. We're heaving starboard-side to the casualty on this heading – not enough sea running to waste time in forming a lee . . .'

He broke off. McKerchar was looking over the rail and down at the surface of the water. 'You could say there's even less need than ever now, Mister' he said expressionlessly.

Ellis saw what he meant before he started running again.

Animal or vegetable oils are exellent mediums with which to modify the effect of breaking seas. Kerosene or petroleum spirit is comparatively inefficient even when released in large quantities but still retains, nevertheless, the ability to dampen smaller waves wherever it lies.

There were no wavelets on the Atlantic swell anymore. No excited little white crests anywhere to be seen in that closing space of sea between *Olympian* and the breached tanker.

Along the starboard side of the foredeck seamen of the Bosun's party were preparing rescue gear as best advance planning and the miserable resources of *Olympian* would allow.

Two cargo nets had already been secured inboard of the bulwark. Even as Ellis arrived their rolled lengths were launched to hang outboard, suspended against the ship's side as rough and ready scrambling aids for any fit survivor. In anticipation of the less fortunate – the injured and the oil-helpless – the carpenter had busied himself earlier in the voyage with knocking together a wood and canvas cradle judiciously weighted with firebars which, theoretically anyway, should submerge sufficiently to maneouvre under a floating man. They'd never had the opportunity to give Chippie's contraption a sea trial yet; to attempt to lift the body-weight of a sodden human being up a vertical cliff while hampered by the height of the welldeck bulwarks. The cylinders of the cargo winches between one and two holds had already been drained and steam called to them; now they turned slowly out of gear in case of need: Ellis wasn't taking any chances on that score.

The pilot ladder had also been rigged and eased to the waterline; heaving lines and coiled ropes lay ready along hatch covers. The seamen worked in uncharacteristic silence, each casting anxious glances towards the drifting tanker. A sense of grim urgency had married with the petrol vapours about them now.

Ellis immediately sought the violated ship when he reached the bottom of the ladder. At first sight she looked even bigger from this lower viewpoint. While showing little freeboard, loaded deep as she was, the *Tunfisk's* midships bridge-structure and after funnel housing still appeared to loom above him, stark against the lighter sky. It was a trick of the night to some extent: they were three cables – over a quarter of a mile from her – though steadily closing: still sliding perceptibly through the water.

She'd been badly mauled despite her only appearing slightly down by the head – petroleum tankers, by nature of their compartmented construction and their lighter-than-water cargo did tend to stay afloat unless, or until, flame and roaring fusion took them. But already he could make out the rearing twisted skeleton where her forward tank-deck catwalk should have been; the glint of moonshine on buckled plating; the blacker-than-shadow cavern of a massive wound in her side. The port wing of her navigating bridge had been blown away, sheered clean by a high-explosive razor – would Second Officer McKerchar be envious then, of whosoever might have been on watch out there when the U-boat struck? No prospect for that particular Dane of dying slowly, adrift on an endless sea. Her foremast leaned at a drunken angle, her port midships lifeboat had vanished . . .

But where were the anticipated survivors? The bones they'd been delegated to collect? Where, f'r that matter, were her boats? Hadn't her crew even begun to abandon *yet*?

He peered frowning at his watch – seven minutes after

Four Bells. Grief, had only such a short time passed since she'd been torpedoed? They might still be trying to save her if they were brave enough – careless enough for themselves. Or still be attempting to count heads; free trapped shipmates; divide the quick from the dead. There must have been casualties within or upon the decks of that debris-raddled midships island. Many of her seaman complement, almost certainly her master and deck officers, would have been in that part of the ship at the moment of disaster. That, combined with the stupifying effect of shock might, for a tightly-disciplined crew, have delayed the final executive order to abandon.

'Mister *ELLIS*. Are ye there, Mister Ellis?'

He swung and stared up towards the bridge. The silhouette of Albert Burton's head broke the line of the starboard wing.

'Aye, sir.'

'Can you make anything out? See any movement over there?'

'Negative, Cap'n'.

There was silence. Then the Old Man's petulant growl drifted down. 'Well *I'm* not bloody waiting!' he lied.

Ellis snatched a quick glance around the break of the foc'sle. The last rank of SC whatever-it-was showed their sterns a good long way ahead now and steadily steaming away from them: already the more distant were hull down in the darkness. He'd never seen the convoy from this far astern; considered them as a separate entity. It was a Bone Collector's view, a new experience for the *Olympians*.

Ellis didn't enjoy it. He hoped he wouldn't be privy to it from that angle again tonight. He had a sick feeling he would, though – always assuming they were granted a second opportunity! No matter how hard he tried, he couldn't rid his mind of the big question; the doubt which must have been with every man aboard. Setting aside the reluctant Danes – even disregarding the likelihood of the *Tinfisk's* disintegra-

102

tion and the possibility of their own incorporation within that grand event – where *was* the resourceful *Kapitänleutnant* Neugebauer in his praying mantis craft right this second? Was he already watching them from beneath the waves through a mirrored Cyclopean eye? Was he an ordinary man or was he smirking a Nazi smirk over the misery of his latest kill? Was he sad, was he impassive – could he really still be remembering that little daschund of so very long ago?

Leather shouted, 'Boat on the falls, sir. Aft by her funnel. They're abandoning!'

'An' about bloody time!' the Captain snapped from high in the sky and disappeared. Ellis heard the telegraph jangle for a touch ahead, then Albert's shape materialised again.

'I'll take her in to two cables, Mister Ellis: no nearer. The water shouldn't burn at that distance, but any closer an' by God we'll be a Christmas puddin' in brandy fire along wi' them if she does blow.'

'Anyone lights a fag now, I'll see 'im in hell,' the Bosun growled threateningly. Somebody sniggered hollowly; even Chief Officer Ellis had to allow the grimmest of smiles.

Already nervous men whirled as Horrible Westall, eagerly clutching a pair of binoculars, suddenly came clattering down the welldeck ladder with all the delicacy of a baby rhinoceros. 'Captain says you might find these useful, sir.'

AB Edwards, one of the older seamen, patted his heart and muttered a pointed, 'Keep going, you fool!' Ellis only just resisted temptation and took the Barr and Strouds instead. 'Thank you, Westall.'

'Can I stay and help, sir?' The apprentice's eyes were almost pleading, fixed on the drifting tanker.

Ellis was going to say 'No': to file Westall out of sight and out of mind back up on monkey island. He didn't. The boy would have felt it too hard; been made aware of his isolation in what was still, to him, a desperately alien world.

Dress him down; yes. Bawl him out for whatever stupidities he would invariably commit – that was all part of making a sea-child into a mariner. But don't let him feel lonely. Don't make him believe he isn't needed.

'I'd be obliged if you would,' the Mate replied. 'They'll need every good hand we can offer to get them aboard.'

He could have sworn Westall grew six inches in that moment. 'Aye, aye, sir.' the boy enthused.

'But don't climb outboard,' Ellis supplemented hurriedly, nursing a sudden vision of half a hundred Vikings drifting patiently into the darkness again while everybody tried to recover Apprentice Westall. 'Don't go down the net; don't take your lifejacket off – and don't, for God's sake, get in the Bosun's way!'

It was a disturbing experience: observing the tanker through the glasses. Instantly magnified by the power of seven, and with the darkness affording less secrecy when penetrated by night-coated lenses, she slammed into visual close-up, yet the distance separating the two ships still deprived him of his sense of hearing; imbued his uncomfortably-intimate inspection with an eerie quality of silence. Doors hurriedly left open but undogged now swung monotonously with each roll of the helpless vessel – only he couldn't *hear* them slam. Fractured piping nodded weakly against blast-distorted rails, steel against steel, yet without a single clank or clatter. Torn iron plates worked continually against buckled iron frames within the compass of her shattered hull, yet Ellis's bewildered ears were denied the grating squeals implicit in such monstrous movement.

But iron against iron? Steel against steel? While simultaneously the glasses revealed that everywhere, from every rent and every split in the breached tankship's carcass, the vapour-lethal spirit continued to gush; to extend its already-massive encirclement of the sea around her.

Urgently Ellis swung the Barr and Strouds to examine the *Tunfisk's* poop and funnel decks. Yes, at least they *were* leaving – and quickly, thank God! But still with that detached and unreal air – mute men running along soundless planking; inaudible wire falls passing through seemingly frictionless blocks; Carley floats being jettisoned from cradles to tumble with silent splashes to the sullen mulch below. One boat packed with survivors almost water-borne, a second easing in agonisingly slow pursuit with figures clustered awkwardly in her sternsheets, struggling to ship the heavy rudder. Outstretched arms clutching from the boatdeck for man-ropes now; crewmen reminiscent of monkeys in orange lifejackets sliding hand over hand down lifelines.

Nearly two cables close, and barely coasting . . . Everyone aboard the hushed and cruelly-unsuitable Bone Collector prepared as best they knew how, though for what they knew not. Sailors and firemen gazed narrow-eyed out to starboard despite seemingly lounging over rail and bulwark with the time honoured slouch of the merchant seaman. The Captain's motionless silhouette high above, again deceptively relaxed with elbows splayed at the bridge wing. The Chief Steward's amateur first aid team of galley and catering hands hovered somewhat less confidently amidships; Bosun Leather was in the well, absently coiling and re-coiling a length of manilla.

'Get away from her,' Ellis urged those abstract images trapped within his binocular lenses – silently, of course. 'Get those bloody boats *AWAY*, dammit!'

Sweep forward again, returning to the massive wound just forr'ad of the tanker's desolated bridge structure; the sea clearly surging and swirling with sluggish persistence into her exploded numbers two and three wing tanks as she rolled to port; gurgling and temporarily relinquishing its oily occupation as she shuddered again to starboard while, all the time, the yellowed spirit still squirted and fountained to reinforce the volatile horror already abroad.

105

Leather started to call, 'Another boat, sir! Roundin' the bows from her st'bd side.'

At first, when Ellis saw the light, it looked just like a fitfully blinking eye: some suddenly-awakened creature peering uncertainly from the jagged cavern within her hull.

But only at first, though. Only long enough to draw breath; cry a shocked and quite unnecessary alarm – unnecessary because, as soon as the light began to expand it could be recognised as flame and then, suddenly, the flames fused into a ball of writhing white heat detonating outwards and upwards into the clear night sky.

Well, *everybody* could see what was about to happen, couldn't they? the avgas carrier wasn't no more than a couple of cables off, by then. So they hardly needed some clever-bugger Mate with three gold rings an' glasses to direct their attention to a bloody obvious thing like that!

The detonation of residual vapour within *Tunfisk's* wing tanks ruptured adjacent, previously fuel-tight cargo spaces. Burning petroleum immediately began to flow from the furnace; a cataract of liquid fire tumbling from the tanker's side, spilling and leaping into the sea around her. Simultaneously the water itself appeared to ignite – a wall of red and orange flame exploding from the inferno, racing fanwise in joyful release; licking and clutching skywards to merge into black-whirling smoke.

Ellis did detect sound then. A steady grumbling roar, the thunder of combustion as hundreds of tons of blazing spirit drew upon the oxygen around; devoured the night airs and thus generated its own monstrous draught. Within seconds the forward tankdeck of the Dane was engulfed, her bridge front already smoking and peeling to scatter whisking fireflies of burning paint which, in turn, were captured by the thermal currents, flung high above her highest decks to cavort in gay hysteria.

'Engine full ahead – Port ten the wheel!' the harsh command slashed from their own wing. 'Emergency ring,

Mister Cowan: double ring . . . MOVE, man, dammit to hell!'

The decision had been in prospect from the moment they'd fallen out of column. The Captain's instant reaction had merely been triggered, not prompted, by events.

'Port ten the wheel – wheel's TEN to port, sir.' At least McKechnie was cool, whether with the apathy of bereavement or not. There were others less experienced, less able to accept the inevitable.

''E's *leaving* them to it!' someone near the Mate said, dully incredulous. 'That bastard's actually leav . . .'

'Belay that!' another voice snarled. It was Ellis's own voice. He wouldn't have recognised it.

The clang of the telegraph startled already shocked watchers at the rails. And again: immediately reciprocated from below. Almost as quickly the deck below them began to tremble, and then to shudder as the triple-expansion engine turned in hissing protest. Slowly – Jesus *ever* so bloody slowly to anyone who knew – they started to swing away with the screw threshing white water.

'Port twenty.'

'Port twen . . . Wheel's twenty to port, sir.'

Sea-fire devouring the water in the vicinity of the lost tanker's wound. Little blue child-flames beginning to advance from the main family now, leaping and flashing ahead in excited encouragement as if beckoning their superheated parent.

Dry-throated, unwilling to watch yet helplessly mesmerised, Ellis swung the glasses aft along the shimmering red bulk of the Danish ship. The first boat to slip from the falls was desperately trying to pull before the advancing blaze, but there was no synchronised swing to the oars; no time to co-ordinate. Merchant seamen in commercially-pressured steamships were seldom afforded the opportunity to exercise the small-craft skills of their forebears. Now an already unwieldy lifeboat – even one crewed by men carrying the

107

bloodlines of the Vikings themselves – clawed for offing with panic-aggravated unfamiliarity; a fearful water beetle skidding unavailing against the surface tension of its pond.

Though almost waterborne the second boat was still suspended against the ship's side by the steel umbilicals of its davits. Even as Ellis fixed it in the glasses – again captured that distant image of occupants who curiously made no sound – the little blue flames appeared to dart within the periphery of his lens; entering from stage left, spreading instantly below the actual craft itself, licking and rearing, inviting their dreadful elders.

It was then that the men tried to escape from the spit-roasting boat; leaping desperately for odd patches of still black sea even as the fire reached up to caress them – only by then there was no refuge open to them because suddenly the fire was everywhere; fire and flame and roaring incandescence all along the tankship's length. Now she floated in fire, shimmered behind fire; blistered and peeled and then began to go soot-black above her waterline of fire.

Next the sea-flames surprised the lifeboat clearing the bow from *Tunfisk's* starboard side: only the fire didn't simply surround the boat and gradually devour it – for suddenly the whole boat itself seemed to explode until in one split second, there *was* no boat . . . just fire. Then with reinforced cruelty the flames chased and gradually overtook the Viking's labouring water-beetle, and Ellis again registered a terrible vision of hunched figures stumbling and beating and moving blindly through instant searing heat before the third and final splinter was swallowed whole, together with its frantic complement.

Chief Officer Ellis did hear the sounds of men in those last few moments, but not for very long and only faintly above the thunder of conflagration. It was in that most appalling moment of all that he at last found the strength – or weakness – to forswear the ghastly intimacy of the lenses: snatching them from harrowed eyes to stand nauseated and trembling.

108

Explosions began to gut the tanker's midships section, sullen detonations rolling across the intervening sea. Ever so slowly her foremast tilted and fell backwards against the oven of the bridge. Tanktops, piping, glowing debris scattered in a ring of splashes about her. Now only her rounded counter remained distinguishable above the furnace; poop decks and high funnel etched sombre within her self-fuelled pyre. The last of her crew to tend the boatdeck, the few left alive on board, chose to leap from *Tunfisk's* taffrail then: already-lost and impersonal matchstick figures when seen by the naked eye; climbing over and standing braced above the liquid golden sea with hands futilely gripping lifejacket fronts before they stepped into space.

A sonorous voice behind Ellis was chanting over and over again: 'Dear Jesus pity them an' show thy true compassion – Dear *Jesus* pity them and . . .'

An overly-repetitive requiem, perhaps. But what else could they reasonably expect from a Chief Cook?

'Compassion?' the more practical Chief Officer Ellis found himself translating savagely. 'Compassion's praying they don't grip their jackets tight enough, Chef. Compassion's praying to Jesus that the fall snaps the poor bastards' necks before the fire gets to them!'

The gap between them mercifully widened as the fire bounded in gradually weakening pursuit of *Olympian* herself: chasing futilely now from patch to patch of petroleum sea . . . until, abruptly, a vast rumble followed by a monstrous fireball rearing skywards. The fainter-hearted were still ducking, shying away from the rails as smoking steel plates hop-skipped towards them like flat stones across a river, but they themselves were safe because Albert Burton had been strong enough to balance his compassion with responsibility.

Somebody shouted harshly: 'LOOK!', and they looked to see *Tunfisk's* bow and stern sections rising together as

109

she finally broke in two amidships; both parts beginning to slide together into the furnace created by her dying.

'She's goin',' AB Edwards muttered, and crossed himself.

'. . . pity them an' show thy true comp . . .'

'Robbo! Shut up f'r fuck's sake!' the Bosun breathed.

Her funnel angled to forty-five degrees now, belching great gouts of steam and soot, slipping faster and faster downwards into the volcano . . .

'Our *Father*, then . . . which art in Heaven: hallowed be . . .'

'MIDSHIPS the wheel.'

'Midships . . . Wheel's AMIDSHIPS, sir!'

Olympian's after end mercifully swinging as she crept to full revolutions. Gradually the holocaust became masked by their own ungainly superstructure until, soon, even the little blue child-fires were falling from view. Now only isolated patches of burning sea remained, winking spitefully to mark the place where the Collectors had waited, but which the Viking Bones had never quite managed to reach.

Litle Cadet Westall was still unmoving; staring out over the bulwarks. In the fire-glow that was left Ellis could just detect the trace of tears on ashen, rounded cheeks. Bosun Leather beat him to it.

'Come *on* then, Mister W,' the old man growled fiercely. 'You an' me: we gotter show them idle sailors how to get all this gear back inboard now.'

The Atlantic wind came over the bow; a clean fresh breeze where, minutes before, had hung the stench of spirit and sudden death. It was difficult to believe in those few bracing moments that, up ahead, Convoy SC something-or-other still lay. Plus the Air Gap; the Front Line U-boats . . . and the uncertainty of the night hours yet to come.

Ellis lit a cigarette with absolute safety and turned for the bridge.

'Stand below the rescue watch,' he said.

Six

'One should never put on one's best trousers
to go to battle for freedom and truth.'

Henrik Ibsen: 1828–1906

10.30 p.m.: Five Bells in the 8 to 12 Night Watch

Climbing the ladders to the bridge again permitted Chief
Officer Ellis – if such dreadful opportunity could be described as privilege – one further uninterrupted view astern
of the place where *Tunfisk* and every last man of her crew
had died.

Now there was no part of any ship to be seen: only that
fire on the water, so hot now that it appeared to suck
together into a waisted, flame-twisting spiral before turning
to smoke reaching ever higher towards the stars. It would
burn for a long time yet, continually fed by sea-springs of
petroleum rising from the tanker's crushed and probably
still-sinking hull.

As Ellis hesitated, again compelled to look, he discovered
that Radio Officer Pemberton was watching too; leaning
over the rail outside his telegraphy room. Oh, casually of
course, like everybody else, and backed by the comfortable
twittering screeches of his trade, but with hands clasped
together so tightly that Ellis could hardly fail to notice the
knuckles white in the moon-fire glow.

'If I can tell a man's state of mind from his hands in this
light, then the U-boat which killed the Vikings can easily
target a ship as big as ourselves,' Ellis thought apprehensively, glancing hurriedly around the near sea upon

111

which the little red-licked waves were playing once more, uninhabited by any taint of oil.

He suddenly registered that there was no jewelled path to the horizon on the port quarter anymore: no far away beauty. Fire had finally taken Captain Falconer's *Valiant Star* just as surely, if not quite as shockingly as it had taken the avgas carrier. The Mate wondered if it had taken Benjamin Falconer at the same time, or if he was still alive and temporarily safe over there aboard the Bone Collector for Column Six. Dripping wet, oil-smoke black an' chewing those metaphorical nails of Albert's.

Talking of Bone Collectors – still no sign of the straggling *Theotokos* even now. Yet surely, if she had been attacked, then someone aboard would have reported a flash, a detonation from astern? Or had she – having once relinquished what was at best the dubious protection of the convoy – deliberately veered from the prescribed route and decided to go it alone? Might the Greeks not have placed their faith in continuing solitude; ignored orders despite repeated warnings from Naval Control on the even-slimmer chances of survival of any but the fleetest of independent sailings?

'We bought a dog when I was home last,' Sparks said without taking his eyes off the fire astern. 'The wife calls it "Ruff" an' the kids call it "Bow-wow". It gets bloody confused.'

It never occurred to Ellis to think it odd that a man might talk of dogs while viewing Golgotha.

'We used to have a cat,' he encouraged, conscious of the nerve-whitened knuckles. 'My wife called it a bloody nuisance.'

It was the first time he'd allowed himself to think about Jennifer. He didn't want to. It was very important not to dwell on anything like that . . .

Pemberton obliged by changing the subject. 'I'm running out of matches for the model,' he muttered. 'Only

112

half way through making the lower bridgedeck; no funnel; no hatch covers . . . an' hardly any matches left.'

'You'll get more in Liverpool when we dock. Not that long now.'

'They're hard to buy: kept for the regular customers back home. Probably rationed by now. Either way I don't suppose I'll be able to pick up enough to make the bloody crosstrees.'

Discreetly Ellis cast a glance around for the U-boat again. Of course he didn't see it. You very seldom did when they were there for real: you only saw U-boats when there weren't any U-boats at all.

'There's plenty in the dry stores: try being nice to Henry Grubb. If you can't bring yourself to go that far, then Alf Leather might take up a collection from the crowd: most've them'll save their used ones seein' you're still considered as half-human – the Sparks, and not a deck officer as such.'

'Spent ones aren't any good: not when they're all charred and black.'

Like the floating corpses of the Vikings would be. It was then that Ellis saw the tears coursing down Pemberton's cheeks; reflecting the receding glare of Valhalla. They weren't the same sort of tears shed by Cadet Westall though – his had been uncomplicated tears: the first tears of innocence brutally confronted. The Radio Operator's were those of a young man who had witnessed horror too many times before: had found himself unable to cope as most of them did, and thus had become obsessed by a nightmare.

And what comfort could Ellis offer: what prospect of a forseeable end to Pemberton's nightmares? His encouraging reference to their being home in a few days – Jesus, that promised little enough relief! Sparks – both of them for that matter – would be heading back out into the Atlantic within a week, a fortnight at the most even if the

Mersey hung thick with the smoke from smouldering wharves and people's homes when they eventually docked, and the blitz succeeded in temporarily delaying their discharging.

So who could Willie Pemberton turn to? And what, for that matter, could he say? 'Please help me – I *cry* every time I watch men burn?'

'I'm going to talk to the Old Man, Willie. Arrange for you to go and see someone about a break when we get in. The Marconi doctor: maybe the Naval Control people.'

Sparks did look at him then. There was a wan smile on his lips at odds with the tear-courses against his cheeks. It wasn't a smile of humour though; simply a wry despondency. 'We're Merchant Navy, Dave. D'you know what they'll say? – they'll say: 'Go away, laddie. Jus' be bloody grateful you're not in the armed services like everyone else your age: that you're not a proper fighting man!''

Cynical maybe, but not entirely removed from the truth. Ellis had met a torpedoed ship's master earlier in the war – his ship, an iron ore carrier, had gone down within thirty seconds of being struck, taking all hands but those watchkeepers swept helplessly from her capsizing bridgedeck. When he and his sole surviving officer – her Third Mate – had eventually been landed in the UK they'd possessed only the clothes they wore. Exhausted; uniforms still stained with oil and seawater; wearing old submarine jerseys and ragged plimsolls donated by the rescue escort's crew, they'd entered the first hotel they'd come upon in search of a good square meal: a sad but resolute celebration of their own deliverance.

The head waiter had refused them access to a dining room liberally sprinkled with patently brand-new khaki and service blues. 'You'll find the Seamen's Mission in Steampacket Lane' he'd informed them with barely concealed distaste. 'We only serve properly dressed civilian gentlemen and commissioned military officers here. And I really must

114

add that it's time you Merchant Navy people realised there's a war on: learned to observe certain standards. Look at yourselves – My God, you aren't even wearing *ties!*'

'We'll still try, Willie,' Ellis said without a lot of conviction.

'Thanks, but I'd rather you didn't. And don't suggest I take the option of joining the army instead, Dave. For one thing, I'm a non-combatant at heart and, f'r another . . .' Sparks did smile openly then: it must have taken quite an effort, 'how am I expected to finish the model if I've got to spend all my time shooting back at the bloody Germans?'

Ellis saw the change and was relieved. From a purely objective point of view – for the sake of shipboard morale, to say nothing of Pemberton's own self-esteem, he wouldn't have wanted any of the others to have seen Willie like that.

He grinned back. 'The Bosun wouldn't agree. Leather would give his right arm for a gun on our poop. He's about as pacifist-minded as Attila the Hun.'

Pemberon switched his gaze back to the sea fire. The smile had gone again, but at least the strain had as well. He didn't seem upset any more; or not from the outside, anyway.

'I don't cry simply because I'm scared, you know? I don't think I am, f'r that matter – no more nor less than anyone else. The tears just happen. Jesus, I can be sitting listening in, maybe working on the model; even reading a book – an' suddenly I find tears streaming down my face. I don't *want* to leave the job: to leave the sea. I'm not a coward, Dave.'

'Where's your lifejacket?' Ellis asked abruptly. Sparks frowned.

'In the radio shack. Beside the key.'

'You're not a coward, Willie,' the Mate said. 'There's plenty of our blokes already wearing theirs down there, and they're not cowards.'

'You're not even carrying yours,' Pemberton pointed out.

'I'm a bloody idiot,' Ellis grinned, turning for the ladder. 'See you later, Operator.'

115

'Hopefully in a happier state. Mate,' Willie rejoined spiritedly, and Ellis felt glad because he could see that Pemberton was at least trying hard.

The Captain looked tired for the first time when his Chief Officer arrived on the bridge. Tired, and uncharacteristically dispirited. Ellis guessed intuitively that their failure to save the tanker's crew had hit Burton harder than he would ever reveal. Being a Bone Collector, it was proving, could demand an even higher premium of sadness than just being an ordinary convoy ship.

Ellis could guess at what was on the Old Man's mind but he didn't ask: there always had been a comfortable *rapport* between them; he knew Albert would tell him when the time was right, and only if he wanted him to know. In the event neither man spoke for quite a while; just leaning and staring ahead together to where the convoy looked like barely-perceptible teeth on the black horizon. It was lonely back here: bloody lonely. Ellis didn't think he would like to emulate the action it now appeared the Greek *Theotokos* must have taken – to go it as an independent. Not at seven or eight knots. It seemed to him that, when faced with the prospect of dying, even the company of the equally helpless offered some small comfort.

Eventually the Captain did speak. There was no belligerent Albert, though.

'Should I have gone in closer?' he asked quietly.

'No, sir.'

'Truth? Or kindness, Mister Ellis?'

'With respect, sir, I don't have to tell you about a shipmaster's duty. There are fifty two of us depending on you to strike a balance between compassion and foolish irresponsibility while you're in command.'

Burton smiled thinly. 'You have a somewhat direct way of consoling a man, Mister.'

'It's not meant as consolation; it's common-sense fact – a

116

hundred-odd men burned to death instead of fifty. That fire came close enough as it was: the time they took to get those boats away, they'd never have made it even if you'd risked this ship and crew to halve the distance.'

They'd finished taking the scrambling nets inboard on the foredeck; now they lay ready-rolled along the starboard bulwarks once more. Situation normal – everybody bloody well waiting for something to happen again. Looking down from the bridge Ellis could see most of the crowd now philosophically resigned to a sleepless night, idling in conversation with the wind plucking at bare heads and the glow-worms sparking defiantly in cupped hands. He could detect the stocky figure of Alf Leather sitting on Number Two hatch cover with one tree-trunk arm outstretched, demonstrating some salty and no doubt totally untruthful story to the rapt white blob which was Cadet Westall's face. He'd seen a painting in an art gallery just like that, once: *The Boyhood of Raleigh* it had been called, or something like that. Ellis couldn't really conceive of Westall as being a second Sir Walter in embryo, mind you, but he was glad to see the boy had quickly overcome his shock at the manner of the tanker's death. And grateful to the Bosun for his part: Leather wasn't so damn tough as his name implied.

'Don't you *know* why it took them so long to abandon, Mister?' Ellis heard the Old Man ask somewhat oddly. 'Didn't you see what they were doing through your glasses?'

He frowned, drawing his eyes from the foredeck. 'I didn't have binoculars until Westall brought them down. The Danes were leaving by then. What were they doing?'

'Bailing their own lifeboats, Mister. Before they dared to launch them.'

'Bailing them *out?*'

Ellis didn't understand. Lifeboats slung high above the sea in davits, even with strongbacks and covers removed for instant access under wartime conditions, would only be expected to fill in heavy weather or torrential rain; in that

117

event the normal practice was to remove the bungs, keeping them ready to hand while permitting the boats to drain automatically. In dry, settled conditions threatening an even higher risk of attack than usual – such as those prevailing tonight – then many prudent chief officers would have ordered the bungs to be re-inserted; pariculariy in *das Todesloch* of the U-boats, where seconds might prove critical following a hit.

And especially aboard a quick-evacuation ship: an avgas tanker, say. Like *Tunfisk*. But – assuming the bungs *were* in place – it still didn't explain the reason for her boats having shipped any water in this unsettlingly calm weather.

'They had to be lunatics,' Ellis muttered. 'Better wet feet – wet anything, come to that – than hanging around on top of a floating bomb.'

'Think of it, Mister Ellis,' the Captain's voice was tight. 'There's not a seaman in this convoy mindful of a drop o' seawater in his boots . . . while she *was* a tanker. Full of spirit when she was struck.'

And then Ellis understood. Suddenly he remembered the curious cloud which had hung above the place where *Tunfisk* had taken her torpedo: and the airborne speckles still keen on his cheeks as they themselves had approached the mortally wounded ship. And he conjured a memory of dreadful images captured in his lenses once again – of how the boats had seemed to explode even though the sea fire only briefly touched upon them: men instantly burning from head to foot though the main flames had barely overtaken them.

'They were bailing pure petroleum,' he muttered. 'The initial detonation must've flung tons of avgas into the sky before it fell back across the Dane's poop; filled her boats: saturated every man on deck.'

'Them poor lads were turned into living candlewicks, Mister Ellis. Climbing into what promised to become tinder-boxes in place of lifeboats.'

118

Ellis stared without really seeing, towards a horizon which he might or might not ever reach. So the Vikings had been forced to delay; they'd *had* to drain their means of escape first. With neat fuel slopping around the bottom boards, even though they'd succeeded in pulling away from the ship it would still only have taken one spark, one carelessly-shipped crutch . . .

'Jesus!' he whispered.

But surely none of those *Kapitänleutnant* Neugebauers under the waters out there – with or without the memory of a gutted daschund – would deliberately wish for a thing as terrible as *that* to happen to anyone: not to any ordinary chap just doing his job?

Not even if he was called Chief Officer David Ellis; and had lived in Salford once. When the world had last gone mad in the name of bloody patriotism.

In the early days he had found himself returning to the corner shop in the periods between voyages; spurred more, perhaps, by a sense of familial duty than anything else. He'd received little open welcome – particularly from Father – yet had devised a certain wry satisfaction from the way in which Ellis Senior exploited his homecomings. Capitalized on his presence to glean a little more community status.

'My very own lad!' Father would introduce him as to all and sundry who called by the shop. 'Guided and counselled by me from the day he were a baby. Now he navigates great ships across the highways of the seven seas, bearing this proud Nation's commerce . . . and on top of that, mark you, he's an *officer*.'

Well, he was an officer, admittedly: though to hold a mate's berth in the British merchant fleet of those days could hardly be held as having scaled the heights of Father's apparently-so-important social ladder: a marline spike, a vocabulary fluent in Anglo-Saxon basic and a ready fist being rather more useful assets aboard a tramp steamer than

119

table manners or a gentlemanly accent. And of course David Ellis never had aspired to becoming one of the newer, more sophisticated breed of seamen who, with telescopes under their arms and uniforms by Gieves, paced the bridges of the four-funnelled Transatlantic liners – the truly 'great ships' of Father's imagination. He didn't dispute the point with Father though: he'd accepted a long time ago that it wasn't worth arguing with Father; not while you were living under his roof, not even if you were the most feared bucko Mate to swing a rope's end the moment you actually went back to sea.

But even then they tended to prove awkward, strained visits, especially at first. Self-consciously lean by virtue of glowing health rather than the then still-inadequate diet of local mill workers: sun and wind-burned – contrasting sharply again with the industrial pallor of one-time contemporaries – and increasingly bearing the confident stamp of authority, the Fourth, and eventually Third Officer David Ellis of the early nineteen-twenties found himself becoming more and more estranged; particularly from the elders who had accepted the deprived slum conditions of his childhood so meekly.

But then another factor began to emerge which left him loathe to sever all ties. The maturing Ellis became aware that a wind of change was also blowing through the shore-bound elements – the younger female-shaped elements in particular. He didn't realise it of course, but ever since the 1918 Armistice the emancipation from those same post-Victorian attitudes which caused his own rebellion had been gathering momentum. A determination to enjoy life instead of simply to exist was becoming prevalent among many of his own age who found themselves in their twenties in 'The Twenties'.

One particularly attractive member of the new generation seemed, to David at least, to personify that zest for living. It so happened that he'd admired her over many years from a tongue-tied distance: in fact ever since he'd first singled her out as a dark-eyed temptress in a certain Primary Standard IV. Lord, he'd even given her a ring once, but only in a secret sort of way – through the medium of a 'Waldo's Giant Lucky Bag'.

So it may well have been the case that his returns to Salford owed nothing to subconscious filial affection. Perhaps David's self-perpetuating confrontations with Father camouflaged a much less complex reason for continuing to spend his leaves at home – for might they not simply have provided the perfect means of renewing his long-term pursuit of the enchanting Jennifer Morden?

By the summer of 1924 young Third Officer Ellis had discovered an emotion previously quite alien to him. Most psychologists would have recognised it as something called, 'Love.'

'What time is it?' the Old Man growled.

'Nearly . . . eleven-o-clock.'

The Captain wriggled his bottom then eased each leg in turn, bending them at the knees with a grimace. 'Gettin' old. Old bones get stiff, standin' up here for hours on end.'

It was the first time Ellis had ever heard Albert Burton refer to age.

'Why don't you nip below for a spell? We won't catch up with the convoy before midnight. I *can* cope, you know.'

'I don't doubt it, Mister Ellis, but I couldn't. I 'aven't got the mental discipline to lie down there in me berth knowin' full well – the way Sod's Law works – that the minute I close me eyes some sausage-eater's going to press a tit an' spoil the whole bloody night.'

Ellis wished it were so simple: that so long as the Master was on the bridge the ship really was invincible. They could breed a race of super mariners who didn't need rest then; and nobody would be able to sink their merchant fleet no matter how old and rotten it was, and there wouldn't be any

121

point left in having a war at sea, and nobody would ever get burned alive or blown to bits or drowned in oil ever again . . .'

Ellis gave a metaphorical shrug. The Allies hadn't got round to producing adequate escorts yet, never mind Master Masters for the convoys, so they still had to rely on the Albert Burtons who weren't invincible at all, just dogged and unassumingly gallant – even though they did covet pilchards and wear pyjamas under uniforms. And grew old more quickly than ordinary men because of the weight of responsibility they carried.

'I'll have the stand-by man bring you a chair,' he said. 'I keep telling you I could get Chippie to rig something permanent if you insist on spending hour after bloody hour out here.'

'Now don't you go gettin' all motherly an' petulant on me,' Albert protested. 'If I 'appened to be a budgie in a cage – *then* maybe I'd need to sit on a bloody perch all night. But I'm bloody not: so I bloody won't!'

Ellis grinned secretly to himself. They helped each other during these informal yet never indisciplined sparring matches: this time he was helping Albert. Justifiably or not, the deaths of the Vikings would stay with the old Man for the rest of whatever life the U-boats granted him: it was up to his Chief Officer, as far as he was able, to prevent that burden adding to the already-taxing weight of command.

No one would be able to help Albert Burton then. It was in the first night hours after landfall, when a man was alone, that the rationalising really began; the 'ifs' and the 'buts' of what might have been. Whereafter, if you were a realist and knew that you had done your best, you got up one morning and went back to your one-sided sea war, and ran the gauntlet of the current Master Race with tolerable fortitude once again.

The Old Man started to shift uncomfortably once more. 'God rot me bloody drum-sticks,' the Mate heard him

122

mutter, and smiled to himself again. Albert's stubbornness had worked him into his usual corner: now there was no way pride would let him ease the ache in his legs by relaxing, even briefly, on a convenient lifejacket box or casing. He wouldn't even allow himself to be seen to slip into the chartroom now, to tackle that revolting tinned-fish supper so rudely postponed by the tanker's death-blow. Not while it might be construed simply as a ploy to sit down.

Ellis didn't go all that much on Hitler's chances of winning this war when he thought about it again. The British might not have bred a Master Race of shipmasters yet . . . but by God they must've produced more than enough with the kind of awkward bloody-mindedness that drove would-be dictators to chew carpets.

'I'll leave you here then; go over to the port wing an' chat to the lookout for a while,' he said pointedly.

Albert brightened visibly. 'Aye? Well, don't feel the need to hurry back, Mister Ellis: the lad could do wi' a bit of company.'

Ellis grinned in the darkness as he left: there were more ways of skinning a cat than by shoving a chair under its backside.

He hadn't been out of Burton's sight for more than two minutes when everybody aboard *Olympian* heard the roar from the starboard wing.

'All right – who *did* it . . . ?' the Old Man bellowed. 'Who bloody DID it then?'

Of course eventually Albert remembered he'd done it himself. And it was a perfectly understandable oversight in the darkness – to have forgotten, in the confusion following the *Tunfisk* incident, that he'd left his plate of pilchard sandwiches balanced on top of the ventilator situated in the after corner of the bridge.

It had just been the right height, too: that ventilator. And secluded enough for any shamelessly deceitful man to select as a spot for a sneaky sit-down.

Seven

‎———————◇◇◇◇◇◇◇———————

'D/F bearings on 4995 kc/s at 2107Z suggest heavy U-boat concentrations to NE and SE your track. 2. This is not repeat not to be taken as urging you to maintain Convoy PCS [Present course and speed] against your discretion'

Admiralty to Convoy Commodore

11.00 p.m.: Six Bells in the 8 to 12 Night Watch

The moon had begun to dim fitfully behind fleeting webs of cloud by the time the Old Man had de-pilchardised the seat of his battle trousers and, having heaved the squashed remains overboard – Chief Steward Grubb's plate included, prowled in simmering and aromatic isolation back out on the starboard wing, daring any man, even Ellis, to approach.

The wind had become more lively too and, while the sea itself still sighed with masochistic pleasure rather than exploded resentfully under the bluff-bowed thrust of the hurrying ship, Chief Officer Ellis could smell that a change of weather was approaching at last.

But would the new conditions reach them in time to give even scant cover from the main force of U-boats which everybody aboard now sensed was near? Because everybody did. There was a feeling, a tangible apprehension abroad in *Olympian* which whispered that *die Rudeltaktik would* be implemented tonight – perhaps now, in the next five minutes . . . perhaps not until four or five-o-clock in the morning, just before the moon-black lightened to watery

124

grey and false hopes were stirring as their last night in the Death Hole was giving way to dawn.

It would happen by then at the latest. The butterflies in each man's gut insisted that it would. And fifty three butterflies, many of them bitterly experienced, couldn't be wrong!

The convoy they were chasing now spread before Ellis' dimly seen, like erect and sombre castles across a desert of pitch, proceeding in lines of quiet determination. Every so often the castles would briefly become elongated islands as the ships altered to yet another zig-zag. Occasionally, very occasionally at that angle, a momentary gleam or a flash would spark among the plodding throng as roll or dip and tilt of porthole or window glass combined to reflect the moon in treacherous betrayal.

There were the signals which gave already-clumsy secrecy the *coup de grâce*; drew the eye of even the most tardy of U-boat lookouts. Of such unavoidable indiscretions were bloody nightmares formed.

Third Officer Cowan's estimated position of 2300 hrs placed *Olympian* still some three miles astern. They had a good hour to run – slightly less perhaps if they cut a few corners from the laboriously weaving track of SC whatever-it-was – before they could scuttle into the rear rank once again to benefit, at least, from the psychological comfort of the herd.

Ellis suddenly became aware of a movement above him – Senior Cadet Moberly had been up there on monkey island, quite forgotten, since before the tanker had been hit; over sixty minutes ago now. At first he became angry with Cowan – the Third Mate should have remembered and called Moberly down. Then he remembered Cowan was already harrassed enough: the Old Man's fury over the pilchard trap was temporary, but his constant presence on the bridge during night after night at sea caused a strain for any young and relatively inexperienced watchkeeper.

During peace-time you could at least make your minor mistakes in private once the Master had gone below for the dark hours; in the convoy war not only did you carry the added responsibilities of station-keeping, signal interpretation and manoeuvring in column – all aspects of seagoing alien to your previous Merchant Navy training – but you also bore them under the continual scrutiny of your seniors.

And anyway: it had been Ellis, not Cowan, who'd sent Cadet Moberly up there in the first place.

The lad came shinning down the vertical ladder at his call. Ellis said, 'Sorry, Moberley: I forgot about you. Nip below for a cup of tea. Take as long as you like unless you hear the whistle.'

The boy smiled wanly, without resentment. 'It's been a busy night so far, sir.'

The Mate turned automatically to glance aft. The sea-fire was a good five miles astern now; still burning to cast a red aura reflecting from the base of the shadowing clouds. When he turned back it was the Death's Head bobbing vacantly above the home-knitted woollen scarf again; not Moberly at all.

Ellis knew for certain then that something appalling was going to happen to Cadet Moberly before very long. But was he also reading, in Moberly's dreadful mask, an omen which encompassed the whole of *Olympian's* present complement – could he even be staring into a mirror in some macabre way? A mirror reflecting his own future?

He would have liked to believe he'd recovered his self-composure instantly, but Moberly coughed hesitantly. 'Sir: You all right, sir?'

'Just thinking . . .' He plucked desperately for a straw of conversation. 'When d'you go up for your second mate's ticket?'

'One more trip, sir. I should have enough qualifying sea-time in by then. Unless, of course, they transfer me to another ship with a shorter run.'

126

'I hope they leave you with me. And you can take that as a compliment.'

The Senior Cadet smiled with obvious pleasure. 'Thank you, sir. D'you want me to bring you a cup of tea after I've been down?'

Ellis forced a grin. 'I've already suffered one mug of Robbo's kai. That'll keep me going till Liverpool.'

He watched the boy go and felt so bloody helpless and concerned for him. He was glad when Able Seaman McKechnie climbed the ladder after having been below for his fifteen minute smoke: at least Cowan had remembered the regular watch when the panic had ended.

McKechnie said 'Hello again, sir,' as he passed and went to the wing to relieve the previous port-side lookout, Sprunt. As Ellis strolled over he was slinging the binoculars around his neck.

'Well, how are the crowd bearing up?' the Mate asked casually.

'A few of the lads have gone back to their bunks,' McKechnie volunteered. 'Most of 'em are stickin' to the upper decks though. It looks like being a long night yet, sir.'

'Then let's try and pass it educationally,' Ellis remarked. 'Tell me a bit about rabbits.'

'How d'you . . . ?' The seaman looked surprised for a moment, then realised that Ellis had seen the New York cable. 'The telegram about Mum an' Vie, sir?'

'You don't need to talk about it if you don't want to.'

McKechnie shrugged. 'I'll be home in a few days: I'll have to face it then. They're gone an' that's all there is to it, i'n't it?'

'I suppose so,' Ellis said, trying unhappily to think of something consoling to add, and failing. He hadn't intended to reopen barely-healed wounds, only some light dialogue which might help both McKechnie and himself.

'How many have you got, McKechnie – rabbits, I mean?'

127

'Six, sir. Angoras.' He took a long, careful sweep of the beam sea through the glasses before lowering them. 'They're the long-haired kind. Well, it's wool, really: though it looks more like hair. We . . . ah, keep 'em in hutches in the back yard.'

McKechnie trailed off awkwardly and buried his eyes in the binoculars again, as though he'd told Ellis as much as there was to know about rabbits. It wasn't McKechnie's fault, it was simply the communication barrier sliding into place: that traditional suspicion which existed between members of the foc's'le and most ship officers – especially Chief Officers. Under normal circumstances Ellis would have been the last to discourage it: British vessels, whether engaged in trade or war, had conquered the oceans in centuries past largely by virtue of that most efficient hostility. It was just that, this time, Ellis himself had felt the need to communicate with yet another lonely man, irrespective of station or rank.

'What d'you feed 'em on?' he tried half-heartedly, sensing he'd already lost the battle.

'Rabbit food,' McKechnie said. Quite seriously. 'Sir.'

'Ah,' the Mate replied, every bit as solemnly so as not to hurt the lad. He turned away. 'Well, keep a good watch, McKechnie. Interesting, though – learning all about rabbits.'

After he'd pushed through the black-out curtain and entered the dimly lit chartroom Ellis still automatically searched for the brass bulkhead clock over the settee. It insisted that the time was fourteen minutes before three-o-clock. It wasn't clear whether that meant morning or afternoon but it was academic anyway – the mainspring had broken nine months ago and it was a safe bet that the parsimonious indifference of *Olympian's* Owners rather than the exigencies of war had caused it to stay that way.

His own watch said it was actually ten-past eleven. He

wriggled his wrist, then listened to make sure the watch hadn't caught some fatal disease from the brass clock, but it hadn't. It still ticked dutifully. Jesus, it really *was* turning out to be a long night.

How brief a period had actually passed since the first knock-and-run-away U-boat sank Convoy Number 12, the Dutch freighter, while he'd sipped cocoa in the galley with Leather and the Cook. Hardly a spit more than two hours altogether, despite his feeling more as if two whole days had taken their toll of nervous energy. So far it had largely been the mixture as before – the undertakers cut one coffin from the cortege, then wait. Then a second . . . maybe a third. And shadow, and wait. And, doing it that way, not only did they steadily destroy the tonnage but they also wore out those who mourned in helpless frustration over the corpses of fellow seamen floating face-down along their wake. They kept up the pressures of the psychological war in parallel with their explosive burial games.

But usually, by this point, the dawn light would have come once more, enabling red-rimmed eyes aboard the escorts again to protect the gradually-shrinking convoy – whereas tonight was different: tonight they'd tolled the bell with precipitate zeal, the white-capped funeral directors in their black-leather jackets. Only Six Bells in the 8 to 12 watch; four ships already interred; prayer books slammed shut again but not, it seemed too likely, put away this time . . . just kept to hand, so to speak; in the ready-use locker.

Maybe that was why the butterflies felt so uneasy about it. Well, sure as hell Ellis's Butterfly felt sick as a parrot.

If butterflies could feel sick as parrots, of course . . .

It was a devil: this waiting period sandwiched between spasms of sheer fright and moments of pyrotechnic-induced awe; particularly while you weren't actually standing a watch yet felt you should be doing something constructive – even more particularly when you also happened to be Chief Officer of the bloody ship.

Ellis toyed gloomily with the handle of the Old Man's teapot, luke warm now yet still ignored by Albert with petulant self-control. He registered his lifejacket suspended from the back of the door alongside Burton's and swinging with the slow roll of the ship. That made him link torpedoes and violence with his own tenuous mortality again, so he quickly forced his thoughts back to the broken bulkhead clock which, in turn, brought him full-circle to the miserly prudence of Owners.

Ellis smiled wryly: they were always favourite for taking a British sailorman's mind off more-immediate perils – his current vessel's Owners. Unless you were contracted to some of the big ocean fleets who had, by the outbreak of war, grudgingly begun to recognise that you were a part-human being, it didn't matter which tin-pot shipping company you'd signed articles with: the chances were they'd pare you to the bone over wages an' vittles an' conditions, and even then appoint some stone-pursed bastard like Henry Grubb as Chief Steward to make damn sure you didn't exceed your miserable Board of Trade due, whether master or most junior deck boy.

Christ, even the war was on the side of the shipowners rather than the crews who endured in their decaying hulls. For as long as hostilities lasted their ships were taken into charter by the Government; maintained by the Government; insured against loss by the Government . . . but did you know that they – your Owners – were also entitled to stop *paying* you from the moment you were forced to abandon? Your articles – your contract of employment for the voyage – were automatically cancelled when that happened, you see. So when you did strike a mine, or a bomb or a torpedo blew the guts out of your probably-unarmed vessel, then legally and officially you ceased to exist as a servant of the company. Right along with the bloody ship!

Ellis felt better having rebelled, even if only mentally, against the iniquities of a sea-going man's lot. He didn't

130

think like that often: not many of those he sailed with gave it even that much weight – they were seamen; it was their way of life; it had been for generations, and that was all there was to it. They would always gripe and complain about conditions, but to suggest the majority of them bore a burning resentment would be to undervalue what they were doing now; out here in the North Atlantic Death Hole or wherever else in the world British freighters were burning and Allied sailors drowned.

He couldn't help reflecting for a moment longer on the most hurtful aspect of all, though: that even in these enlightened days of 1941 too many people ashore still didn't want to know about the exploitation rife within the Merchant Fleet. Not so long as their food got through, and the fuel and the weapons and everything else needed to keep Hitler from their doorsteps.

Curiously it was Bosun Leather who'd summed it all up during the previous voyage. They'd been helplessly watching a tankship burn yet again. Just like the Danes' *Tunfisk* only quicker, more mercifully. There had been no survivors from that holocaust either.

The Bosun had said tightly, 'You heard they got a black market back home now, sir – people buyin' ration coupons on the side, an' that? Well, I wus just wondering how much of the petrol in that tanker would've found its way into some posh family's motor car f'r a few shillings extra on the side? Or to put it another way – what percentage of them poor bastards over there are dyin' just to make a profit f'r some bloody racketeer?'

Chief Officer Ellis glanced at his watch again: 11.13. Only three minutes had passed since he'd entered the chartroom. He began to think about Jennifer again. He didn't want to: he didn't even know what had triggered that line of reflection; he'd tried very hard to avoid thinking about her tonight.

Perhaps it had been talking to Able Seaman McKechnie

131

which had undermined his resolve. Particularly when the subject of Mum and Vie had got confused with the rabbits . . .

Ramsay MacDonald had just formed the first Labour Government ever elected in Great Britain by the time the then Third Officer Ellis finally plucked up enough courage to pursue his grown up Miss Morden rather more forcefully than by simply slipping her a token in a 'Waldo's Lucky Bag'.

Not that politics had anything to do with his decision, of course: he'd still have courted Jennifer even if the Conservative Mister Baldwin had been re-elected Prime Minister . . . no, that general election of 1924 had simply been one of the peripheral events with which he associated the milestones in his personal life and which still came to mind at odd moments even now, eighteen years later. In the middle of the Atlantic for instance, while waiting for something awful to happen.

Come to that another memorable event had taken place at about that time.

He'd been homeward-bound from Shanghai then, in an asthmatic old three-islander called . . . the *San* something-or-other, was it? Well, OK: so perhaps his memory wasn't that good! Anyway, their intermediate destination had turned out to be the port of Hamburg, and Third Mate Ellis had been every bit as anxious as the rest of her crew to sample a few modest European fleshpots before his return to Salford after months of Oriental tramping.

It was when they'd berthed that the notable discovery was made. Ellis had been pleasantly surprised to find that economic disaster was fast overtaking the German Weimar Republic: so much so that even a contemptible British seaman could afford to be Lord for a day on a sixpenny piece while, especially in a seaport like Hamburg, for one silver American dollar a bloke could buy practically anything, or anyone, he wanted. And why not – considering he was being offered 130 billion hyper-inflated German marks to the buck?

Most of them went stupid of course: finished up breaking a few Teutonic heads in the beer cellars along the Reeperbahn – had a few drink-addled British skulls cracked in spirited Prussian return for that matter – until finally most of the crew were bundled back aboard by non-too-gentle German policemen in strangely fashioned helmets, while a few of 'em never came back at all and were never seen again . . . and naturally neither the Old Man nor the Mate even bothered to look for 'em, because the *San* Thingumabob had been due to pay off in Liverpool a couple of days later anyway so any foc'sle hand who jumped ship, whether by accident or design, saved the Owners six months wages. And there were always plenty more where they'd come from.

'An' that had been that!' as they'd all thought at the time. A bloody good run ashore an' the cheapest dissipation you could ever hope to bore your mates with through persistent recounting in voyages to come. Only it wasn't to prove the end of their Teutonic adventure at all, was it? Because as things turned out they had caught a brief glimpse of what was to prove the beginning.

Not that any of those British seafarers who'd taken part in that memorable docking could possibly have interpreted what was happening around them at the time. Certainly no itinerant trampship hand of 1924 could have imagined that the seeds of a dictatorship – one which might well demand his own personal sacrifice in convoy nearly two decades later – had even then been sown in some Munich beer hall. That the post-Armistice resentment and the financial insecurity of the German people was already being turned to political advantage by monstrous men giving comic salutes – and that the most monstrous man of all had, during that very period in which Ellis's crowd ran riot in Hamburg, been preparing the first volume of a black-print for genocide called . . . *Mein Kampf*, was it?

Mind you, if neither Prime Minister MacDonald nor Mister Baldwin could see the need to counter the evil spawning within Germany during those early days of the Nazis, then how could someone very ordinary, like David Ellis, possibly have foreseen that a sailor's luck in being able to exchange a silver dollar for 130-billion reichmarks held such a dark and frightening portent?

And so, on the first afternoon of his return to Salford, he'd blithely dismissed the entire German misfortune and concentrated, instead, on visiting the place in which he might approach Miss Jennifer with some pretence of subtlety – Woolworths Penny Stores as it happened; where she then worked as a sales assistant.

The only snag was that, when he got there, he suddenly realised that shipboard life had hardly equipped him for the pursuit of love, and found he couldn't think of anything to say. So he simply wandered around trying to look nautical and terribly mature and . . . well, in the absence of further inspiration – pretending not to notice her.

Intentional or not it appeared to prove remarkably effective: his tactic of conspicuous disinterest. Admittedly he was aided by the fact that the drive for female emancipation was reaching its peak – the rigid conventions of Victoria's reign had virtually surrendered to the determination of young women to break with the traditional bonds of domestic service; to hold their own in previously male preserves of factories, shops and city offices; even in the military where, six years after the Great War, girls wore khaki uniform as a matter of course, and the bobbed hair styles of the Women's Army Auxiliary Corps hardly caused a shocked glance as they passed confidently by.

Jennifer was quite obviously one of that liberated band. Her hair wasn't only bobbed; it was shingle-cut. She wore

134

the tiniest suspicion of make-up, even at work. And *knee-length* dresses!

One might reasonably assume, then, that any bronzed – and of course, mature-looking nautical chap such as he; appearing impervious to Miss Morden's dark-eyed attractions must, at the very least, have presented an intriguing challenge to a liberated girl.

Whatever the reason, she eventually *did* speak to him first. In fact she smiled with such genuine encouragement that all his secret ambition had immediately found expression. Haltingly he'd asked there and then, right in the middle of Woolworths, if he might have the honour of escorting her to the newest Fairbanks moving picture after she had finished work that same evening.

Well, naturally, by the time they'd accomplished an adventurous thing like that together, even to the extent of holding hands while the projectionist changed the reels – Jennifer reassuringly, he awkwardly – the very naive Third Officer Ellis was metaphorically hugging himself with delight at the success of his own cunning.

It was to be years later before she impishly told him the truth – that he hadn't proved quite so subtle as he'd so imagined. Jennifer had been serving behind Woolworths' stationery counter on that first afternoon. He'd bought five India rubbers, three packets of pen nibs, seven pencils, two bottles of bright blue ink and reams and reams of notepaper – all on separate occasions while preoccupied with the art of 'not noticing' her . . . she had to encourage him to invite her out in the end: if only to stop him spending all his money!

. . . Chief Officer Ellis dimly registered the explosion of a torpedo slamming home a long way ahead and, just for a moment, bowed his head; gripping the edge of the chart table so tightly his knuckles showed bleach white – as white as the hands of Radio Officer Pemberton's had appeared.

But Willie had reached the advanced stage of nervous fatigue, surely? Whereas Ellis had simply received a bit of a shock – he'd forgotten where he was in that minute, that was all. Still back with Jenny when she'd been so pretty and he'd loved her so very much in Nineteen Twenty . . . Four, was it?

Jesus, but he did wish he hadn't allowed himself to think of her right then!

The bulkhead clock still insisted that it was only fourteen minutes to three as he forced himself to walk calmly towards the chartroom door and leave his lifejacket to swing idly on its hook as he passed.

But it wasn't that time of course – it was much closer to 11.30 by now: seven Bells in the not-at-all concealing dark of what was only the first night watch. Still hours of passive exposure to survive before dawn would offer relief.

Yet the already-diminished convoy was coming under attack once again.

Eight

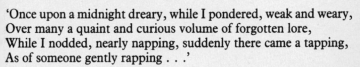

'Once upon a midnight dreary, while I pondered, weak and weary,
Over many a quaint and curious volume of forgotten lore,
While I nodded, nearly napping, suddenly there came a tapping,
As of someone gently rapping . . .'

Edgar Allan Poe: 1809–1849

11.30 p.m.: Seven Bells in the 8 to 12 Night Watch

It came ridiculously to Ellis's mind – that quotation from
'The Raven' – as he hurried once more into the moonglow
washing *Olympian's* bridge.

It kept repeating itself as his eyes, already conditioned by
the red-shaped chartroom lamp, made what little re-adjust-
ment was needed for full night vision. *I pondered, weak
and weary: over many a quaint and curious volume of forgotten
lore . . .*

He had been doing just that, too – pondering. The
memories had been infiltrating his subconscious ever since
he'd handed over the watch to Cowan three and a half hours
ago now; his sometimes wry reflections on what had –
perhaps, for that matter, on what hadn't – gone into the
making of Chief Officer David Ellis. He wondered grimly if
his nostalgia might be construed as yet another omen of
impending disaster? It was said that drowning men saw
their past flash before their eyes – was it conceivable that
those same drowned men might have engaged, however
unwittingly, in that depressing exercise for some time *before*
they fell into the bloody water?

While Poe's brain had created a further chill image:

137

Suddenly there came a tapping, as of someone gently rapping . . . ?

Jesus: such bland description. Yet wasn't it the very stuff of horror? The kind which stretches nerves thin as spider's silk; stirs spectres lurking beyond the swirling mists which mark the edge of sanity in every man?

'Suddenly there came . . . a TAPPING?'

Well, the U-boats tapped before they materialised, didn't they? Just like the nightmarish imaginings of Edgar Allan Poe only now, a hundred years later, the one-eyed bugaboos were spawned out of Krupps steel: tapped and rapped with talons weighing three thousand pounds, drooled compressed air bubbles; bellowed with the power of TNT . . .

'Here, Mister Ellis. Over here!'

Of course Albert assumed he was still night-blind. He wouldn't have guessed his First Mate was enduring the shivers yet again – Poe's shivers too, perhaps?

The rear rank of the convoy wasn't much more than a mile ahead now; Ellis could even detect the occasional froth of white water kicking from under the high counters.

'Someone in the starb'd columns: probably well up front,' the Old Man muttered without lowering his glasses as the Mate joined him. 'Just a flash so far; then the bang. Can't make anything else out yet.'

Ellis made a hurried appreciation of the sky. The clouds were definitely thickening; scudding now rather than drifting across the moon. When he put his face over the dodger he felt the wind moisture-fresh from ahead while three, maybe four-foot waves had formed where previously the swell had been smooth enough to mirror fire . . . but even if the threatening gale did come it would probably be too late. The North Atlantic was still ideal for killing ships: just not so good for any would-be survivors forced to abandon them. The nose and mouth of a comatose man adrift and supported only by a lifejacket hovers a bare

138

finger-span above the surface . . . A slack jaw can drown him as surely as if he'd stayed aboard when she went down.

'Couldn't have been depth-charges?' he tendered, without believing it himself.

'Torpedo,' Burton growled. 'Def'nitely a torpedo.' He grinned suddenly: well, it was more a grimace really. 'Unless some other ship's inflicted with a Chief Steward useless as Grubb, o' course, an' they all passed wind together. Grubb's vittles are bad enough to gasify a herd o' elephants!'

'There couldn't be two Grubbies,' Ellis speculated half-heartedly: more preoccupied with having left his binoculars lying on the chart table in his hurry. Now he was straining to detect the latest casualty without their aid. 'God couldn't possibly have made two mistakes in the same image.'

''E made a lot of Nazis, didn't he?' the Captain argued reasonably. 'Anyone capable of doing that wouldn't stop at one Henry Grubb.'

Strange, really – chatting idly like this despite the urgent need for vigilance. But then, even the shadowy figures on the forward welldeck didn't appear to gaze outboard with the same sense of apprehension now, while that atmosphere of crisis which had oppressed *Olympian* after the first casualty of the night – the Dutchman – had been hit wasn't quite so keenly felt. It seemed they'd become more philosophical in their waiting for whatever was to happen next. It wasn't a unique phenomenon: Ellis had become aware of it before, during previous convoy actions. After the initial panic when an attack began, your fear muted to a dull resignation in between sinkings. Perhaps it was something to do with the human chemistry – adrenalin and so on: that it simply wasn't possible to stay on a permanent high of terror. Perhaps man adapted to every situation despite himself: even to one in which ships and other equally-resigned men exploded around him at increasingly regular intervals.

'It sounds as though you don't take Him seriously,' Ellis commented eventually.

'Who: Henry Grubb?'

'No – God!'

'Ohhhh, I takes Him seriously, Mister,' Albert said with feeling. 'Specially out here in the Atlantic with the U-boats in tow. I bloody have to: in case He goes over to their side f'r spite.'

'They probably think he always has been,' Ellis shrugged. 'The Jerries in the last war even used to have *Gott Mit Uns* fashioned on their belt buckles – "God's With Us!"'

They fell silent, concentrating on the convoy. Eventually Ellis gave up peering and nipped back into the chartroom for his glasses. As he returned he met the Third Mate craning round the wheelhouse door. The Third Mate had his binoculars levelled fixedly ahead.

'Think I can see something, sir. Fine on the starboard bow.'

'Have you reported it to the Captain yet?'

Cowan shook his head. 'I'm not certain: I could be wrong.'

'Report it! Better wrong than . . .'

'Object ahead to starboard,' Burton snapped censoriously from the wing. 'Dammit, Mister Cowan: you should've sighted it; your eyes are younger than mine!'

'Ohhhh, screw *you* too, you miserable old bastard!' Cowan snarled in weary irritability – making damn sure, mind you, the Old Man didn't actually hear him. Ellis pretended not to: it was out of character for the normally placid young 3/O, but the tension got to everybody, even the meek.

The foc'sle lookout's cry came far too late, even making allowances for his lower vantage point. 'OBJECT AHEAD, SIR! Fine on the st'bd BOW!'

'Jesus!' the Old Man shouted in temper. 'Have I gotter shipload o' Blind Pughs pretendin' to be sailors, or has the

140

Third Reich bloody surrendered an' I'm the only one's not been told I c'n go back to sleep?'

Chief Engineer Gulliver came up the internal stairway into the wheelhouse just then, looking hot and oily. He jerked his head, raising a curious eyebrow towards the simmering Albert.

'What's he on about?'

Ellis kept his face straight as he lifted the Barr and Strouds. 'Pretty well everybody. He's not been the same since he sat on his sandwiches.'

Gulliver raised the other eyebrow in company. 'He didn't!'

'He did. Honest.'

'It's not been all bad then,' the Chief said delightedly. 'Even if we get torpedoed now, it's not been a totally wasted night.'

Whatever the mysterious object was, it didn't appear to pose a threat to *Olympian*. Half awash, it was really more a swirl of foam at first: only as they closed did it assume an identity of sorts.

'Ship's boat, sir. On its side!' Cowan shouted, determined to be first this time. 'And other wreckage, it looks like.'

Nobody had said much, but you could sense the feeling of relief on the bridge.

'Good on you, Three Oh,' Ellis whispered as he passed on his way to the Old Man. He noticed the columns were turning to another zig-zag ahead; passing across their bows now from starboard to port. Shapes which must have been the escorts were moving fast out on the convoy's threatened quarter: trying to keep the latest attacker down while their flock cleared the area.

'If we altered now, sir,' he suggested as he came up to the Captain, 'we'd cut a sizable chunk off our next leg.'

'No, we'll hold our course for a while longer,' Burton decided, showing no trace of his earlier pique. Then he turned unexpectedly. 'Engine to slow please, Mister Cowan.'

'Engine slow ahead, sir.'

Albert caught the doubtful expression on Ellis's face as the vibrations faded on the jangle of the telegraph. 'Aye, we'll chance a brief stop: I want a sight o' that wreckage, while there's something else strikes me as odd.'

The Mate frowned. 'Odd?'

'Anything occur to you as significant – about our present position?'

Ellis understood. 'We're coming to the area where that last ship was torpedoed?'

'Aye – and yet we never saw another drop back in support,' the Old Man speculated calmly. 'I'm wondering why, Mister Ellis.'

Ellis gazed grimly after the receding lines of merchantmen. Albert was right: none of their sister Bone Collectors *had* fallen astern on this occasion. Did that mean the most recent casualty was still struggling to keep up with the convoy – or had someone decided there wasn't justification in risking another ship to look for survivors from one which had sunk? If so, then that posed the further question of whether the Commodore had been forced to change the rules because Admiralty Intelligence reports suggested the U-boat threat was becoming even more acute – a factor which would apply particularly to trailing and isolated rescue ships?

Such as *Olympian* herself. A straggler in this very moment.

Burton lifted his glasses, making a further cool assessment of their approach. 'Stop engine. Midships!'

Ellis caught the whiff of pilchards as the little master hung over the bridge front with his toes practically clear of the deck. 'One scramblin' net down on your st'bd side please, Bosun. Have a shaded torch ready: just in case.'

Then they were coasting over what suddenly seemed an

142

even more hostile sea, only this time, the waves were slapping and banging warningly under the bow whereas they'd merely sighed in protest on the previous occasion, when *Olympian* had slowed to attend the tanker's funeral.

Again Ellis became aware of the eerie quality of such silent passage while feeling, quite illogically, even more exposed despite the absence of firelight.

'D'you want me down there?' he asked.

Albert shook his head. 'If there were living souls to pick up, God knows we'd be hearin' them now, Mister.'

The foredeck crowd had hopefully moved *en masse* to the starboard bulwark all the same: craning to observe the surface ahead. From *Olympian's* bridge it was now possible to identify the major piece of wreckage as a ship's lifeboat even with the naked eye. Lying on its side it floated strangely: only half a boat really; split along its keel with the port buoyancy tanks either perforated or blown away. There was something draped across the top of it: something vaguely human in form.

'It's a man,' Ellis snapped, screwing his eyes harder to the glasses. Quickly he scanned the surrounding sea; there was a lot of flotsam recognisable as having come from a ship now: a wealth of splintered hatch boards, a barrel and a chair, a mattress, a deck locker . . . what must have been part of a canvas awning or tarpaulin spread out grey and ghostly in the black water, undulating with the rise and fall of the waves.

And what might have been another man. Once . . .

Chief Engineer Gulliver arrived and stood behind them. 'She were an old 'un, whatever her name,' he said matter-of-factly.

The Mate half-turned. 'How d'you know, Chief?'

'Coal dust on the water. If she'd been a modern job she'd've leaked fuel oil as she went down.'

'You think she's under us, then. She sank?'

'Too many internal fittings around. Once you see matt-

143

resses and so on – look, there's a wardrobe door an' a bit o' table top, is it? You see stuff like that, Dave, an' it's a fair bet the sea's got into her upperworks.'

Everybody was staring over the side now as the broken boat drifted abreast of *Olympian's* stemhead. It was dangerous – too many people concentrating on one small area of sea while there were U-boats about.

'I catch any lookout takin' his eyes off of his appointed arc o' responsibility,' the Old Man shouted abruptly, showing the volatility of an opera star under the strain, 'an' I'll bloody *log* 'im f'r dereliction of DUTY!'

'There's a bloke on the boat all right, Cap'n,' Alf Leather called from below. 'Permission to put a man over to bring him aboard?'

'Touch astern to take the way off her, Mister Cowan,' Albert responded, mild as milk again. 'Pick that poor lad up if there's a chance he's breathing, Bosun: use the torch if you must. And sight if there's a ship's tally on the bow.'

'Aye, aye, sir . . .'

Just for a moment Ellis caught sight of Bill Gulliver's eyes beside him. They were narrowed – not looking down at the boat at all; gazing outboard into the darkness instead. The discovery depressed Ellis out of all proportion – so even their usually phlegmatic Chief Engineer was betraying anxiety tonight, could presumably visualise the white tracks of converging torpedoes just as clearly as Ellis himself; particularly while *Olympian* wallowed there so exposed and defenceless.

The deck began to bounce perceptibly as the screw threshed under astern power and abruptly the slap of water below the bow ceased. 'Stop engine!' the Old Man snapped. He raised his voice. 'Quick as you like now, Bosun.'

Two seamen were already over the side, hanging on to the cargo net just above the lick of the clutching waves. Thanks to Albert's skilled shiphandling less than six feet separated them from the half lifeboat, yet its tenuous rider made no move to respond. Ellis found he was gazing almost straight down at the scene from his lofty viewpoint on the bridge wing.

The man was wearing a standard British B.O.T. lifejacket, but the kapok had exploded from one side of it, fluffed and white and pathetic somehow. He was spreadeagled face down across the scarred grey planking with arms spread and hands gripping fiercely on what had originally formed the gunnel of the boat. His body was immersed from the waist down even when the waves sucked away from his part-craft; at other moments they almost reached his shoulders in their anxiety to claim him.

But he didn't let go. He was buggered if he was goin' to let go!

Not even when the boat drifted closer and one of the *Olympian* seamen leaned right out, lunged and got hold of the back of his jacket, and heaved. He just clung there like a leech and said nothing; refused point-blank to be rescued.

It was then that the Bosun triggered the torch briefly so's the beam slashed downwards, cutting through the surface of the water itself. And someone immediately vomited on deck while the two sailors on the net pulled back with shocked revulsion.

The stubbornly-unhelpful man's intestines waved below the surface like the tentacles of some great pink squid, reflecting the light in sinuous, wavering horror. Whatever dreadful explosive force had split the lifeboat must have cleaved the lower part of his torso also. But if it had – however did he then become so attached to the only part left of his sunken ship? His hands could only have closed with such a grip while life existed; not after death had mercifully taken him . . . Was it conceivable, then, that a half-man, even aided by his tattered lifejacket, had managed to reach the ironically-appropriate refuge of a half-boat, and cling to it before he died? Was the human will to survive so indefatigable that it could overcome such dread mutilation, however briefly?

Come to that? 'Was it bloody well worth his trying to preserve what little was left of him?' Chief Officer Ellis thought as he swung hurriedly away from the rail.

'For surely not even Mister Poe, with all his capacity for hideous imagining, could have envisaged human suffering quite as exquisite as *that*?'

The lost ship's name had been *Menestra*. Leather relayed that much in a steady voice before he extinguished the torch and they allowed the part-corpse to drift astern into the darkness still leeched to its terminal craft – and the more-or-less whole corpse too, for that matter, for the other blown-up man had proved equally intransigent; floating past out of reach and face-down in the sea, wanting nothing at all to do with them even as they'd speculated on the macabre determination of his shipmate.

Menestra. British Port of Registry: Newcastle-on-Tyne.

Olympian herself had been born there once, a very long time ago. It was more than likely, then, that they had both been sired from the same family tree of craftsmen; had baptised their proud new keels with the caress of the same waters. It afforded a sad intimacy with her loss for those who cared about such things; and many of them did because seamen tend, if nothing else, to be a sentimental lot.

It didn't answer the question posed, for which Albert had sought an answer – why no Bone Collector had stayed with her? For as soon as they were under way again, and the waves were once more smashing and flaring beneath the bow, and the funnel puttered smoke and the decks throbbed with revitalised urgency, the Captain had hurried down to his cabin safe, only to return with a sour expression.

'I just looked up the convoy plan,' he growled. '*Menestra* were listed as number fifty-two: second ship in column five . . . Down to 'er marks wi' iron-ore.'

'A dead-weight cargo,' Ellis reflected. 'Liable to shifting: minimal air space in the lower holds: no reserve buoyancy . . . bloody apt, really – a dead weight.'

'Then chances were she kept on going right under when she was hit,' Chief Gulliver commented levelly. 'Makes me grateful we're just a dehydrated omelette pan.'

'So did her column rescue vessel leave 'er because the odds were she went down with all hands – or was he ordered to stand on because the Commodore's learned somethin' we haven't?' Burton gloomed, revealing involuntary pessimism for the first time that night. '. . . like there's more U-boats waitin' up ahead than we got ships in convoy?'

'Oh, come *on*, Albert,' the Chief protested, lightly encouraging. 'Jerry can't have that many subs in the whole Atlantic – an' anyway, we're near as dammit home: they can't hit us that bad now.'

'No? Then what about SC 7 not all that long ago? *They* were less than four days from home – an' you know what happened to them poor fellows as well as I do.'

'Nothing official's been released,' Ellis interjected hurriedly. The manic-depressive course of the conversation was hardly helping but it was hard to stop the Old Man once he was in full gloom.

'That's right!' Gulliver growled, getting nettled. 'I don't listen to rumour, Albert: neither should you.'

'They lost twenty ships, I'm telling you – sixteen in one night,' Burton insisted, wallowing in the kind of masochistic self-indulgence he normally reserved for Grubby Grubb's vittling. 'Same run as us: slow convoy from Breton . . . The old *Assyrian* was Commodore ship – she was sunk. And the *Eaglescliffe Hall*, the *Trevisa, Wandby, Shekatika* . . .'

It *had* happened, whatever Chief Gulliver pretended – or maybe needed – to believe: Ellis was bleakly aware of that. Even the wartime Merchant Navy was still a village once seamen met other seamen ashore. Half the crews on the

North Atlantic had heard whispers of Convoy SC 7's agony, climaxing during the night of the 18th October 1940. It had been a bloody massacre of defenceless ships and gallant men, by courtesy of pre-war government.

'Well, I don't want to talk about it,' the Chief stated firmly. 'It doesn't do no good to speculate on what's past an' done.'

There was a strained silence. Until . . .

'Oh well,' Albert said with infuriating cheer; mercurial as the wind. 'It's a nice night to be at sea, I suppose. And nothin's happened to us yet. Maybe nothin' will.'

Having devastated all senior officer morale, he bumbled off into the wheelhouse to stare critically at the compass, leaving Ellis and Chief Engineer Gulliver gazing speechlessly after him.

'The little bugger!' the Chief grated eventually. 'Ohhh, the aggravatin' little BUGGER!'

'It's strange,' First Mate Ellis thought inconsequentially, 'how we can all remember convoy serial number SC 7 . . . yet here I am, actually sailing over the very same Death Hole here and now, and I can't even recall the tally of *this* one!'

Or was that merely because the night wasn't over? That the losses, so far, had simply been routine? That nothing quite awful enough had happened yet to afford this, his sixth Atlantic convoy, the significance of being even a little bit special?

The pre-sailing conference at Cape Breton some . . . what – two weeks ago now? Well, that had certainly been routine, even to the extent of appearing mundane. No impression given there of intrepid supermen about to embark upon a hazardous adventure.

The Naval launches had collected them from the assembly anchorage at the appointed hour: all the masters of the thirty-odd merchantmen under orders to make up Convoy

Sugar Charlie whatever-it-was – plus Chief Officer Ellis of course; deputising for the temporarily-stricken Albert. All looking uncomfortable and out of place in navy-blue mackintoshes and trilby hats and best lounge suits because, traditionally, few masters wore their uniforms ashore.

Some of 'em didn't wear them that often aboard, come to that. Not in the really dirty old ships like many which made the slow speed North Atlantic convoy runs . . . they were modest and independent men, most of them: matter-of-factly conscious of their authority before God. They didn't feel compelled to dress to prove it.

Anyway, they'd all turned up, along with radio officers scheduled to attend the separate and more detailed on-passage communcations briefing. It had struck Ellis then, in the few minutes prior to the formal conference beginning, how low-key it all appeared: more of a business meeting really, a sort of company boardroom function where the stakes represented mere profit or loss; not the survival or the deaths of nearly two thousand seamen and, very possibly, a whole island.

But that had been his seeing it through the eyes of a newcomer; a slightly romanticised impression. They knew precisely what was at stake; those grey-eyed, weatherbeaten Allied merchant captains chatting quietly in groups around him while the Naval Control people prepared their presentation, but even the murmur of conversation was domestic rather than brave; full of phrases foreign to the ear of any but a seaman maybe, yet still concerned more with ships and ordinary ships' business than death-defying resolution.

'Due to weigh at oh six hundred.'

'. . . saw her abeam of the Heads last night.'

'Needs a lighter more o' dunnage.'

'Red flashing three, six seconds, afore they extinguished it . . .'

'Wants to adjust before he's ready.'

'Hopes to come on the list by midnight . . .'

After they'd been called to order and settled with a self-conscious shuffling of boots and knocking out of pipes and fumbling with spectacle cases and rolled-up charts, the uniformed chairman – the senior Naval Control Service officer – began by asking, 'Well, gentlemen – any doubtful starters?'

There weren't, as it happened. A few doubtful finishers, maybe – like the Old Man of the career drop-out *Antisthenes*, alias, *Magdeburg, Eskisehir, São Vicente,* the *Chinghai* and, unbelievably, *Lafferty's Pride* – who'd probably attended more convoy conferences than any of his peers, yet never actually made it in a convoy – but no doubtful starters.

'Then to business, gentlemen,' the NCSO had said crisply. 'Before you, you will each find a copy of your sailing orders.'

And so it had continued, with the room growing thick with the smoke and some masters staring fixedly at papers while others stretched back and puffed and eyed the ceiling while speaker after speaker briefed them in his own particular field of expertise.

Some of it was hardly pertinent. The Defensively Equipped Merchant Ship officer, for instance: telling them all of the advantages of tracer to pinpoint a submarine's position at night, and to try not to use pyrotechnics or snowflake without good reason, and only to use qualified gun-crew because otherwise they were liable to sink friend or foe indiscriminately . . . and lastly, reminding them that their convoy might be used for practise attacks by friendly forces, and therefore: 'Please, gentlemen, identify your intended target before you fire.'

'But I 'aven't got a gun,' one master said, without wanting to be awkward, while nearly everybody else nodded in approval and wondered why the Defensively Equipped Merchant Ship expert had bothered to attend, when hardly any of them were defensively equipped.

150

'Then you may not sink many U-boats, sir; but look on the bright side. Your lack of weaponry could well preserve the lives of a few of our own chaps at the same time,' the D.E.M.S. man had retorted solemnly, and everybody knew why he'd come then – to give 'em all a bloody good laugh!

There had been other speakers who hadn't made them laugh at all – like the baby-faced RCN coastal escort commander with the flint-hard eyes, who knew they would only have a corvette and one trawler to support them after he'd handed over off St Johns. He didn't smile once when he emphasised the need for strict black-out; good station-keeping; tight security – there was a poster on the board behind him which showed two sailors chatting in a bar on one side, and a merchant ship sinking on the other: all below the legend: *Even the walls have ears!*

Then there was the Intelligence Officer who'd appraised the performance of the enemy's latest long range submarine type: the 'Atlantic' class VII-C U-boat. None of the collected masters about to face such sophisticated killing machines in dark waters took *him* lightly. Not even when he tried to offer optimism as a counter-weight; reminded them we'd closed the Air Gap quite a bit now, since we'd begun to operate from Iceland . . . then rather dimmed the glimmer of cheer by suggesting a bit weakly that, 'Because you don't happen to *see* any friendly aircraft, it doesn't necessarily mean they aren't there, you know.'

Just before ruining everything completely by conceding: 'Yes, I can't deny that the going might be a *little* rough, hostility-wise, in the middle, gentlemen.'

He didn't mention what had happened previously to SC 7, of course. But then, nobody would officially – not until the war was over and historians asked questions; by which time a large number of those listening to him would, in all probability, be dead.

But that was what it was like for the convoy men. The

151

experts tried hard to boost your morale, to give you the good news. But they were bloody loath to give you facts.

There was a young RCAF Liaison Officer from Coastal Command to elaborate on what air cover they might hope to see on either side of the Gap. And a pretty WRNS Staff Communcations Officer young enough to be the grand-daughter of many of those grizzled masters who listened with remarkable attention to her every fascinating word on codes and war call-signs, and light and sound and se-maphore signals, and those personal crew radios which caused so much aggravation in the need for absolute radio silence. The Anchorage Control Officer went into their detailed departure procedures and the sequence of weighing to leave harbour in some semblance of ordered confusion at first light. The Boom and Seaward Defence Officer went through the roll of participating ships, stragglers' routes, the problems of critical speed in formation. A more junior NCS Lieutenant took notes of any last minute require-ments:

'*Duella* hasn't had her convoy box delivered yet.'

'My donkeyman's like to go down wi' the trots. Can you hospitalise him and fix me another?'

'*Carrington Castle* needs a new chart – North Atlantic: Western Portion . . . old one's like a bloody dart board.'

'*Tinkerbell* got a .303 Lee Enfield rifle issued for protec-tion against them VII-C U-boats o' yours. Can we have a few rounds o' ammunition with it?'

'Case o' red flares, please . . .'

'Morphine, if you got it. An' a book of instructions.'

Then finally, of course, the Commodore had spoken to them, and had reassured Ellis as well as many others by his quiet fortitude. He'd talked of the way he intended his convoy to be run; of the need to control garbage dumping and bilge pumping – any clutch of tin cans and potato peelings or patch of oily residues left astern of a convoy were as good as a signpost to a hunter submarine. He implored

152

them to reduce smoke as much as possible; to maintain station at all costs; to keep together when the going got noisy or the ice or the fog or fifty-foot seas tried to separate them. He outlined the actions to be taken by stragglers or broken-down vessels. Only once did he look truly Admiral-fierce – when he warned them against slipping the convoy to go it alone: to succumb to the false temptation of becoming a 'runner'.

Or even a 'romper'. Any ship which raced ahead of the convoy was just as much at risk as a straggler trailing astern.

'Get yourselves torpedoed while committing a foolish error like that, gentlemen,' the Commodore promised, 'and I shall wave to you in a most friendly manner while you disport yourself in the water. But I shall not stop to pick you up'.

They'd listened more attentively to their Commodore than to any other expert there. But after all, Rear Admiral Sir Joseph Chanders KBE, CB, RN, retired – sixty-six years old and still creaking fit, was going with them all the way; not simply advising them on how to behave and leaving them to get on with it as most of the uniformed men on the platform were duty-bound to do.

. . . though to suggest any but a few die-hard merchant masters harboured that sort of contempt for the planners wasn't fair either! Everything humanly possible at Naval Control's restricted level of priorities *had* been anticipated prior to SC whatever's sailing – their genuine concern at the conference alone had amply demonstrated that – so who was Chief Officer Ellis to claim that those harrassed shore-bound staffs were complacently remote; couldn't visualise the half-men and the drowned men every time they removed a torpedoed ship's tally from the route they had considered the safest across the tactical plot.

No. Ellis wouldn't have wanted to be a Naval Control Service officer. The thankless task of planning, followed by a total inability to help once things went wrong a thousand miles away . . . that, to any man accountable to his conscience, must demand a considerable price.

He stirred restlessly in the darkness of the bridge. They were actually here, now – out in the North Atlantic! – yet not even they could see anything in the crystal ball to indicate what the night still held in store.

He swung from his reverie to find the Old Man still in the wheelhouse and the Chief seemingly spirited away. Probably Gulliver had gone back down to his engineroom to oversee the change of watch: it had to be approaching that hour now – nearly midnight. Time for the middle watch to begin. Poe's time of night . . . the dead of night. *Once upon a midnight dreary, while I pondered, weak and wea . . .*

He stood for a few moments longer, gazing into the distance with the rising wind plucking unheeded under the peak of his battered cap. Another passage from Poe kept forcing its way to his mind. He had used to enjoy reading Poe once, curled up and tingling with imagined dread while such a threat offered only childish escapism; but not anymore. Not now, aboard a ship at sea in a war. Not when it was so chillingly apt.

'Deep into the darkness peering, long I stood there, wondering, fearing.
Doubting, dreaming dreams no mortal ever dared to dream before . . .'

Ellis shivered involuntarily. Perhaps it was only when you'd been on too many Atlantic convoys – when you *did* dare to dream Poe's kind of dreams – that The Shivers became so very real.

An all-too-familiar voice squeaked, 'Sir? Bosun Leather sent me up to report to you. Said you might need me to help for a bit?'

Ellis closed his eyes in momentary despair: surely not even Mister Poe could have devised a plague quite as awful as Cadet Westall? Meanwhile, he said cheerfully, 'Good oh,

154

Nine

—≈≪≪≪≫≫≫≈—

'There's times when I hate this bloody job;
this is one of them.'

> *Commander: U-boat Group Seeräuber.*
> *Preparing to attack.*

Midnight: Eight Bells in the 8 to 12 Night Watch.

Because of the delay incurred by offering succour to men
long past being grateful for it, *Olympian* was still two miles
astern of the convoy when Ellis numbly conceded that
Westall really had seen a U-boat.

Chief Gulliver's triple-expansion steam engine was already wheezing to push her along at a deck-bouncing nine
knots by then. *Herr* Benz's or *Herr* Stultzer's, or whoever
else had harnessed 2,800 horsepower inside a steel cigar –
their twin diesel engines were smoothly driving the
thousand cubic yard displacement of the surfaced submarine at nearly twice that speed.

It meant that in under six minutes she would lead them
by a mile; within a comfortable ten minutes she could
overhaul the rear rank of the convoy. She was passing like
an express train overtaking a shunting engine.

Always assuming she didn't slow down to sink them, of
course. But doing that would have added a few minutes to
her obviously pressing schedule.

Come to that – why hadn't she sunk them already? The
old *Olympian* wasn't much of a ship maybe, but wasn't she
still a bloody sight better value than most of the others up
ahead?

157

Ellis felt ludicrously offended in his moment of incipient hysteria. Well, so would anyone else be, wouldn't they: if they'd just been good as told they were completely irrelevant?

Of course as soon as he did roar 'U-BOAT . . . Port SIDE!' everybody rushed to it; him bein' the Mate and everything. Down on the foredeck a tidal wave of bodies surged helter-skelter, right to left, scrambling and slipping over Number Two hatch, shoving and jostling to get there first: some with a silent tight-lipped urgency, others grinning broadly as they hurried; even winking an' joking *sotto voce* to their oppo's, anticipating what kind of laugh they was goin' to get, this time at the Mate's expense.

Until they got there. No one made a joke once he'd got to the port side and looked out.

Third Officer Cowan and Second Officer McKerchar – even the relieving middle watch helmsman, a usually unflappable AB called Manderson, crowded the bridge wing beside Ellis and Westall, leaving McKechnie isolated at the wheel and and holding course with somewhat dazed resentment. Dark figures were hurrying to line *Olympian*'s port side funnel deck rail too by then: most, being senior rates or watch-below officers, smiling cynically, a bit self-consciously until they got there. All standing gaping once they did.

Ellis couldn't help reflecting during his fleeting moments of indecision, on how incredibly evil the U-boat appeared; just running there on the surface, almost gliding through the water and stark black against the northern sky. It needed the twin contrasting trails of grey exhaust and the whip of its Nazi Ensign abaft the conning tower to confirm that man had any involvement with such robotic-seeming menace.

There wasn't any need to look and identify the speaker when a voice from somewhere aft intoned, not without a certain gloomy satisfaction, 'Behold a pale horse: and his name that sat on him was Death.'

158

Then the Chief Steward's querulous snarl. 'Shurrup, Chef! We know you always gotta sanctimonious smart-ass quote. Now bloody SHUT it!'

'Oh . . . Then *is* it not lawful for me to do what I will with mine own?'

'Bloody NO!'

'Saint Matthew. Twenty fifteen!' Robbo the Ecclesiastic Robot announced anyway, without the slightest sign of contrition.

'Out! OUT! Out o' the WAY, lad!'

The Captain elbowed through the bridge group to stand beside Ellis, set fair to explode. Then gripped the rail instead and muttered blankly, 'Damme. It is a U-boat!'

'Yessir,' the Mate agreed mildly, but he'd had a bit longer to get used to the idea of proceeding to war in line abreast with the enemy.

'But what's he doing there?' the Old Man demanded still trying to hoist it all in.

'Not very much.' Ellis lifted his glasses and laid them on the opposing vessel's bridge. 'Not at the mom . . .'

He faltered. 'What?' Albert shouted. 'What's 'e doing NOW?'

'He's . . . waving, sir,' Ellis echoed faintly.

And he was. As soon as the Barr and Strouds – which had already captured burning men and half-men and quite a few broken ships that night – as soon as they focussed on the U-boat's bridge they revealed another sailor gazing back at Ellis. And through binoculars as well! Of course they would've been Karl Zeiss lenses, presumably: not Barr and Stroud. Anyway, as soon as the German saw Ellis watching he lifted his arm in a casual wave. Not a Nazi salute or anything; just a wave of greeting, much as any seaman gives to another when ships pass on their respective business in deep waters.

Already the U-boat was forging ahead, almost stem in line with stem now; the short steep seas rearing and tumbling aft

159

across her rakish stem to cascade in white diagonal plumes down the round of her pressure hull.

The Second Mate had been standing motionless all the while. Ellis caught sight of McKerchar's eyes then; they were fixed unblinkingly on the enemy vessel. Hooded. Expressionless. Recalling, perhaps, a raft on a sun-tormented and increasingly more lonely sea. Ellis decided there and then that, in the unlikely event of their having to rescue survivors from a depth-charged U-boat, he wouldn't place Second Officer McKerchar in control of the afterdeck recovery party.

The Captain whirled abruptly; decisively.

'Get back to the wheelhouse, Mister McKerchar. Whistle the Chief – tell 'im I want every pound 'o steam 'e can produce an' bugger his gland packings. Mister COWAN!'

'Sir?'

'Radio room! Tell Pemberton to send out a general 'S' call immediately – "Submarine warning! Am being attacked."'

'*Attacked*, sir?' The Third Mate's expression was a picture of confusion. 'But we aren't being attacked yet, si . . .'

'Don't be BLOODY silly!'

'Present position two miles astern of the convoy, Cowan,' Ellis interjected hastily. 'It's near enough to give the escorts a line on her.'

The Old Man swung back. 'Right! Whereaway now?'

'Forr'ad of the beam, sir – see her?'

'I see her!' Burton snapped. He raised his glasses and voice together. 'You still on the wheel, McKechnie?'

'AYE, sir . . .'

'Then port fifteen, lad. Come round gradual.'

'Port fifteen! Wheel's . . . fifteen to port, sir.'

'*Port*, sir?' Ellis questioned involuntarily. 'You're not turning away then?'

Albert lowered his binoculars and looked at him. Just for a moment.

'Damned if I will, Mister Ellis! Not while it's likely to be the only chance I'll ever get.'

Suddenly there was tight suspicion in Ellis's gut. 'Only chance? To do what?'

The Old Man seemed surprised Ellis hadn't thought of it himself.

'To *ram* one o' the buggers, o' course!' he said.

'Damned if I will . . . !'

Father had said exactly the same thing. The minute David had told him of their intention to get married and, diplomatically as he'd thought, asked to give their union his blessing.

It had finally happened after four years of courting in which he'd used up all the Woolworths writing pads he'd bought, plus a few more as well, because he'd only been home on five occasions in all that time; yet each time Jennifer had been waiting for him, and each time he'd thrown his arms around her and kissed her and hardly credited his good fortune when she'd told him she still loved him.

That meant it must've been Nineteen Twenty . . . Eight, wasn't it? Yeah, 1928! The year in which he first sailed as second mate, he and Jennifer married, and Hitler and Father both suffered an unexpected setback – Hitler because Jerry had retained some sense; smashed the *Führer* -to-be's initial attempt to dominate Germany, to seize power in the *Reichstag*, by voting overwhelmingly against what was apparently still considered in those days as a lunatic fringe Nazi Party – and the ageing Arthur William because he tried for very last time to dominate his only son, and failed.

'Damned if I'll give my permission,' he'd thundered that evening with Mother busy like a mouse in the kitchen as she usually managed to be when confrontation loomed, and David's sisters, who'd never supported him anyway, ostensibly cleaning in the shop downstairs but actually listening with purse-lipped approval at the drawing room door.

'You chose the irresponsible way of a nomad against my advice: you rebuffed the honest toil of this heritage I built for you . . .' Father's arm had encompassed the whole universe in that moment rather than the few square yards of miserable property that was actually his to endow, but grandiose gestures like that always had been, to Arthur William, the legitimate tools of argument, '. . . for the idle pleasures of a sea-going life. But never, young man: never will I sanction such a feckless union as you propose with Miss Morden.'

'Why not, Father?' David had asked, dangerously quiet, while Jennifer had sat there demurely, knees pressed together and hands folded in her lap and saying nothing, yet with such a determined look in her pretty eye that both Father and Son would have been well advised to heed before irreparable harm was done.

'Why not? Why *not*?' Father had spluttered. 'Then I'll tell 'ee why not, lad! Happen I hold too much respect for that young woman there to concede her the misery of an empty bed for near enough eleven twelfths of every year. To inflict on her a husband who's nobbut a travellin' man – no better than my own forebears always were, to my eternal shame . . .'

'Father's forebears – *Father's* roots? But weren't they mine as well?' Ellis remembered thinking all that time ago. That was when twenty-five years of bearing the brunt of Arthur Ellis's vinegar pique finally exploded, right or wrong.

Not even Jennifer was to bring them together after that night; which, on reflection, must have proved the cruellest irony of all for Father. The only argument he'd ever had with his son in which he *had* shown some consideration for others, had promoted anyone's interests apart from his own, was to prove the catalyst for their final breach.

David Ellis had never spoken directly to his father again; . . . but too many things had happened since their rift, and the now-Chief Officer Ellis of the Steamship *Olympian* had little time in which he could afford to reflect on unhappinesses past. Not right then. Not while his Captain showed intent to commit an act of warlike malice.

One thing he did remember with fleeting sadness though: before death and destruction again took priority.

After they'd stood before the Altar in the tiny Salford church; while the 'Wedding March' played and Second Officer Ellis had led his Bride up the aisle past all her relatives on one side but only his sisters and a few friends of his, because Mother hadn't dared to come with Father so set against it . . . as they proceeded – he stiffly self-conscious in his best uniform with the two new gold rings that had never then kissed salt and her, well . . . simply beautiful – she'd suddenly squeezed his hand whereupon, startled, he'd looked towards the rear of the church, at the last row of pews just beside the door.

And seen Father sitting there. All alone. All uncomfortable in his faded blue worsted suit and his clip-on tie and his familiar celluloid collar, with his gnarled hands clasped atop his walking stick – just sitting, not even looking: simply staring stiffly ahead and pretending not to notice.

Jennifer had gone over to him there and then, right in the middle of their grand procession, and kissed the elderly man on the cheek. Ever so gently.

And whispered, just loud enough for David to hear: 'We do love you, you know. Both of us. And I'm very proud to be the wife of the son you made.'

Of course Ellis never spoke of the event to Father because, by that time, he had committed himself never to address him again and, no matter how hard Jennifer had tried to encourage him in subsequent years, he never did because he *was* the son of Arthur William and had inherited one trait if little else.

163

But he'd often wondered in the dark night watches that followed – why a man so hard and selfish as Father had been crying?

Oh, well: whatever happened now, they were committed to attack. For the next few minutes, as in all the lurid penny-dreadfuls Ellis used to devour as a boy, the hunted would indeed – as the stirring clichés had it – become the hunter.

Mind you, the consequences on this occasion promised, in Chief Officer Ellis's hastily-formed opinion, to depart somewhat from traditional lore. According to most of the fiction *he'd* read, heroes invariably avoided getting themselves killed while being brave. Miss a VII-C U-boat after metaphorically slapping it across the face with your clanking, age-corroded gauntlet like Knight Albert over there was doing, and it mounted one 3.5-inch; one 37-mm; two 20-mm guns and five 21-inch torpedo tubes – including one laid specifically to snap-shoot at ships astern – with which to make damn certain you never returned, story-book gallant an' bloody stupid with it, for a second joust.

But it was a bit too late to point that out to Albert.

So *Olympian's* bows continued to swing faster and faster; steadily converging on a point some several hundred yards ahead and common to the courses of both vessels. Already the Mate could feel the revolutions building as Gulliver's half-naked firemen sweated cobs below without even knowing why, and above and behind the bridge the safety valve on the high funnel began to trill uncertainly as steam pressure came perilously to the feather.

The Captain stepped urgently to the wheelhouse door.

'Ease the wheel.'

'Ease the wheel, sir.'

'Steady . . . Now keep 'er steady as she goes, lad.'

Albert rushed back to the forward rail and peered out towards the U-boat. Aye, she was still there; still holding to the same track with the grey exhaust trails lying along her wake and the man-shadows in her conning tower apparently as contemptuous of impending danger as they'd proved to be of *Olympian's* presence.

'By God, Mister: maybe we *have* got 'im . . .' Burton growled, wriggling now with tension. He leaned out, hands cupped. 'LOOKOUTS: clear the FOC'SLEHEAD!'

'*And* the foc'sle,' the Mate suggested grimly. There might just be a few hardy souls still with their heads down in there, determined to sleep in their watch below; which brought him back to the 'bloody stupid' bit again. Even when new the ship hadn't been designed as a battering ram: if *Olympian* did collide with anything, even something a sight less substantial than a submarine's armoured pressure hull, she would certainly compact her own forward underwater sections to a grue of rusted debris in the process.

Grudgingly Ellis had to admit it wouldn't matter though, not if the outrageous did come off. Even if she herself sank it could still be considered a justifiable sacrifice: exchanging at least temporary reprieve for an indeterminate number of Allied ships during the coming critical months against the price of one old nobody. Well, tactically-speaking one could assume so. Ellis, still bemused by the prospect of Albert's converting their *own* particular *SS Nobody* to instant dreadnought, wasn't too sure of how the rest of the crowd would feel about the sacrifice part either.

Though they *were* all volunteers, weren't they: out here already in the North Atlantic's bloody misery? Signed-on to do or die or whatever despite the lousy food and the appalling conditions, the lack of escorts and the second-by-second threat of extinction. Dammit, man – had one single deckhand or fireman or trimmer down there complained about conditions of service when, little more than an hour ago, Burton had elected to expose them by heaving-to in the petrol seas surrounding the short-fused *Tunfisk*? And hadn't they, for that matter, learned at first hand precisely

165

what happened to merchant seaman whether or not they fought back, once the U-boats had seized the initiative?

Maybe six minutes had passed since Westall first saw *his* U-boat, and *Olympian* steaming flat-out now: battering and smashing through the short seas, rising and dipping to the long Atlantic swell with the black smoke pouring carelessly – downright provocatively in the eyes of any Convoy Commodore – from her skeletal funnel to roll and whirl solid across the afterdecks. Every window, every fitting, every wire stay rattling and dancing and strumming with the excitement building inexorably in the chase.

The submarine – no, the *target* now – still fractionally leading to port and bloody arrogant in its contempt. Still holding to its track; still possible . . .

Ellis felt himself being carried with the sheer euphoria of it: the too-long-denied desire to hit back. Fired by a shameless lust to look, just for once, upon German oil and German wreckage – even exploded German lungs scattering the hostile ocean, he leaned out over the rail beside Burton.

'See there's no one left in the foc'sle,' he roared to Leather on the foredeck, while most of them ogled up in surprise, whitefaced blobs through the darkness, because it wasn't often this First Mate used such a steely, uncompromising tone, 'An' make DAMN sure everyone down there's got a lifejacket to hand!'

'We're not goin' to ram Jerry too hard though, are we?' one faint voice questioned uncertainly.

'Hard? Happen we'll squash 'im like a ton o' bricks onna beetle!' a throaty growl retorted derisively. 'Who's gotten heavy weight to drop on 'em as we pass?'

''Eavy weights? Nay, chain stoppers round the fists, matey: yon's the gear f'r the close-quarter stuff.'

'How's about paraffin an' cotton waste, lads? An' a match – watch they Gerrymans burn.'

'Molotov cocktails, thass it! Bottles wi' petrol in 'em . . Beer bottles! 'Oo's got beer bottles an' some avgas?'

166

'Och, man, we're gaun tae *spifflicate* the bastards!' A particularly rich vein of resentment, captivated by the imminent prospect of real Glasgae-quality violence. 'Ohhh we're gaun tae gouge their fuckin' eyes oot! Pit the boot innem! Rool richt ower the shitty wee bastards an' spit onnem as we go . . .'

'Lord,' Ellis thought faintly. 'And I doubted how *they'd* feel about it?'

Quickly he scanned with binoculars again, bracing his elbows first on the rail but then lifting them clear because the transmitted shudder of Chief Gulliver's pounding engine was making steady sighting impossible.

By God but the gap was narrowing fast between the two hulls; the darkness thinning ever faster by their moonlit proximity. It provided Ellis's first ever intimate view of a convoyman's executioners. Four men on her bridge, all in oilskins and sou'westers – what're they wearing *oilskins* for, as British seamen did? Weren't U-boat men supposed to wear black leather coats and white peaked caps, an' be hung about with Iron Crosses like the super-beings he'd always imagined them as?

Crazy-beings these, more like . . . Less than half a cable under *Olympian's* port bow and the white water smashing on either side to emphasise the juggernaut hull bearing down on them, yet they still persisted in holding course with foolhardy brashness. Only there was nothing foolhardy about most surviving U-boat men. The Death Hole wasn't an exclusive resting place for Allied ships; the Death Hole was open to anybody who cared to call – all the foolhardy U-boat men already drifted and bumped with purple, bloated faces against the deckheads of their crushed machines lying at the bottom of *das Todesloch*. So – no! No, it was more as if they were deliberately provoking Albert Burton. Almost as if they had some other trick to pla . . .

'You make out what Jerry's doin' NOW, Mister?' the

Old Man snapped, more testy than resolute Knight. Ellis screwed his eyes harder to the binocular cups.

'Ohhhh, Jesus,' he muttered catapulted back to bleak reality. 'They're manning their after gun!'

And they were. Two of the sou'westered seamen had clambered down to what, according to that Convoy Conference Intelligence Officer's pre-sailing assessment, must be presumed to be twin 20-mm cannons mounted abaft the tower itself. They weren't one-hundred-per-cent certain yet – the Naval Intelligence people – but the CCIO was *pretty* confident that would be the weapon configuration one might expect to find, particularly in the modified version of the Atlantic VII-C.

'I wonder if he'd've been quite so damn fascinated by technicalities if he'd been standing here, where I am now,' Ellis reflected as the presumed weapon began to traverse towards him, barrels already rising to lay directly on *Olympian's* bridge.

A suspicion stirred. He swung – saw young Westall's flushed face still hovering, overlooked, beside him; oblivious to what happened to gallant boy sailors in real war. 'Get off the bridge f'r *CHRIST*'s sake, laddie,' the Mate snarled. 'Get down that bloody ladder an' take COVER!'

A hundred; maybe only ninety yards now.

Westall collided with Third Officer Cowan at the head of the ladder. Cowan snapped 'Watch it kid,' and hurried over. 'Escort Commander's acknowledged receipt of your 'S' call, sir. Message reads: "Take no offensive action until we arrive."'

'JeSUS!' Ellis muttered again, faintly.

The gun barrels pointing right *at* them now! Cowan looked curious. 'What's happeni . . . !'

'DOWN!' Second Officer McKerchar had rushed out of the wheelhouse and was roaring at the crowd on the foredeck. 'Everybody DOWWWN!'

'Sod *that,* pal!' some anonymous hard-man yelled back,

168

full of fight. 'I gotter twenty-pound shackle 'ere to drop on the bastids.'

Eighty yards! Still holding on!

'Oh, we GOT 'im!' the Old Man was chortling, totally ignoring the guns. 'We've bloody GOT 'im, Mister: right up 'is backside.'

'Then the Lord awakened as one out o' sleep. An' He smote his enemies in the hinder parts . . .'

'ShurRUP, ROBBO!'

'. . . Psalms! Seventy eight, sixty odd.'

Seventy yards! So close now that even without the aid of glasses Ellis could clearly make out the outline of hatches and gratings along the narrow black afterdeck: the circular rails of her gun platforms – the U-boat men's 'conservatories' . . . the slender spires of her attack and sky periscope standards, even the blobs of upturned faces above the angled wind deflector surrounding the U-boat's bridge: all facing aft towards them now but still unmoving. Not even seeming anxious? An' anyway – why *didn't* they FIRE?

Almost as if to please him, bring his apprehension to conclusion, the guns *did* fire. Once! A short burst which exploded the night momentarily yet was over before anyone really had time to accept it had actually happened. Ellis captured a brief image of the spraying hull below them flickering Hollywood-dramatic behind the muzzle-flashes; stroboscobic; bloody terrifying . . . jeeze, he wanted to throw himself down but it hardly seemed worthwhile – there was only a finger's thickness of wood forming the bridge front between him and them anyway.

The newly-returned Third Mate blinked up at the funnel, shocked. Suddenly there were holes in it with wisps of smoke streaming from them, and part of the monkey island had been blown away. Nothing else. No carnage. Almost a gentle warning.

'They've shot us,' Cowan announced dazedly. 'They've damn well *shot* us, sir.'

Still going like an asthmatic express train – well, a fast goods train anyway. Not more than sixty yards of crash- ing sea left between *Olympian* and her sliding quarry.

'Maybe their boss hasn't told THEM not to be bloody hostile till our escorts arrive, Cowan!' the Mate snarled, shaken to the core.

Odd! The submarine wasn't as far to port as she'd been a moment ago.

'Starboard FIVE.' the Old Man suddenly roared: compensating for the fractional change of disposition.

'Starb'd five, sir.' Icy cold from the wheel. Could grief really have killed all fear in McKechnie so completely?

'Starboard *ten.*'

'Starboard TEN.'

Ellis's hands squeezing juice out of the teak rail now with the tension of it. They only needed to fire once more; the guns were still rising to follow the high bridge now surely towering above them – but wasn't something *else* happening down there and ahead? An abrupt flurry of white water astern of the rapier *Frontboote*. More exhaust jetting from her sleek sides.

'Ten o' st'bd wheel on, si . . .'

'Fiftee . . . *Belay* that, dammit to hell – HARD a starboard, man! Bring 'er round: bring her ROUND . . .'

The Old Man dancing up and down suddenly, waving his arms. 'Fit to chew nails', the expression was – he'd used it himself once: 'Fit to chew bloody nails!'

Even as the tired old *Olympian* heeled right over under the screw of what was, for her, a thundering turn, Ellis watched blankly as the U-boat crossed under the bluff bows and pulled out of reach as effortlessly as if her clumsy and suddenly rather pathetic adversary had lain stopped and dead in the water. Twenty-eight hundred horsepower had instantly accelerated the slender hull to well in excess of seventeen knots. Maybe they were able to gear her 'E'-

motors – her electric motors – to the shafts to run in parallel with the diesels: maybe . . .

Whatever her secret, she was already drawing fast to starboard and masked by the loom of the foc'slehead before Ellis had time to blink. And no wonder he did – for could it have been that the commander of that effortless robot actually *waved* again to Ellis before showing him his tail?

'Escorts in sight, sir! Approaching on the port bow.' While the Second Mate's tone hinted of savage betrayal it was crisply efficient. McKerchar hated, but he was efficient.

'BUGGER the escorts!' Albert screamed. 'I want more speed, Mister.'

He ran through the wheelhouse and appeared the other side, leaning perilously out over the starboard wing and flinging something after their fleet-footed enemy.

'The convoy manoeuvring signal book I think, sir,' Cowan whispered. 'He's got the sandwich box in his other hand.'

'Ohhh, shit!' the Mate muttered resignedly, tension evaporated in a curious mixture of disappointment and slightly ashamed relief as he trailed in his Captain's footsteps; hopefully before Albert threw the rest of the bloody ship overboard.

'Call *Apple Blossom* on the Aldis, Second,' he said levelly as he passed. 'Tell him his target's going over to starboard; indicate the U-boat's course – speed seventeen knots. Add: "We intend proceeding to rejoin the convoy".'

'Unless they need our help, eh?' the Second Mate snarled in frustration. Ellis simply shrugged ; he didn't need Mc-Kerchar's resentment; he felt sick and weak and deflated enough already. The gallant adventure was over. Hell, it hadn't even been that – the unquestionably tolerant U-boat commander had been playing with them ever since he'd first surfaced so enticingly beside them. But why? Why had he risked such an apparently pointless exercise in the first place? And why had he subsequently refrained from sinking

171

Olympian; even from using those fearsome automatic weapons of his to devastate her navigating bridge and upperworks? They hadn't been tactically astute – they'd bloody well been spared!

Could it be that such a thing as compassion for the blind-courageous and the lonely existed in the heart of one Black Atlantic Knight: perhaps even one called Neugebauer?

He didn't have to wait too long to find out.

Even as Ellis joined his helplessly fuming Master Mariner on the starboard wing of the bridge, and registered the distant silhouette of their late target leaving them easily astern, a crackle and a metallic screel slashed briefly across the widening gap.

Just before a loud-hailer called, '*Auf Wiedersehen, Olympian . . .*'

'Goodbye . . . I'll give 'im GOODBYE!' the Old Man bellowed, re-galvanised into fury. 'And how does 'e know our name, eh? That's classified inf'rmation, Mister – so how the hell does that bloody cabbage-eater know the name o' my ship?'

'Probably,' Ellis suggested through clenched teeth while keeping a tight grip on his nerves, 'because you insisted on repainting it on our bows the minute we sailed from bloody Breton. Sir!'

The security wasn't what concerned him then, though; it was the inference he drew from the rest of the U-boat's parting greeting which alarmed him more than anything. It might just have answered the first part of his earlier doubts – the question why they'd been spared.'

As far as Ellis knew, the phrase *Auf Wiedersehen* didn't mean an outright 'goodbye' in the sense it obviously did to Albert. Wasn't it a little more equivocal than that?

Didn't it actually mean: 'Till we meet again?' Which, in turn could be construed as suggesting they hadn't been spared so much as granted a temporary stay of execution.

Yet the convoy had come half-way through the critical

dark hours already with only 'routine' casualties; hit and run torpedo attacks. A few ships savaged, a few dozen seamen lost . . .

So *had* Black Knight Commander Neugebauer been as polite and gallant a fighting seaman as he'd initially appeared? Or had their strange sea-meeting contained a more sombre significance?

Was he, for instance, so confident that *die Rudeltaktik* would achieve success tonight – that his sister U-boats were already in position ahead to launch the final onslaught on SC whatever-they-were – that, perhaps even unwittingly, he'd given Chief Officer Ellis a quite specific warning?

Apple Blossom and *Trois-Rivières* had begun their ASDIC search well away from *Olympian's* starboard quarter by the time they'd crept to the immediate rear of the convoy and were within visual distance of homely *Duella's* blue stern light and trailing marker barrel.

The bridge was quiet again after the frenetic near-hysteria of their brief aggression. Weary quiet. A time for reflection and disappointment. McKerchar felt it most sorely, you could tell that. The morose figure of the gangling Second Mate stood lonely and still out on the port wing, daring any man to approach the malevolence of his eye. Even Albert had the sense to keep clear of him. You didn't play tartar with a man who'd once lived with the dead.

Third Officer Cowan had gone down: maybe to search out more congenial company; maybe just to sit waiting in his cupboard of a cabin. Able Seaman McKechnie had gone off watch after handing over the wheel in tight silence. But he must have wanted so very much to kill a U-boat, just for Vie.

Even a lot of the crowd had drifted back into the dank refuge of the foc'sle, preferring that to hanging round on deck and getting chilled to the marrow. Apprehension had to give way some time before the inevitability of the total exhaustion.

Chief Officer Ellis noticed that the wind had freshened even more in the last few minutes of their isolation; now the convoy moved restlessly, uneasily before the rising seas as if the ships themselves sensed that time was at a premium: that soon they would be safe. Or . . . ?

God but he was tired, too. Nearly half past midnight and he'd virtually spent the last eight hours of life on this narrow, hemmed-in platform . . .

Odd! Why did he think of them as the *last* eight hours of his life? Why hadn't he just considered them the 'most recent'? For some reason he thought about Senior Cadet Moberly again, and the hideous dessicated skull he'd imagined bobbing and grinning beneath Moberly's cap. Was this, then, a further premonition of disaster?

Ellis shivered and knew he had to go down: he was too tired, too fanciful. Only he couldn't stop thinking about the U-boat that had played with them; and why it had bothered to in the first place.

The Captain stretched, placid again. 'Ring the engineroom, Mister McKerchar,' he grunted, just loud enough for his voice to carry to the sombre man. 'Tell 'em to come down to station revolutions. Tell 'em we're back home again: the black sheep returned to the fold.'

'JESUS!' Ellis blurted. 'I *do* know why he did it!'

The Old Man swung. 'What the – ?'

'The escorts,' Ellis snarled. 'He guessed you'd send a U-boat warning – he tricked us all, dammit!'

A ship blew up with a flash and a monstrous roar right in the front rank. Then a siren began to boom in a panicking *I am directing my course to starboard* blast even as a second torpedo's track – seen too late by some watchkeeper who'd assumed he was safely surrounded – ended in a flash and a bang and a great ball of flame precisely in the centre of the crawling rectangle.

174

'. . . he used *us* to draw the escorts back from the track of the CONVOY!' Chief Officer Ellis bellowed above the din: sick, resentful – and impotent as a cripple in an earthquake.

A *third* ship exploded and began to burn like a Roman candle; shooting sparks and bits of white-hot steel and parts of men high into the flickering sky.

It was almost One Bell. In the middle watch.

Ten

'The Carpenter's monkey had been fitted with a miniature life-preserver. It swam about and chattered constantly until those of us who had been spared were finally rescued. It provided a great source of comfort to us all.'

Master's report on sinking of SS 'Juryman'.

00.30 a.m.: One Bell in the Middle Watch.

There seemed to be flame, explosion, smoke . . . some violent incandescence occurring in every quarter ahead; snatching fleeting priority for the electrified eye in starkly-etched sequence during those initial seconds of the main attack.

Ellis had already guessed that was precisely what the lucifer bedlam stretching before him signified – that the threat of a full pack offensive against the convoy had finally become reality. Suddenly the comforting and familiar lines of darkened ships they'd just rejoined – just come *home* to, dammit! – were red and flickering and three-way solid, not black and two-dimensional any longer.

They could only stand and watch at first, and wait tight-lipped for their own deck to burst upwards with a roar of fire. There was no immediate executive action demanded of the Captain or Chief Officer Ellis; none from any Merchant officer aboard the still-whole vessels. Unless taking emergency measures to avoid stricken ships in their path, or falling back to pick up survivors, the column numbers must still hold doggedly on, still maintain their air of dignified imperturbability and wait for the Commodore's orders. Lines of metal ducks and rabbits did precisely that – kept steadily passing in strict order before the weapon sights, in fairground shooting galleries.

Olympian would hold course too, until she was called as a Bone Collector. Or as another Bone Collector's client.

'It's started then, Mister Ellis,' was all the Captain said. Almost matter-of-factly; the way he always acted in true hazard when those around him needed strength and an old salt's pique had little place.

Paradoxically it was that very quality of Burton's fortitude which caused most apprehension in his Chief Officer. The Bosun had noticed it too.

'When the Old Man's not flappin' an' wavin' his arms about,' he'd once remarked with unsettling acumen, 'then I *knows* we're in the shit!'

Well – Albert wasn't flapping this time. Strained, yes, and briefly transfixed as they all were when a bit more of SC whatever began to blow up. But, following the initial shock, he concealed all hint of the dread which surely clutched him also: betrayed, for that matter, little more than the merest hint of apprehension at battle finally joined.

Though perhaps that wasn't as surprising as it seemed. Maybe he was simply relieved that it *had* begun at last and that the strains of anticipation were over.

'You'd think they could've waited.' Ellis had to force a grin, knowing words alone would be uttered too gruffly to deceive. 'Until we'd settled back in for a while.'

Albert looked at him perceptively by the flickering glare of the fires, then smiled back. Rather as he'd done previously, when first conceding his own nodding intimacy with fear.

'There's times,' he said, 'when I wish you and I could bring ourselves to be a little more open wi' each other . . .'

He pivoted on his heel: the shutters of command had slammed down again. 'Mister *McKERCHAR*'

177

'*AYE.*'

'I'll take the ship for a while – you keep your eyes peeled for the Adm'ral's signals.'

The Second Mate came through the wheelhouse and stood looking sardonic – sardonic even for McKerchar, that was – at the starboard door.

'Then I'm no' likely to see many,' he warned harshly. 'Goin' by the bearing o' the flash, Captain – I'd say the Commodore ship was the first one torpedoed!'

The Old Man did look shaken then. And old. McKerchar could have been a bit more circumspect. Burton had spent months in affectionate conflict with *Pendragon's* Archie Mulligan when they were both apprentices in the old five-masted *Barossa* . . . that had been even before the First Battle of the Atlantic – the Fourteen-Eighteen one.

Ellis felt angry for Albert, yet it wasn't really McKerchar's fault. McKerchar couldn't have been expected to know, while any capacity for gentleness McKerchar might once have possessed had been drowned in a wartime ocean just as surely as, it seemed, Archie Mulligan might be doing right then.

'Then watch for the Vice-commodore to take control, dammit! *Naiad*: lead ship – st'bd column' he flared back anyway. 'You know that bloody fine, McKerchar . . .'

A further hollow detonation rattled the wheelhouse windows. Immediately a fourth set of masts separated by a pathetic stick funnel began to swing askew half a mile off and part-way up the second column. A gout of blood-reflecting spray hung briefly above them. '*Cleopatra*' someone was coolly analysing down below them and within earshot of the bridge, '. . . or mebbe *Juryman*.'

'Can I be the *only* one unnerved aboard this ship?' Ellis thought desperately. The another voice began to curse steadily, monotonously from the afterdeck and Chief Officer Ellis felt a bit better.

The Captain turned sharply, his first responsibility to those in *Olympian*. There was more to concern him than the risk to a surely-indestructible friend right then.

'Ensure that, apart from engineroom watchkeepers, every man aboard is wearing his lifejacket properly tied from now on, Mister Ellis,' he ordered quietly. 'And that as many as you can spare – those wi'out immediately pressing duties – are assembled ready by their boat stations.'

They'd been through a lot and come out the other side; they and the ship together. The Captain had never specified a measure like *that* before; never betrayed anything but staunch confidence in the future.

Was that yet another omen?

Ellis said, 'I'll go myself.'

A ship began firing starshell over to port and the red columns turned to stark flickering white. Someone else began to imitate him and the whole night turned to day: either panic was spreading – or the U-boats had already begun to run and fight on the surface. They were soon likely to find out: *Olympian* was drawing steadily closer to the line on which the first casualties had occurred, and still no sign of a course alteration demanded by either Commodore or Vice.

The Mate finished, 'I'd like to keep a small recovery party ready by the nets fore and aft: Chief Steward and his catering first-aiders standing-by in the saloon – otherwise we can clear the lower decks of black gang an' spare seamen unless they're needed. What about the cadets?'

'Up here on the bridge. I can keep my eye on 'em.' The diminutive master smiled briefly: a spark of humour. 'Anyway, yon laddie – Westall? He's got a useful capacity f'r seeing U-boats where it seems most of us can't.'

Ellis stepped aft and blew two blasts on his whistle. As he did so he glanced uneasily astern to where Westall had conjured up one undisputed U-boat. There was nothing

179

back there now, other than dark sullen cloud and wind-swept loneliness.

'I'd feel a bit easier if he'd settle for pinpointing the bloody escorts,' he muttered, not amused.

'They're out there, Mister Ellis. Doing their best to protect us, you can be sure.'

More starshell went up, and a giant splutter of snowflake. Ellis turned momentarily to face the burning ships and the dodging ships, and the sea which was almost certainly claiming men like him even as he breathed.

He was fed up with being resolute.

'It's bein' so sure they *are* already doing their best,' he rejoined grimly as he headed for the ladder, 'that bothers me so bloody much!'

He stuck his head through the radio room light trap again as he passed. Pemberton was sitting, writing, headphones clamped in place, half leaning forward over the desk with his other hand on the key.

Ellis noticed absently that a dry battery had been connected to a wire running up the bulkhead and ending in a 12-volt bulb suspended above the transmitter. The overall effect of the tiny star was lost against the harsh brilliance of the main system.

Willie half-turned as he stepped across the coaming, following his enquiring eye. He finished writing, rattled a staccato acknowledgement, then hauled his phones off before swivelling in the chair to face Ellis. He jerked his head at the wire. 'Done-it-myself emergency lighting. If we take a hit they could lose power on the gennies. I get nervous in the dark.'

Ellis had to force a grin: Pemberton deserved one. 'I get nervous in the light – it's like Coney Island out there.'

Sparks didn't quite manage the grin, just a grimace. He ripped the top sheet from the signal pad and reached for the bridge telephone, waving the sheet in explanation.

'*Juryman*; Number Sixty-three: torpedoed st'bd side and abandoning . . . and a Frenchman a couple of minutes ago: I didn't get the name – convoy number Twenty-two. They're hitting us from both flanks, then?'

Ellis avoided the question. 'Before you give the Old Man a bell – anything from *Pendragon* yet?'

Pemberton said, 'Oh, Christ, *she's* not been hit? The Commodore ship?'

'We don't know.'

'Christ!' Willie said again, then shook his head. 'Nothing. You were right, Dave – I should've been a Brown Job. In the desert or whatever; anywhere a long way from water.'

But he didn't say it in a tight-strung manner any more; just reflectively, almost ruefully.

'It's probably hell anyway; sand in your boots day after day.' Ellis looked at the young operator closely. 'I'm in a hurry – you all right now?'

The Radio Officer nodded. 'For the moment.'

Ellis turned. 'Right, then I'll go an' fight the war.'

He hesitated before he opened the curtain. He didn't want to risk unsettling Willie again. 'By the way: maybe you'd better wear your lifejacket from now on. Just in case.'

'Is that an order?' Sparks asked.

'Er . . . sort of.'

'Thank God,' Pemberton said, grabbing for his with shameless alacrity. 'I thought you'd *never* give it.'

It occurred to Ellis then. Whatever the outcome of tonight, Radio Officer Pemberton had already won one battle against the U-boats.

Off-watch seamen and black gang were already more in evidence on the funnel deck as Ellis clattered down the ladder. They weren't clustered nervously around the boats, they were really only standing in groups watching the pyrotechnic display still flickering and cracking above the lines of ships, but the Mate couldn't help noting that quite a

181

few convoy bags were in evidence – the neatly sewn canvas containing those personal effects most cherished by each man – while there seemed little need to pass the word for lifejackets to be properly secured.

Again it underlined the universal sense of apprehension . . . Normally that part of ship was recognised as officers' leisure space; certainly at night, even on wartime passage. Equally, mind you, the welldeck adjacent to the break of the foc'sle was jealously guarded by the crowd as being *their* privileged recreation area – and woe betide any inexperienced young officer ill-advised enough to go down and try being 'chummy': if the Old Man didn't blister him on sight from the bridge, then the Bosun would pack him off back amidships quick sharp. And not too politely!

Just as inflexible a system as that which had always existed ashore – the British social structure: the separation of 'class' according to origin and means – and maintained as rigidly by the lowliest as by superior ranks. All floated out to sea and re-created within a mini-community a few hundred feet long flying the Red Ensign.

Ellis couldn't help contemplating how his father would have understood better than most who had never lived aboard a ship, as he got to the foot of the ladder. His father would have understood all about social divides, that was for sure. After all, wasn't it because of Arthur William's misdirected resentment over them that Father and Son finally fell out? And that because of what they'd made him – because of his blinkered selfishness – that everything ultimately went sour for them all, even for Jennifer and Ellis as a family unit, in the end . . . ?

Mother had died in 1933 – or sort of faded away, really; as ineffectual in her determination to survive as in the defence of her children against Father's paternalism. She caught a cold and, because she was afraid to incur a doctor's bill and Arthur William's displeasure, the cold turned to consump-

182

tive something-or-other and, finally, to death. It didn't even take very long. Mother never had been one to cause unnecessary fuss.

David was thirty years old then and had been married for nearly five of them. He remembered Mother's year of dying as much because it coincided with his first appointment as Mate – aboard a clanking British tramp called the *Tobago Star* – as for its impact on his own affections. Mother Ellis hadn't endeavoured to claim them in life; she could hardly have been expected to do so from the grave.

Oh, and because Hitler was appointed Chancellor of Germany at more or less the same time, and the *Reichstag* was burned as further fuel for the flames of Nazi fanaticism. Within months of Mother's death Hitler had spurned the German constitution, banned trade unions and opposition parties and begun to steer a National Socialist course which would eventually involve a lot of *Kapitänleutnant* Neugebauers as well as the then-brand-new Chief Officer David Ellis in the Second Battle of the Atlantic.

1933, on reflection, had been a pretty rotten year for everybody: especially the German people. And Mother, of course.

But it was later in his marriage that things began to go wrong. One disturbing factor became more and more apparent to David during the Salford leaves – that even after five years of not speaking to Father, Father had nevertheless begun, gradually, to re-assert himself as influence in David's life.

There always had been that inexplicable *rapport* between Father and Jennifer. Whether, in her vivacity, the old man had been captivated by some image of what he would have wished for his own colourless daughters, or whether, in Arthur William's character, the then still-childless Jennifer found some similarity to that of her largely unavailable husband – whatever it was it seemed that each time the sailor did return from sea he found the sense of Father's recent presence hanging ever more openly in the air of the little house they'd bought in Jutland Way.

'He's a widower, now and getting old, darling,' Jennifer would say with that sweet determined persuasion. 'He only comes for tea sometimes. And never when *you're* at home.'

And, of course, she never so much as suggested he should go and see Father and make up. Or that Father should be asked to tea when David *was* at home. She knew exactly how far to press him. Perhaps she even hoped his conscience would eventually complete the task of reconciliation for her.

Well, all right: maybe he should have had the foresight to sever all connections with Salford after they'd been married; God only knew how aware he was of Arthur William's capacity to dominate. But he'd had to consider Jennifer's happiness too, hadn't he? To bear in mind her close affection for parents and relatives so different from his own. He hadn't wished to cut the links which would certainly be of comfort to her during his long voyages, and he hadn't been totally without caution: he'd selected an area much more distant than a casual stroll by an elderly man might encompass.

Trouble was, he'd overlooked both Father's determination and the pre-war blossoming of Salford's Corporation Transport system. Jutland Way shortly became a mere tuppeny omnibus ride from the corner shop – and that new route ended right outside his bloody door!

Father withdrew into comfortable semi-retirement once he'd got round to noticing his wife had passed away. But he still kept the shop on, exploiting David's sisters as counter-maids because they depended on his support completely; never having succeeded, either of them, in attracting an offer to share some other man's income instead.

And so, for the next four years, Arthur William's visits to Jennifer became more and more frequent, while Jennifer never denied him her bubbling and quite inexplicable affection. Increasingly, when David came home, he detected more and more passive reminders of Father's continuing involvement in his life – a pipe left on the mantlepiece; Father's old slippers by the range; a bottle of Father's favourite beer in the scullery.

Little David Ellis Junior was born on the third day of September, 1939. Chief Officer David Ellis was loading in Valparaiso for Surabaya at the time. Grandpa bought the child a giant teddybear from Lewis's in Manchester – the only time he'd ever given a present to anyone, other than a pre-vetted 'Waldo's' Lucky Bag', of course – and lavished all the love on little David that he'd denied his own son.

Oh, yes – and *Kapitänleutnant* Lemp's U-30 torpedoed the British passenger liner *Athenia* off the north-west coast of Ireland that same day. The Germans were to sink a further twenty-five Red Ensign merchant vessels before that month was over. For the men of the British Merchant Navy anyway, the Second World War had started with a vengeance . . .

When David Ellis did finally return home some weeks later, weary of unfamiliar darkened ships and extinguished navigation aids, and nerve-strung by the first tensions of war at sea he'd . . . well, simply exploded with resentment when he'd discovered Father's growing involvement with the child.

It was a foolish reaction, particularly knowing Jennifer's character as he should have done. Calculated to ensure that she, too, would dig her heels in and take Father's side: not because she didn't love David but simply because she was too proud and stubborn – an attitude Chief Officer Ellis could never understand.

There was a long and desperately unhappy scene in which dreadful things were said and immediately regretted but not, at the time, retracted. The outcome was that he stormed black-faced from the house, spent one simmering night in a miserable hotel down by Salford Docks; decided he was damned if *he* was going to relent, and impulsively took the train to Liverpool where he came upon a vessel urgently requiring a replacement Mate for one stricken that morning with appendicitis.

Her name was the Steamship *Olympian*. Then under orders to sail for unspecified waters at dusk.

It was only when he'd first settled into his dank cell on the starboard side of *Olympian's* funnel deck that he became aware of the enormity of what he'd done. But by then the Formby Light was abeam and radio silence frustrated even brief re-affirmations of love. It was too late to redress foolishness; too late even to acknowledge he'd been wrong and that nothing, not even Father, mattered as much as his wife and child.

He could only swear to himself that he would go back home and beg forgiveness – even make it up with bloody Father if need be! Just as soon as the war, and the U-boats permitted.

Olympian had headed for the South Atlantic initially, sailing as an Independent and, as they discovered later, dodging as much by good luck as inexperienced Naval Control, the enemy's commerce raiders then roaming the trade lanes between Pernambuco and The Cape in search of revenge for the Montevideo scuttling of the *Graf Spee*. It was only months later that she was finally routed to the United States coast, and thence via Cape Breton into North Atlantic convoy service.

In those long, isolated weeks Chief Officer Ellis, like every other man aboard, grew more and more alarmed by rumours of the punishment Britain itself was beginning to receive from the *Luftwaffe*. Even reading between the lines of the heavily censored BBC Overseas News broadcasts they sensed the growing horrors of the blitz: civilian deprivation, the very real miseries of evacuation; the persistent and ever-growing threat of Nazi invasion. Ellis found himself

186

becoming desperately concerned for the safety of Jennifer and little David.

But the oddest thing of all was when he . . . well, when he began to feel an inexplicable concern for Father's welfare too.

Just as Ellis reached the funnel deck a ship began firing to starboard and somebody shouted, 'That's not starshell: that's *live* rounds!'

The Mate swung sharply outboard, eyes searching across to their sister Bone Collector, *Stafford Pride*. He caught the next muzzle flash; horizontal and long as a dragon's lick from her high poopdeck, heard the *crack* of the report skittering across the sea between them, caught the rip of the shell going away astern somewhere . . . and then Leather came charging up behind him.

Not alarmed like Ellis was, though. The Bosun's expression was jealous green; reflecting a fury to pale the glare of the action. 'Look at 'em! Bloody LOOK at 'em, Mister Ellis! They givvem a gun an' they have to go shootin' an' showin' off an' . . .'

But then Bosun Leather always had been in favour of being granted the firepower so carelessly bestowed on others.

The Mate snapped tightly, 'More to the point – what're they firing at?'

'They won't hit it anyway. Them bat-blind apologies f'r sailormen couldn't . . .'

'LEATHER!'

'Yessir – What, sir?'

'Can you *see* what . . . they . . . are . . . bloody-well FIRING at?'

Of course *Stafford Pride* immediately stopped firing then, whereupon the amateur gladiators around her antiquated gun dispersed to drift, disconsolately it seemed, to the taffrail where they huddled together, reassuring themselves,

187

no doubt, about what had happened to the surfaced U-boat they'd positively identified, if it really *had* been there on the end of their sights.

Alf Leather's craggy face was a picture of smug self-vindication.

'Don't say it, Bose,' Ellis warned him. 'Jus' don't you bloody say it!'

'I told you so? 'Course not, sir,' the Bosun lied. And grinned broadly.

'Thank God for men like Leather,' Ellis thought gratefully.

He gazed astern into the blackness outside the periphery of the flares, suddenly remembering the long-absent *Theotokos*.

'The Greek that dropped back, sir? The runner?' Leather queried, reading his mind. Ellis nodded. The Bosun's grin faded as he meaningfully inverted his thumb.

The rectangle of SC whatever-it-was continued without any sign of breaking formation. Convoy discipline was still holding. In fact the night had gone almost quiet again, slowly the last splutters of snowflake were dying: even the sea had gone down slightly in the few minutes since the last wave of torpedoings had occurred. The diminution of activity didn't ease the pressure on the watchers, though; it increased it. Like most experienced convoymen, Ellis's butterfly told him it was only a very temporary lull.

He became aware of Leather's lifejacket still dangling casually from the Bosun's hand and remembered he'd left his own up on the bridge. He felt an overwhelming desire to return for it.

'One seaman party to remain fore and aft by the recovery gear, Bose. You take charge forward; Chippie can stand-by at Number Four hatch: McKerchar and I'll come down if we have to stop for survivors.'

'And the rest, Mister Ellis?'

'Boat stations, Alf. And pass the word for lifejackets to be worn at all times; certainly till dawn.'

188

Leather looked at him strangely. 'Captain's orders, sir?'

'Aye.'

'He's stopped wavin' his arms about then,' the Bosun interpreted meaningfully.

'We think the Commodore's been sunk. They should know up on the bridge by now.'

'Christ!' Leather showed shock for the first time.

'Now you sound like the Cook,' the Mate made himself grin.

'Standin' in a cathedral, rigged in a dog collar an' *cassock* I couldn't sound like the bloody Cook!' the older man retorted spiritedly.

Briefly they stared out over the again dark convoy. Only one burning ship from the three assumed casualties of the most recent attack was now in evidence, slowly drifting abeam to starboard: but identification was difficult, the fire being constantly masked by the procession of intervening vessels. It hardly seemed likely to be the Commodore's *Pendragon* – Archie Mulligan's *Pendragon* really – though. It lay near enough a mile away, far out on the flank, while *Stafford Pride* was showing no sign of preparing to stop as she would had it been her own column leader in trouble.

Did that mean the other two were still limping on? Had already foundered? Or were they lying out there on their beam-ends, too low in the water to detect? That was the trouble with convoy actions. Not only did you stand there alone, whether anyone was beside you or not, but you also stood equally bemused whether in the dark or the counterfeit brilliance of day. If you were just an ordinary sailor on deck you didn't know what the hell was happening . . .

'Look, sir!' the Bosun exclaimed, and pointed.

Ellis followed his arm and made out one – no, TWO lifeboats directly ahead of the *Pride*. Just where *Pendragon's* survivors might be expected to have ended up. They looked very small, hardly big enough to save men.

The aged ship with the aged gun abeam of *Olympian*

189

began to fall astern as she reduced speed. It was too dark now to make out activity on her lower decks but Ellis guessed they were lowering their nets, preparing bowlines and stretchers – and each looking expressionlessly out into the gloom while they worked.

He didn't know; he probably would never know until – or if ever – they reached their destination, whether or not doleful Archie Mulligan was shortly to be hoisted aboard. But, speaking as one Bone Collector to another, one thing seemed certain.

'Better get forr'ad and ready to open up shop, Bose,' he said levelly. 'Looks like the pick-up business is picking up.'

Grubby Grubb was completing the conversion of the saloon to a makeshift hospital as he entered; along with Steward Weston, Chef Robbo, one of the galley boys and a couple of volunteer deckies. Ellis noticed that the straight-backed dining chairs had already been unshipped from their deck chains and lashed securely against the after bulkhead. Now the two long tables designed to separate deck and engineer officers – social division again: even at mealtimes, and within the one strata of class – had been covered with mattresses while spare canvas boat gripes lay loosely, somewhat ominously, on top of them.

'Thought we may get a few lads aboard needin' a bit o' repair work, Mate,' Grubby condescended, looking superior at Ellis's uncertain frown. 'Liable to lash out: kick a bit.'

'Oh,' the Mate muttered faintly. Traditionally either the Master or the Chief Steward served the basic medical needs of the crew, but he'd never visualised Grubby Grubb as a full-rigged surgeon before.

There were piles of clean blankets stacked in one corner; cans of spirit, supplied by the Control authorities before they sailed from Breton, to decontaminate oil-fouled survivors; a five gallon drum of Jeyes' Fluid and a bag of purplish Condy's crystals as rough and ready disinfectant. Knives

190

from the galley, bottles of iodine, cotton wool, scissors, rolls of elastoplast, makeshift splints . . . the nightmare plethora of holocaust anticipated.

The galley boy was tearing old sheets into strips for use as bandages; Slimy Weston, eyebrows meeting in ferocious concentration, was laboriously wading through a book called *Emergency Medical Practice For The Seafarer: 1912 Edition*.

'It keeps 'im occupied,' Grubby explained, showing a remarkable and uncharacteristic tolerance. ''Course, we'll not let him get 'is hands near open wounds or nothing. Even if we dipped 'im in that drum o' Jeyes Fluid over there, Slimy'd still be unhygienic.'

Ellis eyed the Chief Steward surreptitiously: there seemed to be a new spirit in the man. It was as if the old Grubby Grubb of previous convoys – of tonight's, in fact – had changed completely. As if, somehow, he'd resigned himself to circumstances and become a better man for it.

But he had not changed completely.

'I heard the Old Man sat on 'is sandwiches,' Grubby sniggered. Ellis couldn't help smiling to himself: thank Heaven for a *bit* of normality.

The first explosion from ahead rattled the stacks of chairs against the bulkhead. Then another, and another.

No one moved in the saloon. It was a bit like a statue dance in the Seamen's Mission – everybody fixed rigidly as they were; half-ripped sheets motionless; Slimy part-turned through a page on arteries; Grubb's mouth frozen in beaming malevolence. All with the one common factor: all listening intently.

Then a fourth detonation, echoing through the hull.

'It's all right, they're depth charges,' Ellis interpreted, feeling the relief as a gush of blood to the head. 'They're keeping one down somewhere out front.'

'HalleLUjah, Mister Ellis,' one of the deckies grinned: crossing himself exaggeratedly.

'That's *my* bloody part o' ship,' Robbo snapped, piqued. 'You leave the relig'n to me an' stick to what you knows, Caine. Like harlot women an' strong drink.'

'You arrange with the Lord to supply 'em, I'll be happy to stick to 'em, Cookie.'

'That's it then,' the Chief Steward rubbed his hands and looked pleased. 'All ready to serve the customers.'

'You've done a good job, Henry,' the Mate said unreservedly. It was the first time he'd ever had occasion to congratulate Grubby in nearly two years of voyaging. 'Now get your team to their boat stations and see they're wearing their lifeja . . .'

'We got to make sandwichis for the lads yet,' Grubby protested. 'Tea and sannies, Mate.'

Ellis gaped. 'You've got to what?'

'Make sandwichis. F'r the crew.'

'You quite sure you're feeling all right, Henry?' Ellis asked faintly.

'It's what you said earlier,' Grubb admitted: a picture of liberal conversion. 'I realises I can't take it with me if we do get torpedoed. It's like, well – one in the eye for 'Itler if the boys eat it first, i'n't it?'

'Lord,' the Mate muttered with a new respect. Talk about resolution? If Grubby Grubb was prepared to offer extra rations, then *Olympian's* Chief Steward hadn't merely changed: he'd mutated.

But bewilderingly he found himself in the middle of a catering department conflict.

'Not me,' the Cook said emphatically. 'I don't mind layin' on the odd pot o' tea, but I'm buggered if I'm makin' fifty-odd sannies in the middle of the night f'r them gannets out there.'

Grubby started to go red in the face. 'If I'm prepared to put up the bread, cheese an' scrape, Chef, then where's *your* love-thy-neighbour bloody input? *YOUR* Holy-bloody-goodwill to all men?'

'Weeping may endure f'r a night, but joy cometh in the morning,' Robbo retorted complacently. 'Psalms three zero: five. It means they'll get their bloody breakfast at the usual time.'

'There may not *BE* a mornin', the way things are goin' just now! Them poor lads is all out there on deck; frozen to the marrow. Famished an' weak from lack o' food.'

'Not fifty-odd rounds've cheese san'wich an that's *FLAT*, Chief Steward!'

'Maybe they won't all WANT one! Maybe some of 'em won't have the bloody *MONEY*!'

There was a deathly silence in the saloon. Only the throb of the engine and the creak of the saloon chairs stacked against the bulkhead broke the hush of the make-shift hospital.

Eventually Ellis found his tongue. 'You mean you're going to *charge* them for a sandwich, Henry? You just said it yourself: there may not even be a morning – yet you're actually proposing to charge them extra for their own food?'

'Only tuppence a throw, Mate,' Grubby defended weakly. 'Just at cost price, so to speak.'

More dull explosions rattled the saloon from ahead, and the light flickered briefly. Ellis spoke restrainedly, very precisely. 'Presumably, while you can't take bread and cheese in a lifeboat, you can take hard cash? The Owners must be very proud of you, Chief Steward – to say nothing of Hitler and Grand Admiral bloody Dönitz!'

'Pre-sinking sale: everythin' mus' go.' Slimy Weston sniggered, and his aged shoulders heaved wheezily.

'In fact *you*, Henry Grubb,' Ellis pronounced after deep and careful consideration, 'are without a shadow of doubt the most miserable; the most useless; the most leprous; the most conniving, consciousless, penny-pinching bast . . .'

The next explosion was louder. Much louder. This time the lights went out for a full five seconds before cutting back in.

Henry Grubb never did learn whether the Mate disapproved of everything about him, or merely certain shortcomings in his character. By then Chief Officer Ellis was gone from the saloon and half-way up the bridge ladder. Running.

Even before *Olympian's* own siren began to blare a frantic emergency avoidance signal.

I am directing my course to port!

Eleven

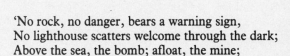

'No rock, no danger, bears a warning sign,
No lighthouse scatters welcome through the dark;
Above the sea, the bomb; afloat, the mine;
Beneath, the gangs of the torpedo-shark.'

John Masefield

01.00 a.m.: Two Bells in the Middle Watch

Momentarily Ellis found himself disoriented as he breasted the top of the ladder even while the ship's siren exhausted itself in a splutter of steam. His night vision this time had suffered from the harsh glare of the saloon; the bridge deck was already lying over to starboard as *Olympian* swung ponderously under full rudder and – the most disconcerting element of all – those neatly ordered lines of ships which had formed their forward horizon for over two weeks now presented a higgledy-piggledy skew of slowly moving leviathans: a confusion of black-masted dinosaurs sliding and passing and roaring warning of their unexpected comings with throaty, vaporous alarm.

He heard the Old Man's measured order. 'Engine to slow. Ease to ten the wheel.'

'Ease to ten the *WHEEL*, sir.'

The telegraphs jangling above the cacophany: McKerchar's competent snap. 'Engine's on slow ahead, sir.' A figure materialised from the gloom of the far port wing. It was Cadet Moberly. 'A ship's been torpedoed up in column four, sir. The Polish timber carrier, I think. She must have her rudder jammed to port an' presumably they can't stop her engines . . . running diagonally through our section of the convoy.'

Ellis hurried to the bridge front, still fighting for vision. 'Whereaway now, Moberly?'

The Senior Apprentice gestured and Ellis registered the glow of fire without apparent source. 'Dead ahead, sir. *Duella's* in the way at the moment.'

A blister of white water erupted a mile ahead, followed by another and a third until a curtain of spray briefly punctuated the horizon – more depth charges. A Hotchkiss gun began firing out on the far flank, and then there was the sharper *crack* of a 4.7. Someone threw a scatter of snowflake and the jostling masts and funnels again detonated into sharp relief.

'Getting busy,' Ellis remarked calmly for Moberly's sake. He knew it had begun this time. There were too many incidents occurring in too many sectors all at once. The convoy was fighting for its life.

Duella's drogue had been towing well to starboard of her counter while she was under turning moment; leaping and skipping in flurries of white from crest to crest over the steep, rearing seas. Now it began to centre under her counter again as she steadied. The temporarily screened blue stern light came into view once more.

'Midships,' from the Captain. 'Anyone see 'er yet?'

'*MIDSHIPS* the wheel.'

'Negative, sir.'

Still vessels all over the place, total confusion. 'How the hell did we get like this?' Ellis asked grimly.

'Vice-commodore ordered an alteration to port, sir. We'd just begun the manoeuvre when the torpedo hit. Some ships were forced to change to st'bd; others went even harder to po . . .'

'*THERE* she is!'

'Wheel's amidships, sir.'

The rogue casualty came clear on *Duella's* port side,

196

lumbering from right to left. There was fire on her after-decks, streaming astern in a shimmering haze with the only-too-familiar fireflies whirling and spinning in her wake. A blanket of smoke rolled over her taffrail into the sea. She'd lost her mainmast: now there were only three in eviden . . .

THREE?

'Christ!' the Mate muttered. 'There's two of them locked together. There's been a collision.'

The Old Man came rushing through the wheelhouse to see better. *Duella's* marker began to skip across *Olympian's* bows again. Burton snapped, 'Starboard *TEN*. C'n you see who else is involved, Mister?'

'Sir,' Westall urged. Ellis looked down and saw the binoculars in Westall's hand. 'Thanks.'

Magnified, the conjoined vessels immediately demonstrated their separate identities. The torpedoed timber ship – the larger of the two – was listing dangerously to port; virtually lying over and supported by the smaller and nearer of the casualties. Ellis could see the towering stack of the Pole's after deck cargo beginning to crumble as its foundations, already eroded by the force of the explosion, burned furiously; huge baulks of Canadian spruce tumbling and sliding to smother her helpless companion. Their bridge structures appeared to have merged – unstable already by definition of being a high-loaded timber carrier, the run-away must have begun to capsize at the critical moment of having past her unfortunate victim.

'She's hit the *Joan M*!' Ellis identified the victim and felt sad. She was that tough little 1905-built steamer which had straggled for eighteen solitary hours without protection while SC whatever had still been en-route for the ice, yet managed to catch up triumphantly despite the fact that there was more steam swirling outside her ancient hull than retained within her corroded boiler tubes.

Now the helplessly-linked hulls were slowing, but also

197

beginning to spin in a monstrous mid-ocean reel, a gargantuan pirouette as one steamed remorselessly ahead, presumably only with dead engineers at her controls: while the other kicked a furious flurry of astern water in a vain attempt to arrest their mutual onward passage. Unless he could free himself from his collapsing burden quickly, the Joan M's master had no alternative but to go astern and pray to God! He couldn't hope to launch boats into seas still crashing past at such a pace.

Through the lenses men were already sliding and leaping from the Pole to the little British vessel's deck: men along with timber and parts of ship and life-rafts tearing away from lashings . . . an avalanche of urgency. Suddenly Ellis could even see figures clambering across the tight-rope-high snarl of wreckage from bridge to bridge.

The locked ships began to wheel alarmingly. 'They're bloody comin' back across us!' Albert complained. He whirled. '*FULL* ahead! HARD to starb'd!'

Someone's 4.7 began firing up ahead again: sharp, cracking reports leaving a singing in the ears. More starshell. A dull, not-immediately-identifiable explosion from God only knew what part of convoy. Immediately ahead of *Olympian*, *Duella's* master had apparently elected to dodge left: she started to slide left. Albert was already committed to a starboard turn. The gap between the so-far inseparable sisters opened steadily with the locked ships dancing square in the middle.

'Christ but I'm gettin' fed up!' the Captain snarled.

A hooter blaring desperately out on the right flank. One . . . two . . . thuree . . . *SIX* short blasts. The Mate shouted 'Sound signal f'r torpedo approaching the convoy from *starb* . . .'

BOOOOOooooom!

A massive geyser of spray climbing from the outboard side of a stubby silhouette in mid-Column Five. Immediately she began to sag by the head, while, out there too, the desperate avoidance began. Abruptly coloured light signals flicked on a long way away and over to the right – the Vice-commodore desperately attempting to cope with events from the ill-equipped *Naiad*. A few ships not totally preoccupied with dodging dutifully repeated them until the convoy took on a slightly festive appearance.

McKerchar came out of the wheelhouse. Ellis noted the Second Mate wasn't wearing his lifejacket either.

'Columns to execute fifteen degree turn tae port,' McKerchar announced dryly. Then grinned. The Mate had never seen the Second even smile before: he understood why, though. Very clearly.

'I can't!' The Old Man kicked the bridge front: sudden rage overtaking him. ''Ow did *HE* know?' His arms took in the departing shape of their once leader. ''Ow did *Duella* know that daft bat o' a Vice was goin' to rush off to *PORT*, eh?'

The burning Pole and the belaboured *Joan M* now lay apparently welded together less than three ship's lengths ahead and slightly to port. Albert Burton in *Olympian* had two alternatives. There were U-boats all around the convoy and closing now; if he stopped and became separated from the protective gaggle they would present a perfect target. If, on the other hand, he carried on when the 'execute' signal was given, *Olympian* would still be careering to starboard while everybody else went the other way, particularly their line abreast companion, *Stafford Pride*. It promised to be rather like driving a lorry diagonally across a busy one-way street with eyes tight shut.

Ellis snatched a glance through the Barr and Strouds. The smaller vessel had adopted a substantial list towards the Pole; steadily she, too, was being dragged bulwarks-under by the massive top weight of the casualty. They could hear the scream of tortured steel and the grinding of iron plates as the *Joan M* still struggled to free herself, and Ellis guessed with sick foreboding that there must still be engineers labouring below in the ever-more angling and near-Victorian world of that almost foundering tramp.

The Christmas tree lights flicked off throughout the convoy. Simultaneously the last snowflake extinguished and darkness fell abruptly as McKerchar called an expressionless, 'Execute, Sir.'

'Ohhhh, *STOP* 'er.' The Old Man snapped tightly. 'But keep the wheel to port an' bugger it!'

A sudden crackle of . . . *small* arms firing, could it be? Some hopping-mad skipper with a Webley or a shotgun even, having a go at a surfaced U-boat running down between the columns? Ellis pulled the glasses from the glare of the linked ships and briefly swept the ships ahead as the lines began to swing. No U-boats to be seen yet, but things *were* different: no longer were they moving together with the tears an' sweat-earned skills of two weeks constant practice. Subtly the convoy was losing cohesion. It was the time the undertakers watched and waited for: the time they could close on the coffins . . . ASDIC would be beginning to lose its power of hearing: ships were sinking, hulls breaking up with submarine rumblings: the escorts would be living on the cold discipline of their commanders and the nerves of their crews, tempted to dash hither and thither in frantic pursuit.

The shiver of the engine had died away as *Olympian* pulsed unpowered yet again through the short seas. Ahead, the long silhouette of *Stafford Pride* cut silently across their track and, further over to starboard, the last ships in each line – the Bone Collectors-designate but not yet employed – wheeled in weary, draggled obedience to the will of the rectangle. One, almost invisible against the black horizon, lay even further astern than themselves as it stood-by the unknown casualty from mid-Column Five.

'Clear to go ahead again, Cap'n,' the Second Mate called with a touch of sarcasm. Ellis wondered yet again why he behaved like that? Was he really *so* resentful of those who

200

had not yet suffered so grievously as he; or was it simply a veneer to mask his terror at the prospect of repeating his experience?'

'We'll wait a minute now,' Albert said, mercurially placid as ever. 'If *Joan M's* goin' to abandon, we might as well be first in the queue for the gratitude.'

More depth charging . . . more mountains of water: ghost-pallid this time without their pyrotechnic theatre light. Everyone knew it was the briefest of respites. Where *were* the bloody U-boats?

Quickly back to the welded ships as *Stafford Pride* cut behind the fire. Almost stopped now, the Pole's after decks were blazing fiercely, thousands of tons of desperately-needed timber providing kindling for her valueless incendiary death instead of for the frames of fighting planes, the stocks of Bren Guns; the decks, the rails, the myriad parts of ships to replace and multiply her a hundred times . . . and Mercy help them on the British deck: that heat must shrivel skin, make clothing smoke. Surely they weren't still hoping to save her, so why didn't they abandon?'

'By God!' the Captain said at Ellis's elbow. 'I do believe 'e's goin' to do it.'

'Be a bit more specific, Albert – do what? Launch her boats; scuttle her . . . haul himself clear?' It was odd, just drifting there and waiting for a torpedo while another ship decided whether or not it was going to give up the battle and sink. Certainly Chief Officer Ellis didn't feel afraid for himself now: more a sort of resignation in a way. Maybe it was because he finally accepted that the U-boats would keep up the pace, that the anticipation was over; his fear of past nightmares briefly neutralised by the adrenalin generated in this current one.

A brilliant flash from the convoy, and the rumble of the torpedo-strike. Then another, almost in the same instant yet much further to starboard. How many had that been since the final phase of the battle began, what . . . less than an hour ago? Six ships? Seven? Multiplied by, say, sixty men apiece? So there already had to be over three hundred seamen either struggling grimly to keep sundered hulls afloat, or coughing blood and oil; perhaps blinded by the pitting of blast-impelled coaldust or simply gasping with the onset of hypothermia in the chill black waters – or already dead, of course. Slack-jawed, vacant: without dignity or marked grave.

'Bloody Merchant Navy. Don't even have a proper uniform, half of 'em. An' hardly a pub down the waterfront where a decent shore-livin' bloke can get a quiet drink when them scruff-arsed convoys get back . . .'

An elderly man had once said that to Ellis. Just in passing conversation on a bus. Ellis hadn't said anything. It hadn't seemed worthwhile at the time.

A huge burst of flame and sparks rising high into the sky from the Polish ship as she shuddered and nestled down on the trapped *Joan M* with a giant screech of protest. Albert snapped, 'Right: that's it! Engine half ahead, Mister McKerchar. Port twenty.'

He started to turn away. 'We'll go in for 'em, Mister Ellis. Have the nets rea . . .'

'Look,' Ellis said quietly.

With a wriggle and a great squirting of steam the little British tramp steamer hauled astern from her grasping consort, rolling crazily as most of the starboard wing of her bridge and quite a lot of her upperdeck rails and ventilators ripped away. Almost immediately the other vessel began to capsize, revolving faster and faster into the sea now separating them. It was an awesome sight from *Olympian*: from the decks of the *Joan M* it must have stopped every heart with a clutch of dread.

Gigantically the timber carrier lay into the Atlantic with her deck cargo exploding and hissing and flinging gouts of boiling water in vast arcs. Just as her still-smoking funnel wearily touched water her bows began to rise until she was suspended vertically, overshadowing the clanking, wheezing freighter; then she started to slide backwards and downwards and even aboard *Olympian* they could hear her bulkheads going like the kettledrums of God.

A moment later and she was gone, while baulks of timber began to shoot from the sea; a flight of monstrous arrows erupting and soaring above the *Joan M* to fall back with great splashes and sometimes strange metallic bangs as they diverted erratically sideways on re-entry, spearing through the water like mini-torpedoes themselves to strike in frustration at the rusty hull of the tramp.

When that was over, and the *Joan* appeared to float in the middle of a Canadian river log jam while her crew, aided by a somewhat dazed group of Polish survivors, began to tackle the few small deck fires caused by their inadvertent loading of some of the burning cargo, Albert cautiously steered *Olympian* close enough to shout across the gap.

'Yer glands. They'll need a bit o' doin' to make 'em pressure-tight again,' he roared at the part-navigating bridge opposite. 'What about a temporary tow, Captain?'

The *Joan M's* master – for it could only have been he who would have had the courage to wear baseball boots, sealskin Eskimo trousers, a bright yellow oilskin jacket and a very British bowler hat – hung perilously above the still-erupting sea from the limits of his sagging wheelhouse, and nonchalantly waved dismissal to the clouds of steam wreathing from his boiler-room vents.

'If yer really wants one, Capt'n,' he bellowed back with indestructible self-confidence, 'Then I'm only too 'appy to give yer one . . .'

Most of the action was still taking place in the van of the convoy as they resumed course: the flashes and bangs; rumbles and abrupt nerve-tensing splurges of airborne brilliance flickering and echoing back across the sea with dull Wagnerian majesty. To Ellis it seemed an unreal experience at first – like watching some vast and shadowed ampitheatre in which portentous events were being played out that had nothing at all to do with themselves.

But as they crept closer to the convoy he became aware that no longer were they last in line. Now the silhouette of a limping freighter steamed slowly out between them and what had previously formed an empty westerly horizon; all alone and trailing smoke yet gallantly refusing to give in. The Bone Collector for Column Five still steamed perilously alone in search for drowning men, while the *Joan M* puffed phlegmatically in *Olympian's* wake, as apparently careless of her hazard as if she was cruising the Bristol Channel. Two others lay dead and very low in the water astern, dark and drifting: stark reminders of reality by their listing attitudes of abandonment. *Olympian* had once again become incorporated within the cast of players.

By then, as if to underline their involvement, they were also nosing through the wreckage marking SC whatever's continuing sacrifice. The heart-familiar flotsam of sea war: hatch boards; another empty and this time quite-undamaged ship's boat; a whole section of bridge wing still spiralling steadily in a coal-dust vortex. There were gratings and buckets and vegetables, and a canvas seabag and dunnage and pieces of packing case – most curious of all a giant inexplicably-inflated beach ball scudding aimlessly before the wind in red and white-striped jollity . . . and half a shattered lifebuoy still attached to its water-activated light which declared, as they slowed briefly:

. . . *rinda: Newcast* . . .

. . . it was shaping to be a sad, bad night for seamen's families on the Tyne.

But it was only when they'd closed to within a quarter mile of *Duella's* blue stern light that they caught the first promise of horror extraordinary.

Of course it had to be the child who saw them before anyone else. 'That lad's certainly got the eyes of a cat,' Chief

204

Officer Ellis was forced to admit. 'It's just a pity he's only got the brain of a bloody cat to go with 'em!'

'*BODIES* ahead, sir!' the Junior Cadet screeched. '*Hundreds* of them – an' the . . . they're NAKED bodies, sir!'

'My God!' the Captain muttered, white as a ghost this time. But he knew Westall's ability, and took him at his word. 'Stop engine, Mister McKerchar. We're surely called to attend the Devil's work tonight.'

Slowly they coasted towards the distant group of pallid torsos bumping and drifting in mute togetherness on the North Atlantic swell. It was a deadful riddle that plagued each and every man in those long moments of their approach – what could possibly have occurred to explode a cargo of apparently denuded men? Could some ghastly freak of blast have stripped death of the last elements of modesty? Why, for that matter had the convoy steamed so callously by without even hesitating to search for sign of life? Surely such a grand disaster would have demanded the deployment of every nominated rescue ship?'

For indeed there *were* hundreds of carcasses, just as Westall claimed. An army division of corpses; a whole troopship of corpses: all bobbing and swaying and reflecting the battle ahead as they rose before every wave to reveal the glint of flayed white fat and red-raw flesh in macabre contrast with the Stygian sea.

Yet there had *been* no troopships in the under-defended ranks of Convoy SC whatever-it-was or, as a matter of certainty, SC whatever-it-was wouldn't have found itself so appallingly under-defended. Hardly any fighting men aboard at all, in fact: just Merchant Navy personnel. So . . .

Chief Officer Ellis, for all his remaining doubts about Cadet Westall's imaginative power, felt nauseated as the castaway cadavers drifted closer and took detailed shape: made even more dreadful as they finally focussed within his glasses by appearing to have been, well . . . quite deliberately mutilated?

It was a full minute before he began to grin. 'That Norwegian in Column Four. I think she's the one that's been sunk, sir.'

The Captain, still strained by the prospect of the awful recovery to come, snarled, 'Dammit, Mister – *SHE* wasn't a passenger ship; no more'n any o' the others.'

'No, sir,' the Mate replied. 'But she did have refrigerated cargo spaces.'

Best quality free-range Texas beef. The Bosun managed to hook three whole deep-frozen sides of it before Albert Burton fixed young Westall with an even deeper-frozen eye, then commanded with enormous self-restraint, 'Full speed, Mister McKerchar. We will rejoin the convoy. Now.'

Bone Collectors? By God they were for once, richly rewarded. Bloody patient they'd been, risking their necks so many times before with no results whatever.

But as Robbo the Cook said, perhaps employing a little Biblical licence in his thanksgiving: 'Cast thy bread upon the waters, mates; f'r sure as eggs is eggs – thou shalt find it multiplied after many days.'

It had been many months, not days, before *Olympian* and Chief Officer David Ellis finally returned to UK waters.

They'd known something was wrong even as they came inward past the Formby Light and seen the pall of smoke hanging over Merseyside. They'd heard the guarded commentaries on the Blitz often enough: it was to be mid-1940 before any of them saw its results.

'Go home immediately, Mister Ellis,' Albert had said quietly, after they'd berthed astern of a burned-out hulk and the Birkenhead stevedores were clambering aboard. 'See to your wife and baby while I stand-by the ship.'

But Captain Burton had never married, other than to the sea. He'd only had his ship to love and to worry about; and sometimes men like Grubby Grubb to provide his comforts and his meals – and the nearest he would ever get to domestic argument.

David had not received a single letter from Jennifer since he'd sailed, so fool-impulsive after what had been such a childish argument. No communication; nothing to ease his remorse, his fears for her and little David – nor, for that matter, his quite illogical concern for Father.

It might have been that her letters, forwarded care of *Olympian's* Owners under rules of strict wartime secrecy, had simply never caught up with him during the ship's South Atlantic adventuring. Certainly he'd never been confident that his would reach *her,* despatched as they'd been from such far-flung territories. While ships carrying mail were even then being sunk in convoy, irrespective of which way they were heading, as Dönitz's U-boats extended their range further into the Atlantic from bases established after the fall of France.

But that had been the optimistic explanation. Maybe the real one was simpler – perhaps Jennifer had never written to him at all?

There was nothing dramatic to see when he finally arrived at Jutland Way. No great piles of smoking rubble or snaking firehoses or the steady roar of flame. Just a cleared site where half a dozen houses had once stood, and over which the weeds and grasses waved in cheerful green contrast to the surrounding acres of untouched but smoke-grimed brick. Even dead, the place where he and Jennifer had lived and their baby had been created, seemed less desolate, less depressing than the rest of Salford as Chief Officer Ellis recalled it.

It must have happened in the early days of the blitz: not long after he'd joined *Olympian.* He understood then why she had never written and, somehow, it brought peace to one tiny pocket of his mind even though the rest of him was numb. The reason was important, though: he desperately needed to persuade himself that she had loved him too much to permit Father's selfish insensitivity to destroy them; to deny them eventual reconciliation as it had denied David Ellis, himself, so many childhood freedoms.

David did hope that she had believed the same of him. But she would know now: and his faith in that conviction was to help a lot in the months to follow.

He'd walked through the weeds and stood in silence, just remembering. An elderly special constable came past on a bicycle with a steel helmet slung over his shoulder and his gasmask bag dangling from the handlebars. He reminded Ellis a bit of Father. He had the same brown moustache; the same determined chin.

He'd stopped and wheeled his bike over, looking uncertain.

'You . . . ah, knew 'em, did you, sir?'

'A bit,' Ellis had said. 'Not as well as I'd liked to have done.'

The constable looked relieved. 'It were a long time ago now.' He frowned. 'Four . . . Nay, five month anyway.'

'Yes,' Ellis said again. 'I guessed that too.'

'Seven killed in this row that night – three where we're standing now.'

Ellis wasn't surprised, somehow. That there had been three of them.

'You were here?'

'I was here,' the policeman's eyes were hard. 'I helped get them out. It's a bloody awful job.'

'I'm glad I don't have to do it,' Ellis had said, and meant it.

'Funny how you remember things.' The constable took his helmet off and wiped round the brim. 'They were all together under the stairs in this one. The husband had tried to shelter the woman and the baby . . .'

'The husband? Wasn't he an old man?'

'They all look old,' the other said grimly. 'Plaster dust, broken glass, loss of blood – they all look old by the time we get them out.'

208

'Oh,' Ellis had muttered, and thought about Father and how he had tried to protect them both when he'd heard the bomb coming down. Maybe Father had even tried to protect him, his absent son, too; in a remote sort of way. And bloody well failed as he'd always done, to fulfil even that most important trust successfully.

The constable had hesitated before he'd left. He must have noticed the little silver MN badge with its crown in Ellis's buttonhole.

'Merchant Navy, are you, sir?'

Ellis had nodded.

'It must be hard for you,' the elderly man commented. 'Bein' out there, an' not knowing what's happenin' back here. Got any family yourself, sir?'

'No,' Chief Officer Ellis had said softly. 'No family at all.'

The telegram, the official notification, had been waiting for him aboard *Olympian* when he'd returned aboard that night. It had followed him through a chain of indifferent, over-worked Agents half-way around the world. No one in the Owner's offices had thought to check its receipt.

He'd never gone back to Salford since. Not even to visit his sisters. Or the little shop on the corner.

'Home, Mister Ellis.'

Chief Officer Ellis stirred. 'Not really. Not anymore.'

Albert looked at him oddly. 'Eh?'

'Just thinking,' Ellis said. 'Sorry.'

'I was sayin' we're home again. Back in column an' three sides o' beef to the good.'

The Mate looked round. Nothing had exploded or fired a shot or blown a whistle for several minutes. The new lull wouldn't last for long. The decimated convoy still continued to progress at less than seven knots towards the edge of *das Todesloch*.

They were waiting again. It was nearly 1:30 in the morning.

209

Ellis left the Old Man leaning on the rail thinking dreamily, perhaps, of roast beef and Yorkshire pudding enough to feed a Royal Court, and walked through the wheelhouse. The Second Mate was by the compass. Ellis noticed he still wasn't wearing his lifejacket even after watching the timber ship sink. But then, neither was Chief Officer Ellis for all his good resolutions.

He tried to think of something cheerful to say that wouldn't be countered with contempt by McKerchar but he couldn't, so he just continued through and out to the port wing, feeling the wind fresh in the welcome darkness. Young Westall was out there all alone and gazing fixedly outboard; hunched, frightened and undoubtedly homesick. Ellis felt sorry for the lad; it hadn't been his fault – about the corpses.

The child didn't move when Ellis came behind him: pretending to concentrate like he always did when the Mate was around. Still . . .

'Don't let it put you off,' Ellis said with uncharacteristic sympathy where Westall was concerned. 'Just because the Captain gets a bit funny, don't let it stop you reporting anything you see.'

'Thank you, sir,' the little apprentice muttered. Typical, really: usually when the Chief Officer spoke to a cadet the boy would at least turn to show a bit of respect. Westall didn't – just stayed there all puffed up in his kapok lifejacket like a bloody fat penguin, staring out over the sea in an obvious huff an' . . .

'There, Sir!' Westall suddenly shrieked, and threw his arm out to point.

'God Dammit, Westall!' Ellis exploded, finally driven beyond any reasonable limits. 'Give you one bloody inch an' you HAVE to take a bloo . . .'

But Westall was almost screaming now.

'S'a TORPEDO, SIR. . . . ! Comin' right TOWARDS US!'

Twelve

01.30 a.m.: Three Bells in the Middle Watch

'We have reason to believe that Jerry has recently deployed a new version of their G7 torpedo in his Atlantic boats,' the Admiralty Intelligence Officer had told them at the pre-sailing conference. 'The current Mk-A derivative runs on compressed air, typically betraying a quite discernible bubble track in favourable sea conditions. The modified G7-E's are, however, propelled by electric motors creating little surface disturbance. I rather question, gentlemen, whether you will receive adequate visual warning of the approach of a Torpedo Type G7-E.'

So it could be reasonably assumed that a G7-A had been launched towards the Steamship *Olympian* on this occasion, then. Not even Junior Cadet Westall's lynx eye would, it seemed, have had time to detect the closing trail of some up-market, battery-powered job.

'Just about what you'd expect, though,' was the bitter thought which flashed through Chief Officer Ellis's mind as he first registered the flash of effervescence cutting the troughs of the black waves. 'Old, superseded weapon stock being used against obsolescent ships like us. A prudent war: an economical war . . .'

'TORPEDO TRACK TO PORT!' was what he actually bellowed.

The Captain's instant, trusting reaction. 'Hard a port!'

A reflex command already practised through a hundred nightmares. The standard recommended drill – always turn towards, never away from, an approaching torpedo which meant, in effect, altering course towards the position of the attacking U-boat as well. Chief Officer Ellis, in common with most merchant crews, had never quite understood why it was, then, that the DEMS authorities sited guns only on the *sterns* of those few freighters favoured with some means of defence. Chief Engineer Gulliver reckoned that the pre-war Hague Convention had decreed – fully supported by the German delegation naturally – that to site a weapon forward on a freighter must be considered a hostile, to say nothing of a provocative, act.

Mind you, Hitler also claimed that the sailing of ships in escorted convoy was a downright provocation in itself. While for any lonely merchantman to use its radio to appeal for aid if sighted by some innocuous *Kreigsmarine* surface raider or circled by a curious periscope – apparently implied a *bloody* hostile act to poor, persecuted old Adolf's mind. In fact, if you thought about it from a simple seaman's point of view, it seemed pretty damn difficult *not* to provoke Hitler into defending himself from the vicious depredations of Allied merchant ships like *Olympian* and the *Joan M* – and with what had presumably, in the terms of the Hague Convention, been considered as non-aggressive U-boats. Invisible, non-hostile G7-E torpedoes.

. . . Albert burst from the port wheelhouse door and lunged for the wing.

'WHERE?'

Ellis and Cadet Westall pointed dumbly together. The phosphorescent trail could be clearly seen now; cream sliding through rucked velvet; maybe a half cable off and still streaking towards them. It was heading directly for the break of *Olympian's* foc'sle at that moment.

212

'GRIEF!' Burton whirled. 'Keep yon wheel hard OVER – the whistle, McKerchar! Torpedo attack from port.'

'CLEAR the forr'ad DECKS!' Ellis roared: suddenly aware of the faces averted below him. 'Everybody aft, Leather. JALDI!'

ssssZZZOOOOO . . . ZZZOOOOO . . . Steam and condensation belching from the brass foghorn still more-or-less secured to the colandered funnel, ripping to wisps of teased-out cottonwool by the wind. The two bow lookouts literally tumbling down the starboard foc'sle'head ladder; clattering boots chasing racing boots as the Bosun's crowd evacuated the welldeck . . . the mainmast beginning to lean against the after horizon now as the pressure came on the straining rudder.

'Swing, you creaking old bitch: swing!' Ellis heard himself praying.

. . . ZZZZZZZZ . . .

Only seconds passed: seems like bloody hours . . . Dear God – a familiar muffled report from Column Two: ahead and to the left. Then a frightened glimpse of yet another all-too-familiar waterspout seeking the sky above the silhouetted ships – the first of the U-boat's spread of eels found a target! Abruptly a cascade of snowflake from mid-convoy, detonating more shockingly than the torpedo.

To hell with other's problems – jus' stare back to bein' hypnotised by your own.

'Round,' the Old Man's mouthing, not even he able to do anything other than pray. 'C'mon *ROUND* me darling lady . . .'

Twenty yards off now; piercing through the rearing ugly crests and heading straight for the overhang of the cumbersome broadsiding bow. Ellis seemingly wading through treacle; grabbing young Westall by the hard-packed kapok jacket as if in a dream; forcing him down to the deck and flexing his own legs at the knees – he'd heard lurid horror

213

stories of men spitted by their own thighbones under the smash of a ship's deck lurching upwards on detonation.

'Charlie!' a voice yelling from the funnel deck, 'Seen me convoy BAG f'r . . .'

The track of bubbles vanishing right UNDER the flare of the bow. 'Everybody hold tight,' the Captain ordering in a calm, clear voice.

'. . . nothing else happening!

Nothin' . . . bloody-well . . . happening!'

Chief Officer Ellis still had his eyes closed thirty seconds later. Until . . .

'You tellin' them about King Kong then, Mister Ellis?' Slimy Weston's intrigued enquiry wheezed from the top of the ladder. Ellis, still unconsciously maintained his anthropoidal crouch, screwed round and blinked. The old steward was balancing a huge tray of sandwiches along with a big brown-enamel pot of tea and gazing with enormous interest at the odd goings-on on the bridge.

'Good film, that King Kong. Saw 'im in New York, sir – on top o' the Empire State Buildin' an' bein' shot at by them aeryoplanes.' Slimy hesitated, worried by the Mate's horrified expression. 'S' alright, sir – on the *pictures* that was. Not f'r real.'

The Captain was already racing through to the starboard side to see where the torpedo was heading next.

'Dunno how they got 'im to climb *up* there, mind,' Slimy shook his head, marvelling at Hollywood's ability to train giant apes to commit suicide in the furtherance of celluloid drama, then waggled his bristle chin at the tray and beamed, 'Chief Stewid's compliments, sir. Everyone aboard's got one f'r free. There's pickle onnem, an' plenty o' . . .'

'Midships the wheel. Stb'd *TWENTY!*'

Albert was hanging out over the wing when Ellis got there; trying to sight the departing trail of compressed air

214

bubbles vanishing into the seas on their quarter. Previously *Olympian's* wake had adopted one giant curve as she'd lumbered diagonally across the line of advance: now the confused water astern was adopting a dog-leg attitude as she began to return to her original course.

In that second the vessel from Column Two which had taken a hit moments before was slowing on their port bow, wreathed in steam and smoke. *Stafford Pride*, already whistle-warned and still swinging to point the direction of the attack, now presented a narrowing silhouette some twenty degrees abaft *Olympian's* beam. It meant she would just be coming in transit with the running torpedo – steaming into a hypothetical line extended from the spot where Chief Officer Ellis stood transfixed, and the estimated position of the streaking missile.

'NO!' Ellis prayed. 'Not after it's just missed *us*!'

The flash seemed to originate below the break of *Stafford Pride's* centrecastle: probably within her Numbers Two or Three holds. Ellis registered a shutter-fast image of a section of welldeck plating and rails and a whole winch lifting vertically on a balloon of shimmering expanding heat before their sister Bone Collector's bridge front, then the rumble of the detonating warhead rolled across the intervening gap while, ever so gracefully, *Stafford Pride's* foremast keeled over and through the hanging spray feathering across her afterdecks, hissing under the snatch of the wind.

Instantly she began to list heavily to port with the seas still leaping the length of her moving waterline. Smoke seeped rather than poured from her exploded hatches forr'ad but steam was already blowing off in a stream of white from her angling funnel. A rectangle of golden yellow shone like a beacon high in the shadowed bulk of her – her engineroom skylight stripped of black-out painted glass by the force of the blast.

No one said anything right away.

Olympian was coming back on course and still swinging. Ellis dragged his eyes from *Stafford Pride*. The first casualty was almost abeam to port now and lying dead in the water, her decks already slanting; settling fast by the head but at least maintaining transverse stability for the moment. Also there appeared to be masts moving slowly outside of her – someone else preparing to stop and take off her crew if abandoning seemed inevitable.

The Captain assessed the heading. They were to right of course and still swinging. He was quite calm. 'How lies the rudder, Quartermaster?'

'Twenty to st'bd, sir.'

'Midshi . . . Belay that: keep her as she is.' Albert looked over at the ship which had been leading the stricken *Pride*: it was continuing as if nothing had happened. 'What're they doin', then?'

'Bugger all,' the Second Mate called sardonically. 'Keepin' their heids down, Captain. Bastards!'

But they'd seen it happen before, on other voyages. Not often: but it did happen. And this convoy was really shaken now: nine ships sunk within the past five hours, was it? Plus three further stragglers in the *Joan M*, the long-vanished Greek *Theotokos* and, hopefully, the unidentified steamer they'd passed earlier which must still be struggling somewhere back there. Unless, of course, she had finally foundered, leaving her stubborn crewmen to fend for themselves in the North Atlantic night.

That non-stopper was a further indication of the way the U-boats were temporarily winning the morale as well as the tonnage battle – Ellis had already detected the first signs of fragmentation earlier. Now the once-geometric lines of vessels had gaps in columns, were untidy in their dressing, had lost their Commodore and thus their professional direction. No one knew what was happening outwith their immediate circle of equally apprehensive sisters. The escorts were seen only fleetingly while, in an ironic way, the

216

certainty that the Royal Navy was doing its gallant damnedest to protect its charges only emphasised the hazard – even increased the strain on the merchant seamen as ships still continued to explode in the night despite their efforts.

'Sod 'em!' Albert swore. 'Then we'll have to be mother. Ten more to starb'd, laddie – Engines to slow, Mister McKerchar.'

'Want a sannie, Cap'n?'

Slimy had appeared solicitously at Albert's shoulder as if by magic. His rheumy eyes betrayed the truth, though: that he'd been more intent on getting a good look at the goings on than his master's comfort.

'NO! – What's onnem?' Burton growled, watching the turn of the ship.

'Cheese . . . Aren't you bringin' her round a bit too fast, Cap'n?'

'S'always cheese. The Chief Steward bloody knows I hate cheese . . . An' mind yer own business, Weston.'

'I c'n put a tourneyquet on,' Slimy said superiorly. 'I read the book, I did. And I c'n fix a broken leg.'

'You're goin' to bloody 'ave to,' the Captain muttered through clenched teeth. 'Just as soon as I've throwed you down that bloody ladde . . . MIDSHIPS!'

There was a massive explosion somewhere deep down inside the listing *Pride*. Immediately the engineroom skylight blew out and the yellow glare extinguished along with all other glimmers of light.

'Making water in 'er stokehold,' someone muttered from below the bridge. 'Boilers have blown. God help any poor bastards still down there.'

'Bet it's bloody cold,' someone else said apprehensively. He must have been looking at the sea right then. Much the same thought had just occurred to Chief Officer Ellis. The men aboard *Stafford Pride* were about to find out.

They could see steam and coal dust jetting in a steady stream from the funnel, while the ship shook herself and began to lie over faster. She was a couple of hundred yards off by then and close enough to see the first life-raft tumbling over the side to hit the water.

'Stop engine.'

Ellis took a last look ahead. A shadow had broken from the port flank of the convoy and was seemingly heading north west. A runner at last, then? A master who had decided to chance it alone? It was dark again: it was always dark when you were scared as hell and needed light. It was only light when you were scared as hell an' desperately wanted everything to be dark.

'I'll go down then,' he said. 'See if the foredeck crowd have stopped running yet.'

'Port ten . . . Go away, Weston, an' tell Chief Steward Grubb with my compliments to stick 'is cheese sandwichis right . . . MIDSHIPS!'

'Where's bloody Cowan?' the Second Mate grumbled. 'If we're tae pick up survivors yon after deck's my responsibility.'

'Wheel's amidships, sir.'

'Chief Stewid to stick 'i cheese sandwichis, sir. Aye, aye, sir.'

Slimy shuffling away with that peculiar throaty chuckle. Third Officer Cowan finally coming through the wheelhouse to relieve McKerchar for the after welldeck. McKerchar stalking off without a word, looking petulant.

Cowan grinning broadly even though a ship was sinking almost alongside them. 'I had to go to the heads, sir. Comin' out I met the Bosun. He said, "One c'n tell you're an officer, Mister Cowan. I had eight sailors out there on the forr'ad welldeck when that torpedo come – not one of 'em had the class to look f'r a toilet before he relieved 'imself."'

Albert's bellow. 'Mister *COWAN*!'

The Third Mate stopped grinning. 'Yessir. Coming, sir.'

Ellis slid down the ladder handrails. It was almost like a factory shift changing. No one would have guessed from

218

their determined normality that any one of them – all of them – might be dead within the next sixty seconds. And that if they weren't, then they were about to pull drowning men and, more than likely, appallingly injured men too, out of the sea while they all behaved as though it was an everyday occurrence.

He couldn't help wondering whether ordinary people living at home in this Year of Our Lord, 1941, had even the first conception of what it was like to be a North Atlantic convoy man.

The cargo nets were already rigged and the ship just coasting through the water when the Mate reached the foredeck. The night was even colder, the sea seemed even nastier now. Every so often a wave would atomise against the windward side of the hull and come scattering and spattering spitefully across the backs of the men leaning to stare intently into the continuing darkness.

Occasionally a rumble or a crack would come from ahead. From this low vantage point Ellis noticed how high in the water above the line of the eastern horizon the ships sat as they moved slowly away yet again. It occurred to him then that he was getting a U-boat's-eye view of the convoy: not so much looking down at the sea as up from it.

They were close enough to *Stafford Pride* now to hear occasional shouts; mostly sharp urgent commands. They could hear the ship herself too: groaning, with a sound of great things moving and shifting inside as she got more tired of fighting and lay further and further on her side. Torpedoed merchantmen – other than those carrying high centre of gravity deck cargoes like the Polish timber carrier – tended to settle on an even keel with the weight of the cargo in them; it was the stricken warships which more often turned turtle under their top hamper of guns and heavy superstructure. *Stafford Pride*, it seemed, promised to be an exception to the rule. Unsecured objects were already

219

sliding and bouncing down her decks as the angle of heel increased. The steady roar of steam or compressing air escaping from somewhere blanked the squeal of blocks as they tried desperately to get at least one boat away before the list made it impossible.

'Maybe we should have launched ours,' Ellis thought guiltily, but he knew they couldn't contemplate a lifesaving operation like that. The time demanded to recover them would place *Olympian* at even greater risk, while they couldn't just abandon them to drift. By God but every ship in SC whatever might well need its boats for itself tonight. No, speed was the essential factor. Anyone who needed a passage aboard the Bone Collector would have to swim, splash or be towed in their jacket: tonight's complement would be boarding strictly tourist class.

'That's it – they're jumping for it!' Leather exclaimed suddenly. 'McKechnie an' you, Sprunt; shin down the nets. Rest of you stand by with heavin' lines for the moment.'

They were, too. One boat was half way down from the listing boat deck with a few men in her, canted forward as her bow falls were allowed to run too quickly, but otherwise figures were scrambling and sliding down half a dozen ropes trailing from her rails. As each man entered the water he could be seen trying to kick away from the steel side already overhanging him, then flounder in the rough direction of *Olympian*. A Board of Trade lifejacket wasn't exactly designed for Olympic-class swimming.

Ellis made out one figure being helped down her pilot ladder by his mates. He moved painfully slowly, one rung at a time with the wooden treads already beginning to float in a snake below them as the distance between sea and bulwark narrowed inexorably. She was going fast now, yet only minutes had actually passed since she was hit.

Nobody said much on Ellis's deck. Parts of packing cases and sections of cargo matting blown from *Stafford Pride's* holds began to drift in close to *Olympian*, hardly moving

220

astern. They had stopped maybe a hundred yards off the sinking vessel.

There seemed to be a lot of men leaving the *Pride*. Ellis remembered the two boats from *Pendragon* which she'd picked up earlier. Lord, this would be their second torpedoing; their second abandoning in one night. Albert must've been thinking the same thing. His voice came clear from the bridge.

'See you pick up the Admiral if he's around, lads,' the Old Man called. 'I've always 'ad a secret fancy to be Commodore ship, even theoretical.'

There was a bit of a laugh, but what he'd really meant was 'Please God, see that miserable ol' bastard Archie's there as well, and safe an' sound.'

Someone else had a slightly different idea.

'If Cap'n Mulligan's on 'is way over, sir, can I shove 'im off again wiv a boat 'ook?' old AB Edwards shouted back at Albert. 'I sailed wi' 'im in the old *Verity* back in '31.'

'No you can't,' Albert retorted from above. 'I'm claiming the privilege of rank. It'll be the look on Archie's face when 'e finds e's been saved by me that's going to make the whole bloody war seem worthwhile.'

There was another ripple of uneasy laughter; then they heard the first retching from the darkness, and registered the frantic splashing close by. And began to collect their very first genuine bones.

'Every man for himself' was supposed the tradition.

Well, it didn't seem to work that way when they abandoned the *Stafford Pride*. If they were fit and young and had bothered to learn to swim they could have easily made it alone, despite the cold and the shock of being hit. But there weren't many who tried: most of them stayed around the sinking ship at first, to assist the injured and the less-well fitted for immersion in the middle of an ocean in the middle of the night.

221

'Father would have been out of his depth here,' Chief Officer Ellis thought with black-unconscious irony. And it was true. The system had finally collapsed. Everyone had found a common bond for the first time ever. They'd suddenly discovered that there were no social divisons; no upper or lower classes in the North Atlantic. A fireman, a mate; a master or a cabin boy . . . rank holds little significance among the oil and the filth and the fear and the valour.

You couldn't tell rank when it floated flush with the surface anyway. You could hardly confirm a man's existence, never mind his status. Ellis discovered that, even though it was possible to see the last crewmen leaving the foundering vessel herself, it became more difficult to detect them once they'd slipped into, and merged with the water. While even a small wavelet is tall enough to obscure a swimmer, the actual seas were running considerably higher now. A glimpse of what might have been a head lifting to a crest was immediately lost as it sank into the trough. They approached in secret through the darkness until you were virtually looking down at them.

So suddenly the turbulent sea around *Olympian* seemed filled with flailing arms and slowly paddling arms and simply drifting arms. And the spluttering and coughing and gurgling as voices began to make themselves heard . . .

'Easy there . . . 'E's got a broken leg.'

'Where's the Chippie? Chippie was over there a minute ago.'

''Ang on to that, Skipper. Wi' the rest o' the leeches . . .'

'Joey. Over *here*, Joey!'

The first hands clutched at the nets and climbed unassisted from the water; slowly, yes, but only having to be helped over the bulwarks themselves. And after a fit of

222

hunched, explosive coughing or maybe spewing in the scuppers, they turned right back to the rail again and leaned over to help their mates.

But then the bad ones started to materialise. The hurt ones.

Someone began screaming from the darkness. 'Heavin' line. Gie's a heavin' line or ah'll no' be able tae haud him.'

Able Seaman Edwards gave a mighty swing and the line snaked into the gloom. Ellis got on the end of it and two men were towed into view. One had his arm round the shoulders of the other. 'He's burned awfy bad,' the Cuddling Man shouted. 'Ah darenae put a bowline round 'im.'

The Cuddled Man began screaming again, and Ellis thought 'Dear Jesus, how can we bring such pain aboard with even the pretence of kindness?' He whirled. 'Chippie's contraption: lower it to the water!'

It went down, eased from the barrel of the winch and with a man straddling it. Ellis heard him swear as the cold of immersion hit him, then the Cuddling Man and the Straddled Man eased the Cuddled Man into the submerged cradle, and all the time the Cuddled Man was whimpering in terrible agony.

'Heave away easy,' the Mate appealed. The Bosun engaged the clutch and the winch clanked and wheezed and chugged as gentle as a rising thistledown until the whole thing was aboard.

Someone else came up behind Ellis and looked down at the Cuddled Man, who was black and shiny with great strips of crisp skin hanging like sodden rag-tails. Only the eyes were white; staring up at them with an awful terror above a melted nose.

'Jesus!' the Chief Steward muttered, for it was he. He shouted, 'Bring a blanket: see it's wet. Get 'im into the saloon,' then lit a cigarette and held it ever so carefully to the Cuddled Man's lips. The Cuddled Man stopped whimpering, and the end of the Player's Navy Cut glowed feebly.

223

The Cuddling Man fell inboard across the bulwark and crawled on his hands and knees to see his oppo. He was black too, but *his* skin was still stuck in place.

'He disnae smoke,' he said.

The Chief Steward tenderly offered the cigarette again, and it glowed again. ''E bloody does now!' Grubby answered.

. . . more men. The cargo nets now a mass of moving, clambering bodies all being seized and eased across the hurdle at the top; yet, glancing briefly up, the ship was quiet and normal with the tall silhouette of the pepperbox funnel puttering easily away, and the angular, unpretty shed of a wheelhouse moving slowly against the sky; and the silently watching figures of the Captain and Third Officer Cowan, and the two Cadets as U-boat look-outs just cutting the line of the wings. It had to be harder for them, and for the engineers and firemen waiting at their posts below, without anything moving, and nothing but the anticipation of what might arrive within the next few vulnerable seconds.

A tall man came over the rail and Ellis moved to steady him. He was either a fireman or a trimmer judging by the black on him, until he said, 'Thank you – ah, Chief Officer?'

'Ellis,' Ellis said.

'Of course,' the Commodore replied. 'We did meet briefly at the conference, didn't we?'

He began to shiver violently. Ellis asked uncertainly, 'Do you want to join the Captain on the bridge, sir?'

'Later,' the Commodore replied politely, and turned to help another man. 'I'm enormously grateful to you, Mister Ellis. We all are.'

Ellis hesitated, but he had to know. For Albert.

'Captain Mulligan, Commodore?'

Admiral Crighton shook his coal miner head. Even the

grey had turned to plastered fronds of pitch. 'He didn't leave *Pendragon*. There were . . . too many men trapped.'

Someone said tightly, 'She's *GOIN'*, lads!'

Everybody stilled; just for a moment. Even weary men half straddling the rails between hell and a survivor's version of Heaven however poor, froze with turned, motionless heads. No one spoke.

Stafford Pride rolled over like a gigantic, spinning log. They could see the hatch covers ripping from the boards as the sea levered beneath them; the mainmast and gouting funnel smashed flat against the rearing waves to keep on going beneath while derricks and spars began leaping and up-ending from the sea around, and the water poured into her glowing forward holds with a vast hissing and steaming and exploding of white hot things until even they were drowned.

Her rudder and propellor were last to go, pointing as they were to the sky. And then there was only a steady bubbling and frothing . . .

. . . but no one had time to watch for that to end.

A man had swum all the way by himself, and quietly waited in the water, just hanging on to the net while others climbed. Eventually he pulled himself out, and slowly hauled himself up with his arms. He waited patiently at the top of the net again, not wanting to be a nuisance.

'I'm goin' to have a bit of a job gettin' inboard, mates,' he mentioned conversationally in the end.

'STRETCHER!' Leather bellowed, and they lifted the man into it when it came. His right leg was severed at the knee.

The next man Ellis helped aboard wore a brass-buttoned reefer. The arm extended for assistance still showed the glint of four gold rings.

225

Chief Officer Ellis said, 'I'm sorry,' and the *Stafford Pride's* master asked, 'How many saved so far?'

'We're trying to keep a tally,' Ellis said apologetically. 'It's difficult.'

'I had fifty-eight of a crew,' the Skipper muttered. He ssemed to have difficulty in orienting himself; kept feeling for the rail. 'Plus thirty-two from the Commodore ship . . . Ninety, is that?'

'Yes sir,' Ellis said. He didn't think there were ninety or anything like ninety men either aboard or still in the water. There appeared to be something odd about the master's forehead and one ear but it was hard to tell in the dark. 'Are you all right, Captain?'

A grimy, dripping figure still swollen in kapok materialised to take the Captain's arm. 'I'm Danskin: Second Mate o' the *Pride*.'

'How d'you do,' Ellis said, feeling foolish a bit too late.

'I think the Old Man's blind,' Danskin whispered. 'Looking over the end of the wing when the torpedo hit. Lost a bit of his skull wi' the blast.'

'Did the Chief get up from the engineroom?' the *Stafford Pride's* mutilated Captain persisted doggedly. 'Ninety men to account f'r,' remember. We must get them . . . we must get . . . them we must get . . .'

A bit of something awful fell out of his forehead to the deck.

'Oh, Christ,' Second Officer Danskin said, and began to cry.

'STRETCHERRRRRR!' Ellis screamed . . .

Bosun Leather greeted the *Pride's* Bosun coming over the top. 'Told yer you'd fuck it up, Bert: gun or no fancy gun.'

'Christ, it's you,' Bert growled. He turned around and went back down the net a bit. 'I'll wait f'r the nex' ship, Alf Leather. If they woul'n't trust you wiv a gun, why should I trust you wiv me life?'

226

'Cause I got a bottle o' Navy Tot in me seabag,' Alf grinned.

'Welcome me aboard, matey!' Bert said.

The *Stafford Pride's* lifeboat drifted past upside-down. There were men hanging to the grab lines all round it. They were singing 'Ohhhhhh, I DO like to be beside the seaside!' Her Third Engineer, still attired in a pristine white boiler suit, was balanced precariously on the inverted keel, conducting with a spanner.

'Well? Do yer WANT bloody saving or don't yer?' AB Edwards shouted over. The interrupted conductor turned, wobbling. 'Nobody gets saved till the bastards learn to sing in tune.'

Edwards' heaving line hit him right behind the ear. He was still grinning, everybody else was cheering, as he fell off into the water . . .

The convoy was a good half mile ahead now. Still the occasional splutter of snowflake, and the rumble of distant charges.

Suddenly there was a massive flash, and a long, echoing explosion. Ellis caught Albert's face lit stark above the dodger, then whirled round in time to see the sick-familiar fireball rolling and clawing its way into the sky above the break of *Olympian's* foc'slehead.

Someone echoed, 'Mary, Mother o' Jesus,' and for once it wasn't the Cook.

The Captain called down calmly. 'Looks as though they've got the other tanker, Mister Ellis. Do you anticipate bein' much longer?'

Ellis looked over the side. There were only a few heads in the water now, plus what must have been a few corpses floating well away from the net.

'Not long, sir.'

'Grateful to you, Mister Ellis.'

It was all so bloody low key, so polite now it had finally happened: now they were a properly-qualified Bone Collector.

The well deck behind him was packed with men coughing or just flaked out and silent on the hatch covers. Ellis guessed that Second Officer McKerchar's after deck would be the same. Nearly all of the survivors were shaking to some degree as the cold and the shock of what had happened overtook them. Slimy Weston was wheezing about with a word of encouragement here; a warm blanket from a great pile carried by his attendant junior steward there. Chef Robbo's imperious bulk was following, dispensing Biblical comfort and condensed-milk-laced tea in great steaming mugs. Some of *Olympian's* black gang were lighting cigarettes and holding them to trembling lips. It was the Merchant Navy looking after their Own.

Apart from the Commodore. The exhausted, twice-torpedoed and Very Important Man was offering chocolate and Horlicks tablets to whoever had the strength to chew while he could so easily have been on the bridge with Albert's silver-plated tea-pot and even a pilchard sannie if he'd wanted.

While, talking of pilchards, Grubby Grubb was also moving through the inert figures, picking the more seriously injured for transfer to the saloon. He looked so competent; so obviously the right man for the job despite his other failings.

As he came near Ellis he announced quietly, 'Yon burned man, Mister. He died.'

'I'm sorry, Henry,' the Mate answered in a low voice.

The Chief Steward squinted back at him against the flickering pyre of the distant tanker.

'He wasn't,' he said. Flatly.

* * *

There was only one man left in the water now. He'd been there a long time, encouraging the others, getting colder and colder but never taking his turn on the net. Now Ellis could tell he was dead, the way the waves lifted him against the hull despite everything McKechnie and Sprunt could do to fend him off, yet he only floated there with his head lolling back against the collar of the jacket.

'Let him go, sir?' McKechnie called wearily.

'Bring him inboard,' Ellis shouted harshly. 'Get a bloody bowline down, Leather.'

They brought the drowned man over the bulwarks as gently, as tenderly as any of the living, and laid him on his back on the deck. Ellis looked down at him, and the drowned man looked up at Ellis. And Ellis then saw the three gold Chief Officer's straps on his battledress epaulettes under the sodden orange lifejacket . . .

He had probably been about the same age as Ellis. And had quite possibly lived in some city which he didn't really like but had nevertheless felt compelled to return to when he was at home, just as Ellis had. Once. Certainly he would have spent his adult life at sea: certainly he must have tasted the excitement, the misery, the rage and the pride that Ellis himself had felt in the tattered Red Ensign they'd both served under – but perhaps that was where they had ceased to be duplicates . . . For perhaps the drowned man had been able to love his Father dearly, and without effort, whereas Ellis had only desperately wanted to. And surely, had he been married, his wife and child would still be alive and thinking of him in that very moment.

Perhaps, if God had been truly charitable, it would have made more sense had it been Chief Officer Ellis lying there on the drowned man's deck and staring up, instead of down, at his professional image.

But there again, perhaps – if God had possessed any charity at all – there would never have been a war to kill either of them in the first place.

The still-alive Chief Officer turned and called to Albert, 'Forr'ad side's clear to go ahead, sir.'

McKerchar's confirmation echoed faintly from aft.

The telegraph jangled, and Ellis began to walk back up to the bridge as the deck stirred below him once again. It was almost two-o-clock in the morning.

Another dull explosion rolled back from the convoy, and another distant whistle began the first of four sad blasts: *I have been torpedoed* . . .

'Dear Lord, will tonight never end?' Ellis thought.

The drowned man's head fell to one side as the ship rose to the seas, and a trickle of saliva and salt water ran from his open, vacant mouth. He watched his fellow Chief Officer, Ellis, go with blank incomprehension.

For surely tonight had ended already . . . hadn't it?

Thirteen

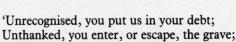

'Unrecognised, you put us in your debt;
Unthanked, you enter, or escape, the grave;
Whether your land remember or forget
You saved the land, or died to try to save.'

John Masefield

02.00 a.m.: Four Bells in the Middle Watch

It was odd, how it did all end . . .

Just as he was walking up to the bridge Ellis registered a flash from somewhere behind him, more-or-less blanked out by the corner of the saloon. He never actually heard any explosion; merely felt a wave of pleasantly warm air curling round and picking him off the ladder and hurling him against the starboard vegetable locker. When he blinked again there was blood in his eyes, and blood in his hair . . . his head hurt.

He heard someone bellowing from a great distance, 'Jesus CHRIST, Neugebauer, but that's a bit thick – all said an' done it *was* only a bloody DOG!'

'Imagine anyone else aboard knowing about Herr Neugebauer,' he thought, amazed at how small the world they lived in was.

Someone knelt down beside him and cradled his head. It was Able Seaman McKechnie. Well, McKechnie knew all about rabbits, but Ellis wasn't too sure how he was on the why's and wherefores of curious flashes and hot winds in the night.

McKechnie said, 'Who's Mister Newgybuyer, sir?'

'Why. D'you know him too?' Ellis asked, even more surprised.

'No – *you* were shouting for 'im . . . at 'im. I dunno.' McKechnie seemed rather confused. 'Can you sit up, sir?'

Ellis sat up. The blood kept running into his eyes and McKechnie began to tie a handkerchief around the top of his head to hold the scalp back down and staunch the flow. He tied it with knots in each corner like the old men always wore when they watched the cricket matches at Old Trafford before the war. It seemed to help a bit.

There was a lot of shouting from somewhere, and steam was blowing off in a steady roar. Ellis moved his hand on the deck and it scrunched in a sort of powder. Bloody filthy: Leather's squad on the deckwash soon as the day men turned-to.

'Coal dust,' McKechnie said off-handedly. 'That's better. D'you want to try standing up now, sir; while I go an' find you a lifejacket?'

'Why,' Ellis asked, very slowly; very deliberately, 'is there coal dust on the deck in the first place, McKechnie?'

'I suppose it come from the bunkers. You know – when the torpedo hit us, sir . . . ?'

Senior Cadet Moberly was wrestling with the tear-off ignition strip on the first of the *I have been torpedoed* rockets when Ellis struggled on to the bridge. It couldn't have been more than two minutes since the hit. Probably Able Seaman McKechnie, with his already proven capacity for coolness, had been the only one aboard able to bind his skull like an old man's at a cricket match, and generally treat the whole event as an occurrence hardly conversation-worthy. Especially the 'torpedo' bit.

'Captain's gone out to the port wing, sir,' Moberly called, his voice thick with excitement.

232

'Where's young Westall?' the Mate snapped, suddenly frightened for the child.

'Captain sent him down to the radio room, sir. With a position report to Comescort an' telling them we've been torp . . . Lord – you're *bleeding*, sir.'

Ellis began to run. There was enough light from the blazing tanker ahead to make out Cowan in the wheelhouse, looking mystified as hell and desperately jiggling the foremast switches on the lighting board.

'Why are you doing that, Cowan?' Ellis snapped.

The Third Mate said dazedly, 'The masthead warning light. One red: I have been torp . . .'

'There's no bloody power in the ship, man! Christ, I've just had my bloody head smashed in an' even *I* c'n tell THAT!'

'Oh, God, I'm sorry,' Cowan said, near to tears.

Ellis rubbed the blood from his eyes, feeling guilty. 'No: I'm sorry, Three Oh. The gennies must've crashed out when . . . You tried for a reply on the engineroom phone yet?'

'No, sir.'

'Try now! Then get on that whistle – four blasts. Not that there's much around to hear it.'

A pencil rolled along the window ledge and rattled to the deck. They'd developed a perceptible list to port: the ship also felt as if she was down by the stern.

'Wheel's ten to starboard an' stuck fast, sir,' Thomas the watch helmsman said uneasily.

'Is she still under way? Sorry, I didn't have time to notice.'

'Don't think so, sir. Think the main engine stopped along wi' the gennies.'

'Stand-by where you are just now.'

'No answer,' the Third Mate muttered, shaking the dead phone. 'Chief was up here a couple of minutes before we were hit. Maybe he's still on his way down there.'

233

'Keep trying.'

'What about the whistle?'

'Westall c'n blow the . . . ohhhh sod the bloody whistle!'

The Captain's voice was sharp with warning as Ellis hurried from the port side wheelhouse door. 'Careful, lad! Watch where you put your feet.'

Ellis called, 'It's the Mate, sir.'

Albert swung round and Ellis felt happy when he saw the look of relief on Albert's strained face. 'You're all right then, Mister Ellis,' was all he said though.

Ellis walked carefully round the gap where the planking had been blown upwards from below. Most of the outer wing had gone too: he could see white tops to the waves just about where the navigation sidelight screen had been. Had the torpedo struck on the other side of *Olympian* it would have obliterated the precise spot where the Captain stood for three quarters of every hour at sea.

'I was in the chartroom,' the Old Man said, reading his mind. Then he scowled: a flash of the old spirit. 'Not sittin' down, mind. I jus' wanted to look at the chart.'

'Naturally', said Ellis.

'I've sent an 'S' call: told 'em we're assessing the damage.' Albert stopped abruptly, peering. 'You *have* been hurt!'

Ellis shook his head. That hurt too. 'I was at Old Trafford. Watching a cricket match.'

'You were where?'

'Nothing. A silly thought.'

The Captain lifted a hand and rubbed his forehead absently. Ellis noticed the arm was trembling violently: maybe shock still found them both wading through a treacle world of indecision. And he'd got angry with poor confused Cowan?

They weren't unique. Only minutes had, in fact, passed since the explosion but there was still that strange sense of

234

the slow motion passage of time. No one had yet arrived on the bridge for orders. No one had even had time to report casualties. And if they'd been struck in the bunkers, then the chances were that the black gang losses would be high.

Who'd been on watch down there? Third Engineer Cramond? It was his first trip in *Olympian*: a quiet lad whom Ellis had hardly spoken to. Funny – how you could live within yards of each other for weeks, yet not really know anything about each other even then. At least four others in the stokehold or round the engine . . . Ellis heard McKerchar's voice snarling at Cowan from the wheelhouse. So McKerchar had survived so far. He resisted the temptation to look back: he didn't think he could face McKerchar right then; he'd rather face reality.

Carefully he picked his way to the after end of the bridge and stood beside Burton, frowning down and trying desperately to think. To help the Captain think.

Most of the wooden planking had been stripped from the funnel deck between the funnel itself and running aft to a point roughly abreast of the Second Engineer's cabin. Now they could see straight through the twisted frames to the curling steel edges of a massive rent in the ship's side. Red hot ash was already spilling from it in a steady stream as the list perceptibly increased, falling with a discernible hiss directly into the sea. A hundred tons of bunker coal was beginning to cook.

Both port boats had vanished from the boat deck just astern of the torpedo hole. Now only the shattered bow section of one was left balanced like a Jules Verne moon rocket on top of the engineers' wash space. All the funnel guys had gone; one good push and the funnel could very well go too. And nearly all ventilators and deck fittings and rails along the port side had been wiped out as if by a duster from a blackboard sketch.

Mercifully most of the off-watch crew had still been down on the welldecks tending the survivors, or in the saloon assisting Henry Grubb; otherwise there could well have been fifteen, twenty men around that area when the torpedo struck, waiting near their boat stations. Now only one body lay crumpled on the edge of the hole, one arm dangling over the glow of fire from within. Other figures were beginning to appear though; picking numbly, uncertainly among the debris. So far they'd been lucky.

'Jesus,' Ellis whispered nevertheless.

'She'll last awhile, but she's finished, Mister Ellis,' Albert said ever so quietly.

'You're abandoning her, sir?'

The Captain looked at him and smiled a sad smile. 'I suspect she'll abandon us eventually. But no, not just yet; not in a hurry. We'll need to make the best of whatever time she affords us – how many men have we aboard now?'

'Fifty-odd of our own, plus over seventy from the *Pride*. Say a hundred and forty.'

'And only two lifeboats servicable. Two thirty-person capacity boats.'

The Mate stared astern into the blackness. Unless one of the escorts came for them – assuming the escorts *were* still afloat themselves, then the only vessel they knew of which followed for certain back there was the old *Joan M* . . . and, of course, the U-boats. The low-on-fuel boats just reaching the end of their patrol endurance and about to return to the VII-C bases at La Pallice or Brest. The ones *die Rudeltaktik* still nevertheless planned to utilise, though: the ones which trailed the eastbound convoys at their most economic speed, and swept up the stragglers and the crippled. And the more audacious or tardy of the Bone Collectors.

'We've also got the Carley Floats,' Ellis said. He made a grimace; it was supposed to be a gallant grin. 'We'll need to wear our woolly vests on the Floats, by God.'

Cadet Westall came to the door, tremendously excited, and shouted triumphantly, 'Sparks got a message through with his emergency batteries, sir. And a reply. "Escort will join you for early breakfast. Stick your finger in the dyke for three zero minutes longer. Medical officer will board if you decide floating can get to be a habit. End of message"!'

'Thank God for the Navy,' Albert breathed. For he'd known as well as Ellis did that most of them would die on the Carley Floats before the dawn light came.

Ellis did grin then, without trying. 'They'll get a helluva shock when they find we've got an Admiral of our own.'

The Captain gently touched the ship's scarred teak rail with a snarled hand; it was a sad caress, but a proud one.

'She'll stay afloat, Mister Ellis,' he said with quiet confidence. 'She's seen us through too many bad times to let us down now.'

Chief Officer Ellis was still grinning bloodied relief when the second torpedo struck *Olympian*. Port side again, but aft this time. At the break of the poop and just below the survivor-packed after welldeck.

This time he heard the explosion – saw the flash, heard the monstrous detonation of the warhead, watched disbelievingly as men and parts of men, and ship and flailing rigging and spray and hatch boards and powdered milk and eggs and . . .

Olympian lay right over to starboard like a stricken dinosaur falling on its side, and then arched gigantically back to port under the weight of the cargo still in her. Little Cadet Westall, only a moment before having felt so important at having borne the sole good news from the battle, was impelled helter-skelter downhill from the open door of the wheelhouse, shrieking past Chief Officer Ellis's vainly-clutching hand, to disappear straight through the already gaping end of the bridge wing and into the black threshing sea.

'It's funny,' Ellis thought as if from a distance, perhaps subconsciously unable to absorb the full horror of it. 'I could've sworn Senior Cadet *Moberly* was the one who was

237

'going to die.' But then he realised Cadet Moberly probably would anyway now, and covered his face with his hands.

For perhaps thirty seconds nobody else moved. The ship came upright again and shook herself, and then began to sink very fast indeed by the stern. Someone on the funnel deck began screaming; a steady, never-ending keen of agony. Long orange and red flames were soaring from the exploded bunker now; adding the tinge of Inferno to Holocaust seascape.

Albert Burton's leg was broken. Ellis could see that even as the Old Man dragged himself up to the rail again: the glint of bloodied fracture pierced clear through pyjamas and trouser.

This time there could be no doubt; no delay.

'Abandon SHIP . . .' the Captain bellowed instantly, and his voice was as strong as a China Seas typhoon. 'ABAN-DOOOOON SHIP . . . Pass the word ALONNNNG!'

He half-turned, pallid despite the fire-bane. 'Go down and save all you can, Mister Ellis. But bear it well in mind to save yourself as well.'

Ellis thought of the Drowned Chief Officer still lying on the forward well deck, and what he might have said about that. 'I'll start with you then. So where's your bloody life-jacket?'

He saw the nearest thing to a triumphant smile you'd ever see on the face of a condemned man. 'Along wi' yours,' the Captain said, 'in the bloody charthouse.'

Already the sea was smothering the taffrail. Only the blackened Red Ensign projected to show there still *was* any stern to the ship. Corpses from the carnage of the after welldeck were floating off to spiral slowly in boiling foam. The Atlantic had suddenly adopted a milky hue, along with the coaldust mulch. 'We really *are* making an omelette by our dying,' Ellis reflected in disbelief. 'Powdered milk and powdered eggs – we're the highest-protein shipwreck in the world.'

238

He touched the Captain's hand and saw tears in the old master's eye. 'I'll get you looked after, but I'll be back,' he promised. 'If I can.'

He whirled round. 'Mister *COWAN!*'

The Third Mate came running from the wheelhouse. '*YOU* should be gone, Mister Cowan,' the Old Man roared. 'I gave the order to abandon *SHIP!*'

'Ohhhh, shut up!' Cowan snapped, having saved it up for months. Then he grinned. 'I gotter save you first. Sir!'

'Lord,' Ellis thought, 'There's greatness in all of us.'

McKechnie came out then with two lifejackets. He growled, 'How d'you no' do what you bluidy well preach, you two?' and dropped one over Albert's head. He thrust the other at Ellis.

'See you, Mate – you go down there wi'out a jacket an' they'll laugh at you.'

'Where's yours then, McKechnie?'

'Ah'll get one.'

The bows were rising higher now. Suddenly Ellis found he couldn't see the convoy. There wasn't any horizon ahead at all; it was all blanked out. He slipped the lifejacket on and began to run, securing it as he went.

He noticed, with unreasonable disappointment, that Senior Cadet Moberly had already left the bridge. He hadn't expected that of Moberly, somehow.

As Ellis went down the ladder they were tying a bowline under the Captain's arms and cradling him, protesting blackly, towards the starboard wing.

'Ease away on the falls. Tight that guy forr'ad. Tight that *GUY!*'

The boat deck was a mass of milling humanity. Both boats were already swung out and almost to the boarding rail, yet there was no rush to fill them. Stokers, seamen, catering staff all waited uneasily while only a bare handful actually clambered aboard: then each turned as he entered

239

and reached out, whereupon there was a ripple of 'Stand back there . . .' and 'Gie the lads a passage, Jeemie.'

The wounded men and the shocked men were being brought from the saloon to be eased across the gap. The boats were filling quickly, but only the halt and the sadly-mutilated were finding space within. There were a lot of broken bones already collected by the Bone Collector: there were many more now since the torpedoes.

The ship gave another lurch and a bit of an anxious cry arose, then she steadied a few degrees nearer the end and slowly even the optimists began to drift away to investigate other means of survival.

In the absence of any of the mates, Fourth Engineer Knox was ready by the tiller in Number One boat. Ellis called urgently, 'Engineroom, Fred – anyone get out?'

Knox shook his head.

'The Chief. Was he down there?'

Knox nodded. His lips were white-tight compressed. Ellis got the impression that he was heartily glad none of the deck officers was around to take command of the boat from him. But Fred Knox had already been sunk once – had kicked his way through a door the last time to get off the ship. And there would be a lot of frightened men in the next few minutes.

There was a sudden sharp explosion from the port side. *Olympian* shuddered, while the flames reared higher in the sky. The whole boat deck flickered and danced under the glare of it.

'Keep one place free in the boat, Fourth,' Ellis shouted above the roar of escaping steam and crackling fire and banging, screeling blocks. 'Soon as you get her in the water, take her forward under the starboard bridge wing. The Captain's hurt and I want him safely away. Understand?'

Knox nodded uncertainly, wishing the boat was away. Ellis felt disillusioned and angry: you never really knew how men would react until the sea swirled at their feet. 'Christ!'

he thought savage. 'That's an *ORDER*, Knox!' he roared. There was nothing more he could do. He didn't have the heart to delay on account of those other shocked, already-wounded men in Knox's doubtful care.

Knox nodded frantically and began to sob. Ellis swung away, sickened. Then . . .

'No more in Number One – Lower away handsomely,' a commanding voice in the background rapped. 'Get that bloody rudder shipped there in Number Two!'

Ellis saw Moberly then. The Senior Cadet had taken charge of every man on that boat deck just as though he'd been doing it for years. Ellis began to run aft with confidence again. He didn't feel quite so angry about Knox's having let the officers down: he certainly didn't feel disappointed in Moberly any more.

A few crewmen were releasing the Carley Floats and beginning to square up to the inevitable when he reached the after end of the funnel deck and stopped, appalled.

From there he was staring right down into red-reflecting water where the after welldeck had once been. And where the second torpedo had struck. Only now there was only the grue and the flotsam and the mutilated corpses of men all mixing together and swirling in the eddies created by *Olympian's* foundering. It was a charnel house of unimaginable horror. Ellis stepped quickly back from the rail and trod on something rubbery: a tennis ball?

He glanced down and found a human brain exploded from its skull.

Robbo the Chef stepped out over the galley coaming while he was still retching. The Cook was trying to eat an apple and carrying a great big box of tinned pilchards at the same time. He stopped when he saw the Mate, and said cheerfully, 'Sea sick, or sick o' the sea, sir?'

The water was beginning to lap at their feet now. With all the dreadful things in it. They didn't have long.

'Just sick, Chef,' Ellis said. 'Of the bloody war, I s'pose.'

Robbo waggled the box. 'Jus' goin' to put these in one of the boats f'r the lads. Then it's me for the bathin'.'

'Got a tin opener in there?' Ellis asked. He seemed to have held much the same conversation with Chief Steward Grubb a million years ago.

'I'm a chef,' Robbo said superiorly. 'Trained to the hilt. Cunard White Star remember, sir? The secret o' good vittlin's inna tin opener.'

A wave smashed against the hull below them. They were drenched with spray. It wasn't surprising: there was only two feet of freeboard left where they were standing. There would have been fifteen a few minutes before.

'No comforting homily before we go?' Ellis asked.

Robbo frowned a giant frown. 'Homily?'

'I thought you would have come up with some appropriate epistle from Saint Paul Robbo. I'm disappointed.'

'You mean the relig'n stuff?' The Cook's frown cleared and he sniffed dismissively. 'Oh, I'm finished wi' all *that* crap, Mister Ellis.'

'Finished?'

'Yeah, well,' Robbo waved the apple vaguely in the direction of the bodies and the fast-encroaching Atlantic. 'I fancied it might stop this happenin' – if I ingratiated myself with Him a bit. But see what thanks I get? Christ, sometimes you'd wonder who's side 'E's on.'

'*Gott Mitt Uns*,' Ellis murmured.

'Sir?'

'It doesn't matter, Robbo. Good luck to you anyway.'

'I wondered about takin' up pornography 'stead o' relig'n next trip.' The Chef wandered off up the sloping deck carrying his box of pilchards and muttering to himself. 'Now *that's* a hobby c'n take a man's mind off of 'is worries.'

The deck was down by a good twenty degrees by the time Ellis reached the midships point again. It was hard; climbing uphill like that. Sailors didn't usually have to climb hills, their muscles weren't accustomed to it. But there again, not many sailors went for strolls around sinking ships either. All the sensible ones got off before they reached the critical stage.

A lot of them were doing just that as well. All along the rails groups of men were drawing a last deep breath and checking for the tenth time their jacket was secure. Some seemed to grin fiercely before they let themselves over on a line or a length of firehose; others were shaking openly and unashamedly. Some were being encouraged by their mates:

'G'wan, Charlie – like a bathe at Blackpool, it'll be.'

'There's people pay a fortune ter cruise Cunard an' that, Syd. Bars; dancin' halls; swimmin' baths. Jus' the same here – 'cept the bath's a bit bigger, an' it's outside the ship!'

'Get in, Eck, or I'll bloody *THROW yer in!*'

Some, a few, just clung tightly to the rail and stared with unblinking eyes and ashen faces down at the water. They were the men no one would have time to help: the men who would stay rooted to the spot until they were either washed off or dragged down with her when she foundered.

As he walked Ellis became conscious of a strange noise; a keening melody rising from the ship. It possessed a curious, cruel beauty: like some great cathedral organ playing a quite random Devil's score; an eerie, steadily rising dirge even above the wind and the shouts and the roaring escapes of steam.

It was the air within *Olympian* gradually being compressed as the water entered her secret spaces; and as it compressed, so it found its way through sounding pipes and tiny vents and great big ventilators: all pitched to a different note, all blending to orchestrate a piping lament. A unique fantasia of wind to mourn the death of a ship . . .

243

The sloping ladders from the funnel deck into the bridge structure were almost vertical now, but Chief Officer Ellis managed to climb them.

Sparks was still huddled over the key when he pushed the blackout curtains aside and entered the angled radio room. It was the only part of the almost-dead ship with electric light – the little bulb shone like a star against the cold green-painted deckhead.

'I had a feeling you'd still be here,' Ellis said. 'Get out, Willie. Now!'

'They're not acknowledging,' Pemberton said through clenched teeth. 'My SOS . . . the bastards aren't listening any more.'

'Aerials are down, Willie. Check your instruments.'

Sparks flicked the aerial meter switch a couple of times, and muttered 'Shit!'

Ellis took the young lad's headphones off and hung them carefully on the hook. 'Out. An' that's an order.'

Pemberton turned in his chair against the tilt of the deck. He was sweating: frightened and sweating. 'I'll stay here.'

'You once told me about your nightmare, Willie: about being trapped in a sinking ship?'

'I can't face the water,' Willie muttered.

'You're going to get it anyway,' Ellis shrugged. 'Out there, or in here.'

He reached over the table and picked up the matchstick model of *Olympian*. The Radio Operator stared in alarm. 'What're you doin' f'r . . . ?'

'Taking it with us.'

'It'll get bloody ruined,' Willie shouted.

'Think about it, Willie,' Ellis grinned. He tilted the model to an angle, and then lowered it stern-first.

Pemberton looked embarrassed, then got out of his chair and tugged at his lifejacket.

'You lot up top have managed to sink the real thing, one

244

way or another,' he said morosely. 'Christ knows what you'd do to a bloody model.'

Ellis left Pemberton in the capable hands of Robbo the Chef, then fought his way to his cabin.

He went straight to his convoy bag and took out the only photograph he possessed of Jennifer – he'd never had one of little David – and put it in his pocket. He didn't bother taking the bag itself, he didn't think there was any point in that. His head was really hurting by then so he rummaged for a couple of aspirins and tried the tap. It was dry.

He left the aspirin on the side of the basin, and lit a cigarette. He never even glanced round the cabin that had been his home for eighteen months: it had just been another ship in a line of ships, really. It stirred no pleasant memories. But then, he'd lived in Salford with Father for nearly eighteen years. He'd no pleasant memories of Salford either.

By the time he closed the door firmly behind him he had to sit on his bottom and toboggan down the length of the officers' alleyway – the angle of the bow was so steep.

When he reached the funnel deck again nearly everybody had gone, and those who hadn't, wouldn't. There was nothing more he could do, and now perhaps the drowned Chief Officer wouldn't have as much cause to be contemptuous when they met again.

He half-slid, half-scrambled to the side of the ship' listening to the creaking of the funnel and the thrumming of the remaining starboard guys. It would go any minute . . . but so would *Olympian*.

He'd partly scaled the rail when he heard the whimpering.

From the funnel? Surely not!

Ellis scrambled and slid back to the centreline again, and listened. There really *was* a whimpering.

Just forward of the funnel and situated flush with the

245

deck was a small iron grating: a ventilation grating really; rusted up and never been opened for years.

He wriggled flat on his stomach and peered down between the bars. The roar of ingressing water was very loud, while the heat forcing its way out from within the flooding engineroom struck his injured scalp an almost physical blow. He didn't draw back because there was also a pair of eyes in there; white eyes in a black man's face, staring up in mute appeal and blinking occasionally, a bit like Al Jolson in his make-up.

There was just enough light from the bunker fire to make out the rest of the whimpering man after a few seconds. He had no uniform to speak of, though he could have been an officer. His flesh was parboiled red between the charred black, and he was crouched at the top of a once-vertical ladder as high as he could go before the grating prevented his final escape.

Ellis could also see, with difficult-to-conceal horror, precisely why the Parboiled Man *was* parboiled – a main steam pressure line had burst halfway up that tortuous escape route. Anyone climbing it must have had to force himself deliberately to pass through a jet of super-heated steam.

Ellis began to try to force the rusted grating open with his heel.

'Who are you,' he asked to make conversation and conceal his own fear.

'Bill,' the Parboiled Man whimpered. 'Bill *Gulliver*, Davey lad.'

Ellis had to close his eyes then. Dear Jesus Lord Our Saviour – Chief Engineer Gulliver! In such a hideous form. He said desperately, 'Please . . . I'm trying to get you out. Can you help, Chief?'

The hand which grasped the bar from below was a black-red melted claw. As soon as it closed, Gulliver shrieked and drew the claw away.

'LEAVE IT!' Ellis nearly screamed himself. The ship gave a huge lurch, and things started carrying away below decks that should never carry away, while other heavy objects started to trundle and roll aft down the now perceptibly-increasing slope. Ellis began kicking frantically; clawing at the steel with rusted flakes spearing under his nails.

'Hurry, Davey,' the Parboiled Whisper came. 'HUR-RRRRRRYY . . .'

Eventually he'd forced it open just a crack: barely enough to drag a slim man through, never mind a gross apparition such as Chief Gulliver.

But then there was the enormous rumble of a bulkhead collapsing somewhere underneath them, and the deck started to slide . . . DOWNWARDS!

'PLEEEEASE . . .!' Gulliver screamed. 'Not now – not after all this.'

'Oh, Jesus,' Ellis was whimpering too. 'Give me your hand, Bill. GIMMEE YOUR HAND!'

The claw came through the gap and Ellis hauled with all his strength – and Chief Engineer Gulliver just fell away: a black starfish fading on a long diminishing howl through the steam and the smoke and the shiny steel pipes that had once been his pride and joy.

And Chief Officer Ellis stared at what was left in his hand, and it was all the flesh from Chief Gulliver's arm: stripped clean from the bone as the cooked meat from a medium-roast Sunday joint.

When he finally rolled himself under the starboard rails and allowed himself to fall into space, the great iron sides of the late Bone Collector *Olympian* were already rushing past him into the North Atlantic with the speed and the roaring of an express train.

Epilogue

~~~~~~~~~~

'What passing bells for those who die as cattle?
Only the monstrous anger of the guns.'

Wilfrid Owen: Anthem For Doomed Youth

02.30 a.m. and forever: No Bells. Not in any Watch.

When Chief Officer Ellis came to, the first person he met
was Second Engineer Ballantyne. He hadn't seen the
Second since he'd been playing draughts with Westall in the
smokeroom at the start of last night's 8 to 12 watch.

Ballantyne didn't say anything: offered no encouragement whatever to a man mixed up along with himself in the
spew of a still-sinking ship. But Ballantyne was dead, with
one arm missing. Probably had been since the first torpedo
opened the engineroom. It hadn't even been his watch, the
middle watch. He'd had no need to have been down there at
all when it happened.

Ballantyne, who hadn't been wearing a lifejacket, sank
again as massive blisters of air began to explode in great
gurgling hummocks of foam on the surface; breaking over
Ellis and whirling him helplessly in the mess of congealing
milk powder and clinker ash and broken planking and stuff.
The hull was still sliding and thundering downwards less
than ten feet away; he could even see the rust scale and the
heads of rivets like hundreds of bug-eyed monsters staring
back at him along the faded, scabrous Plimsoll Line.

He tried very hard to stay on his back, to gaze up at the
bows coming down on him in fascinated horror – the
masochism of the child regenerated: terrified yet still com-

pelled to challenge fear. Like his early Salford days as an awful urchin among awful urchins visiting corpses as a dare: when every step closer to whatever unknown thing might this time be contained within the poor, cheap coffin offered tingling anticipation of some degree of horror not yet experienced.

He found himself staring up at the starboard bridge wing as it bore down on him. And then it came rumbling past to enter the water so close he could read . . . *lympian: Liverp* . . . on the lifebelt still in its cradle. And as the after end of the wing on which Albert had spent so many years impacted against the frenzied surface, so the scant wooden framing imploded and the sea rushed and frothed and clawed for final possession.

Ellis saw Second Officer McKerchar again in that moment. Looking as he was, in along the level of the bridge deck, he found himself briefly staring straight through and into the wheelhouse . . . and McKerchar was there! Wedged diagonally, quite deliberately, in the doorway with his hands in his pockets: just facing astern – which meant almost straight downwards now – with his back against what would normally have been the leading frame of the door and one boney leg bent, foot firmly placed against the after frame.

He wasn't wearing a lifejacket even then; McKerchar. He never had intended to abandon *Olympian* if she was torpedoed: Ellis should have guessed that much after having been allowed, just briefly, to see into McKerchar's tortured soul that time before the Vikings were cremated.

Second Officer McKerchar obviously hadn't been prepared again to risk the lottery of either being rescued or dying, even reasonably quickly, of exposure. Not in the North Atlantic, which was every bit as awful a place to drift forever upon as the Pacific. With or without a sheath knife to help you live a little longer.

The shrinking ship was moaning now, with her ventilat-

249

ing dirge. WHOOOOOO . . . she lamented as Second Officer McKerchar and his intimate knowledge of the *Scottish Daily Express's* view of the war as it had been on Tuesday the 24th of September, 1940, roared and racketed with ever-increasing speed below the boiling surface of the sea.

WHOOOOOOOOOOOOO . . . !

A man was still trying to drag himself over the bulwarks and drop clear as the forr'ad welldeck passed Ellis, going down. It could have been Able Seaman Edwards or it could have been one of the many men from *Stafford Pride* or *Pendragon* who'd been through all this before. He held his arms towards Ellis in a gesture of mute supplication, which was a pretty pointless thing to do; then the hatchcover blew from Number Two as the pent-up forces became too great, and the man disappeared inboard again just before white water detonated over the top of the submerging bridge structure like a tidal wave overwhelming some mighty dam.

The foremast smashed almost flat into the maelstrom as her angle of sinking reached the perpendicular. Only the foc'sle was left now, with the great steam windlass which had weighed a thousand anchors in its time. Ellis began to cry for her then . . . just as the rusted, unkempt bow with the rough-painted defiant letters *Olympian* passed him on its way to the bottom of *das Todesloch*.

The ship took him down in the giant whirlpool left by her passing. And the vortex spun him round and round along with chairs and charts and love letters and corpses and locker doors, and Robbo's discarded Bible.

He met Senior Cadet Moberly down there, and found his premonition had been right after all. The boy must have stayed too long on the boat deck helping others get away. Ellis felt terribly sad about that; but not surprised. Moberly had been a Merchant Navy officer, even though he'd also been a child.

250

The salt of Chief Officer Ellis's submarine tears mingled unnoticed with the salt of the sea.

There was an arm round him when he came to again. And Bosun Leather – whose arm it was – said, 'All you needed wus to make a "pop" as you come up! 'Course y'know they'll call you Corky Ellis from now on, sir.'

Ellis found he'd been dragged half-across a splintered hatch board. He blinked the blood and water partly from his eyes as they came to the top of a wave. There were the heads of men all around, seen briefly in the moon shimmer before sucking from sight again into each succeeding trough.

There was also a terrible hush now the sounds of the sinking ship had gone. Only the coughing and the retching and an occasional cry broke the steady hiss of the sea. Once the silhouette of a lifeboat rode into sight, but it was a long way away and far too far to swim to even if it hadn't been overloaded already. There only seemed to be the one lifeboat, though. And there was no way of knowing whether or not it was Fourth Engineer Knox's.

Radio Officer Pemberton came drifting by in his lifejacket but he was dead after all, even though he hadn't been trapped. The matchstick model of *Olympian* was still clutched firmly in one hand but Ellis guessed it would be broken by now. Sparks always had been a stickler for detail.

Dimly he heard a *crack* and then a distant explosion. Then another one. As the next crest lifted him he saw the stumpy shape of the *Joan M* about half a mile away and burning. Two U-boats were cruising confidently on the surface, one to either side of her, sinking her with gunfire. Worrying at her, like wolves gathered around a corpse. It was the first time in the whole war that he'd ever really hated *Kapitänleutnant* Neugebauer.

'Bastards!' was all the Bosun said. He seemed very short of breath for such a strong man.

251

It was their last chance of survival gone, unless the escort arrived.

Robbo the Chief came swimming past next. Leather made the effort and called, 'Thought you'd've been walkin' by now, Cook.'

It was a much-belaboured joke already. It didn't matter though. Robbo just called, 'Embroidery, Alf. That's f'r nex' trip,' and kept on swimming into the darkness in the rough direction of home.

''E always wus an optimist,' the Bosun said, and went very quiet.

The *Joan M* sank eventually, and the U-boats went to hunt for bigger game. The convoy had faded hull down by then, what was left of it. Only the petroleum from the torpedoed tanker continued to light the sky. Otherwise it was quite a pleasant night to be at sea, really.

After a bit longer the escort came, the tiny trawler called *Trois-Rivières*, and cruised slowly through the area stopping every so often to pick someone up. She stopped by the distant lifeboat and Ellis hoped that meant that at least Albert was safe. He guessed Chief Steward Grubb would be. Somehow he had the feeling that Henry would have wangled his way aboard by hook or by crook.

Eventually the trawler went away. She never came near Ellis. The North Atlantic was a big ocean, and the head of Ellis a very insignificant object. He began to feel cold, and desperately wished it was time to die.

Leather's head fell back in his lifejacket, and Ellis changed arms so's his cradled Leather instead of the other way round. 'Come on, Alf,' he said. 'They'll be coming for us soon.'

'Just a nap, sir.' The Bosun smiled beatifically, 'Christ I could go a bacon sannie.'

When Chief Officer Ellis regained consciousness the next time it was dawn.

The Bosun was dead by then, and Ellis gently eased his arm from around the old man's shoulders and allowed him to drift away.

He wasn't cold any longer. Just tired, and his head still hurt a bit.

When the ship came he could have sworn he saw the name *Olympian* on the bow as it loomed over him.

They were careful as they lifted him out of the water. They must have rigged some kind of contraption just like Chippie's: certainly it was very comfortable.

They laid him on the deck, and then Albert came and stood over him and looked down all petulant and mock-aggressive as he always did. And said, 'You been a long time comin', 'aven't you, Mister Ellis?'

Ellis felt sad then. He'd hoped Albert had got away in the Fourth Engineer's boat and been rescued by the escort, but it seemed that he hadn't after all.

Chief Gulliver came next. All parboiled and black, but fresh as a daisy otherwise. 'It's woodpeckers, Davey. Not *owls* that eat suet.'

Then Sparks came by, and Third Officer Cowan. And little fat Westall trying to look studious, and Senior Cadet Moberly, still with his drowned skull but smiling peacefully now. Then the Chef and Slimy Weston, and Second Officer McKerchar who naturally just looked severe at the Mate's tardiness in joining them.

Able Seaman McKechnie stopped briefly. Vie was hanging lovingly on to his arm, and he was gently fondling a rabbit and looking happy again. Ellis was terribly pleased for McKechnie.

The way Ellis was lying on the deck, with his head fallen to one side, he could just see the convoy – what *was* it called? SC . . . SC what-was-it . . . ? Anyway, he could just see the dogged columns of dead ships out there through the freeing port. *Jollity; Joan M; Tunfisk; Stafford*

Pride; Hecuba . . . Such gallant ships, yet such ancient, ugly ships.

Bosun Leather came and stood beside him then. And you could tell he was Merchant Navy by every cut of his weatherbeaten, bloody-minded jib. And Ellis felt a bit sorry for old Hitler: starting a war he couldn't win.

Then Jennifer came as he'd prayed so desperately that she would. She looked so incredibly beautiful when she kissed him. And little David was with her. And Ellis knew everything was all right . . . everything would be all right between them now, for ever.

Especially when Father knelt beside him last of all, and took him by the hand. And said, 'We're all Family now, son. Come and join the Family.'

They couldn't find a Red Ensign to cover Chief Officer Ellis with, so they had to use the Greek Merchant Ensign.

The Chief Officer of the *Theotokos* cried quite unashamedly when he saw the British Mate was dead. But he was a Greek, and Greeks can be very emotional on occasions; and they'd had a bad night of engine trouble and tension since they'd fallen astern as Bone Collector for *Hecuba* during the very first attack by the Undertakers.

But Chief Officer Ellis didn't mind. SC whatever-it-had-been when it existed had been an Allied Convoy anyway.

And besides . . . he'd found his real Family at last.